CW00555059

NIK THE

SWIFT

CHRIS SPECK

ISBN-13: 9781739330835

'Not everything you steal belongs to you.'

INTRODUCTION

In the middle years of the eighteenth century the country was once again threatened by destabilising forces. The Jacobite Rising of 1745 was the last gasp attempt of the Catholic Stuarts to regain the throne from (who they believed to be) Protestant usurpers. People in Yorkshire were justifiably alarmed, and contributed feverishly to subscriptions for raising defences against the swiftly advancing rebel army. The good citizens of Beverley turned out in their droves to support the cause, led by their memorably named mayor Suckling Spendlove. The rebels were expected to pass directly through York in their progress south from Scotland, and Archbishop Thomas Herring was among the most vocal in leading the stand against the insurrection. Suspected Jacobites in the city had their horses confiscated and were confined to their homes. Even after the Rising faltered, anti-Catholic feeling lingered on for months thereafter. A mob smashed the windows of both the Bar Convent, and the house of the Town Recorder who was thought to be a Jacobite sympathiser.

Even outside of times of national crisis, in this period things were especially tough for those with limited agency over their own lives. Harshest of all was the situation of those in servitude. People of colour from the West Indies were brought to the East Riding as early as 1600, and some worked in the great houses of Beswick and Boynton a century later. In the 1760s, the famous abolitionist Ignatius Sancho – himself born onboard a British slave ship – wrote to Yorkshire novelist Laurence Sterne, urging him to take up his pen to oppose the Atlantic trade; 'think in me you behold the uplifted hands of thousands of my brother Moors.'

Women from poor backgrounds fared little better in terms of autonomy. Stories of female robbers on the roads were cooked up, exaggerated, and regurgitated to reinforce societal roles and patriarchal authority. Of the tales circulating in the early 1700s, few were more remarkable than that of Mary Frith (fancifully nicknamed Moll Cutpurse). Her life of criminality and gender non-conformity assumed mythic status in the hands of scurrilous writers. If we're to believe their accounts, ungovernable, tomboyish tendencies in her youth compelled Mary's family to ship her off to New England. But, she jumped overboard and promptly returned to London where she led a larger-than-life existence characterised by criminality, cross-dressing, drinking, smoking (unheard of in her time), and prostituting herself to men and women alike. Amid this confused meld of fact and fiction, the message rang clear that upending social norms led only to dissolution and despondency.

Other accounts suggest that (in some cases at least) eighteenth-century society could be more accommodating. In 1719, The York Mercury reported that a woman in London had been 'brought to bed of a child' despite having served dutifully as a coachman for sixteen years in the family of Lady Anne Hervey, much to their 'inexpressible surprise'. But rather than being ostracised for this deception, the woman was made decent by being married to another servant in their household.

Dr Daniel Reed
Coventry
22 June 2023

CHAPTER ONE

The East Riding of Yorkshire.
York. September 1744.

"Would you like some more tea, Mr Underhill?" says the woman with pinned-up blonde hair from across the table. She has long fingers, high cheekbones and blue, earnest eyes. This is Miss Ploughman, a mistress in a big York house at Acomb. She is not so far different from a lady that he knew a long time ago.

"I think I have had enough, Miss," he replies smiling with a slight nod of his head. The two of them sit in the front room of a large house in a well-to-do York suburb, the serving girl has supplied them with tea and a number of scones. It's a surprise that Richie Underhill is here.

"I wasn't expecting you until next month," says the mistress. Her voice is steady and educated, bright even. Miss Ploughman should be married by anyone's standard, but she inherited money from a wealthy father and can afford to run a house without a man. It's the sort of thing that can go on in a city like York. Richie comes from a little village south of here called North Burton, and Miss Ploughman wouldn't do well there, not without a husband.

"I'm here because I had a change of plan," he explains, "my business has brought me back to York. I anticipate I shall be here for a few days only, and then be on my way. I trust this is satisfactory to you, Miss Ploughman?" Richie Underhill did not always speak like this. He was once a village lad, and his name was not always Underhill either. It isn't Underhill now. The woman smiles.

"I am happy with our arrangement, Mr Underhill. I have always been happy with it. This time you might like to stay in York a while longer, the races are on in a few days and, I have heard there is a new play at the theatre."

"I thank you, Miss, for your hospitality as always but I would rather keep to my business." They have an agreement, these two. Mr Underhill is meant to be a cousin from Kingston Upon Hull who visits once in a while, but actually he pays for the room he rents, a room he never uses and which, Miss Ploughman keeps spotlessly clean. Mr Underhill is an associate of her late uncle and a bit of an enigma. He is tall and handsome with a ready smile and well-tailored clothes, he always has a pleasant smell and yet, there is something lost about him. She knows nothing other than he does business in York on occasion, but what this business is, she is not aware. She has a liking for him because there is an element of mystery. She has seen that he carries a black mahogany pistol under his cloak. It excites her.

"I must check on my inventory, Miss Ploughman," by this he means his horse.

"I'm sure Kat will have it all seen to properly. She's a good worker and fine with all the animals." The tall man nods as he stands.

Mr Underhill walks through the corridor of the large house, past the wooden staircase and through into the big kitchen where the cook is scrubbing at clothes in the huge sink. He tips his tricorn hat at her. Standing by the back door is the gruff, aging houseman, in his jacket that is meant to be smart and with his moustache bushy and proud. Miss Ploughman's house is not so grand, she only has a few servants, and this fellow is not nearly the finest by York standards. He steps out of the way and Richie passes through the backdoor and down some stone steps, along the garden and to the bottom where there stands a whitewashed stable with a black door. Sitting outside and polishing silver tack is a short haired woman with an ill-fitting jacket and trousers. This is Kat. This is the reason Richie is in York. He does not look at her as he goes through the stable door and closes it. A few seconds later, she steps inside. Despite the sun, the wooden stable is dark. Mr Underhill's black horse is in the stall in the middle, and there's another at the far end. The footman would have brought it here when Richie arrived an hour or so earlier. He wanted to see Kat straight away but he must keep up appearances and so tea with the lady of the house was necessary. Richie is facing away when the stable lass enters.

"It's been six months, I was starting to think something had happened to you," she says. He turns and his face breaks into a wide smile for the lass with messy hair and eyes that twinkle.

"I have something for you." In his hand is a leather pouch which he throws to her and she catches.

"Is it my birthday?" she asks.

"You've earned it, over the years," he replies. She opens the little drawstring and takes out one of the small lumps of metal from inside with her finger and her thumb.

"It's gold," she says.

"Aye, an ounce of it in small pieces, all yours. I want you to pack up within the week." She cocks her head.

"Pack up and go where?"

"That's not my concern. All I need is for you to go, get away from York, and start fresh. You need not be a stable lass anymore with gold in that quantity, neither."

"I like it here. Mr Temperton is a bastard, but nothing I can't handle. I like the alehouses. Miss Ploughman is as good a mistress as any. I want to stay."

"Not possible."

"Why?" Richie takes a deep breath, and his blue eyes look down on the scruffy lass.

"You and I go back a long way, Kat, but we have to cut any bonds that are between us."

"You left me here to watch the place, do you want me to stop doing that?"

"This was a safehouse for us previous, but I think it may no longer be. I'm being hunted, and, it's only a matter of time before whoever it is traces me back to here, and to you."

"How do you know?"

"A little bird told me." Kat's face becomes serious.

"I'm not Miss Ploughman, Richie. You don't get to feed me shite." He looks down in apology.

"I'm sorry. A contract has been taken out on me. A place I had in London was attacked by someone last week. If they can track me there, they can track me here."

"The first smell of trouble and I'll be gone, Richie." She uses his real name because she is the only one who knows it.

"It won't be that easy. You won't know they're coming till they are here. However good you are."

"There's nothing to connect us."

"I want you out of danger."

"I can look after myself."

"I know, but I want you safe. Please."

It has been more than 20 years since Richie first saw her with those same, beautiful, frightened eyes looking at him from the back of a carriage, on her way to hang in Bridlington. He set her free that sunny day and gave her a guinea too. Events brought them back together up in Scarborough and then again when he needed someone he could trust to work the livery of a safe house to keep a watch. It was either that or jail in Hull for Kat. She has worked the stables for a few years now and has not put a foot wrong since then. It seems she has gone straight.

"I don't know where to go, Richie," she says. "I like working, it's easy, I don't have to worry about what I'm going to eat."

"You can find something else. You're rich."

"What if I like it here?" Richie steps forward and looks down from his six-foot four height at her. His eyes are sharp and there are crows' feet wrinkles from the side of them.

"I have one last piece of business here in York."

"What?"

"It's not for you to know." She has a wise head does Kat, even if she has done a good many stupid things.

"What's done is done, Richie. You go turning over stones and a snake will wriggle out and bite you."

"I'm ready for that."

"If you've nothing to tell, why come back here?"

"To give you the money and so you know that I won't be coming back here again, but others looking for me will. Could be that they know we are friends, if that's so, you'll pay for it."

"I'll take that chance," she says. "Miss Ploughman is good to me. I'd rather stay." In the darkness of the stable, Richie Turpin takes a step forward, so he is closer to her yet.

"I won't be able to protect you," he says. There is a sense of apology in his voice.

"You've already done enough for me, Richie," she says.

"I'm tired of saying goodbye. Seems like that's all I've done for a good while."

"That's life on the road," her eyes are bright and wide.

"I wish you well."

"You also, thank you for the gold."

"Aye, don't spend it all at once."

She grins and he can see the familiar gaps in her teeth.

Perhaps twenty years ago, when Richie was a young man and first free, and first a man of the road, he drank here in York, along the Ouse in the alehouses where nobody needed to know his business. This is his river. He fought bare-knuckled in the King's Arms, played cards in the top room of the Green Man and the Globe, went to the races and won more than he lost, went again and lost more than he won. He could ride for three days south to just outside Leeds, rob a stagecoach with his face covered over by his black scarf and be back before the weekend, with a satchel full of guineas. If he needed a change, he'd go north, past Pickering and to the Great Forest of Dalby where he hunted deer deep between the trees, and sold the meat to a butcher in one of the villages nearby. Richie knows the poaching, but unlike when he stalked the forest of Dalton Park back near North Burton, if a gamekeeper or another at the theft of wild animals should chance upon him, rather than run away, he could talk them out of a squabble with his pistol or, if the man was a dog with a bone about his business, Richie could smash his teeth into his head. He's not afraid of that sort of thing.

He stands on Skeldergate Bridge and looks down at the high river water below, the boy he was all those years back, the one who didn't care if he lived or died is not gone, but he is changed. Richie became another, he took his dead mother's name, Turpin. He still does not care if he lives or dies, but he cares for the lives of others who have associated with him, and who could be hurt by it. Richie has heard that a hunter is closing in on him, someone with skills, someone well paid to finish him off, and with no hangman's noose involved.

Some distance away, under a wooden crane, long river boats are unloaded by figures he cannot make out properly because of the smog. York is not the port it has been, the boats would rather trade with Kingston Upon Hull or Leeds where the merchants will buy more for a better price. There are rich folk here in York, with their big town houses and fancy hats, and they won't drink the ale that the burly landlord brews down in the King's Arms below; they need sweet French wine that is really from Holland, or gin that actually is from Holland, and they will pay for it too. It all comes in from the river docks down here, and when it does, the pottery and the leather and the grain goes out. Some landings are controlled by the city but the majority are run by the wealthy families of this town. If you were to speak plainly, you'd call them gangs.

Richie taps down the stone steps towards the Kings Arms alehouse. There is a man he is to meet here. Once he's spoken to him, that will be his business done in this city. The alehouse is busy on a nice autumn day like today, customers are outside with their beer pots and tankards, though it's not yet two o'clock, it's Saturday and some consider this an excuse to drink. This is York, however, and any day at all can be an excuse to drink, even a Sunday. Richie walks up the steps and squeezes past two women who smell of the river, inside the bar itself there's the dull loud chatter of folk at drink. This is what Richie wants. He moves past more lads with wooden pots of ale in their hands to the back of the pub, there's the smell of sweat and hops, fish and beer, the floor is covered in sawdust. This part of the river floods often and so the pub is not as well furnished as others in the city, this suits the clientele, Richie pushes on through the drinkers to the back. He's taller than most and there are comments about his size. 'Big bastard' and 'long legs', and profanities, for all the benefits of being six foot four, there are a few disadvantages – it's harder to go unnoticed.

There's the man he's to meet standing with his back against the far wall of the inn, he has a tankard in his hand. This is Mark Willow, a five-foot but smartly presented drunk who comes from a well-to-do family. He spends most of his time in the alehouses along the river, and sometimes in the posher establishments in the city itself, or down Bishopthorpe Road. You would be forgiven for thinking him a buffoon and a clown, and a rich one at that, for he's loud when he's had a few, he's stupid too. He knows the great and the raucous of this city and the rats as well, that's why he knows Richie. Back in the days when drinking was cheaper and Mr Willow slept with whores and also smoked opium, he was involved in an altercation just south of the river. Rough gentlemen of the road would have taken his wallet with a kicking thrown in for good measure, but a young Richie Turpin, fresh from the rob at Selby rounded the corner to see a fellow worse for drink being set upon by lads, too many to count. He waded in with his big, heavy farm lad's fists and it only took him a minute to frighten them back into the shadows. Richie was angrier then, but less dangerous. These days, the two share commodities. Richie provides money and Mr Mark Willow provides information. He's a friend also, even though money changes hands, they are cordial. The two shake and in Richie's palm, hidden, is a penny which Mark Willow spirits into his pocket.

"How are you keeping, Mr Willow?" he asks.

"Sadly mediocre, Richie and I have been in better shape." Richie stands up next to the little man and towers above his small frame.

"What have you heard?"

"Nothing."

"A guinea?"

"Still nothing."

"Two guineas?" Mr Willow turns to make eye contact, just so he knows the deal is on. There's no need for the money first. He knows this man.

"There's a price on your head."

"I know that much, who?"

"He's Dutch, has experience in the Africas from what I hear. A hunter to be sure. He wears a monkey's finger bone necklace. Grey beard and hair but not so old. He's been paid to find you - and kill you too."

"Who by?"

"A woman of wealth, that's all I know."

"Local?"

"I don't know exactly, Richie. The East Riding for sure. Who have you upset?"

"Nobody," he replies. Mr Willow blows his lips at this as if to indicate it's impossible. In his world, there is nobody he has not disturbed at some point in time. Richie is not like that at all.

"Do you know who he's looking for?"

"A man named Underhill." Richie sighs when he hears this. He's been sloppy. Someone knows his alias.

"Who gave him that name?"

"God knows," answers Mark Willow. He takes a pull on his tankard and the beer froth gives him a white moustache. "There are people in this city who know that you are the highwayman, Turpin. I have heard that's who he's hunting." The tall man wrinkles his nose.

"Turpin was hanged in 1739, some five years past." says Richie.

"Well, our hunter knows that he was not. Perhaps he knows too that the man they hanged, John Palmer, really was John Palmer and not Dick Turpin at all." Richie licks his lips that are suddenly dry. The trap is forming around him.

"Can I trust you, Mr Willow?"

"Not for much longer, Richie. Someone is coming for you, you'd best be ready."

"I'll be back tomorrow," he whispers.

"I'll find out what I can." Richie holds out his hand and Mark Willow shakes it, in the bigger man's palms there are two guinea coins hidden, the payment he promised.

"Until tomorrow then," says Richie.

"Aye. What time shall we say?"

"I'll find you." Mark Willow nods. He knows he will never see Richie again. The tall man makes his way out of the busy pub through the crowd of drinkers. Eyes are on him, from the day watchman to the rough dock lads and the gin whore standing by the door. He doesn't meet their stares.

Richie has to get out of this town. He needs to make sure Kat leaves too, even if he has to drag her away.

It's early evening when Richie gets to the big house on the edge of Acomb. He does not need to return here and has already explained to Miss Ploughman that he will be away for another month and has paid for his lodgings till then, she will not fret, nothing will have been lost. Nor has he left anything of concern in the little room, just a cloak to make it seem like he may return. The expensive black horse he arrived on was too conspicuous for him to keep, he has already left it closer to the river where some keen-eyed thief will have it, the beast was stolen anyway.

Richie is there to make sure that Kat is ready to leave, and, if she is not, he is going to petition Miss Ploughman to have her removed at once. The storm is brewing over Mr Turpin here at York, as it always does in the end, there is no need to lament days lost. This is what happened in Lincoln and in Whitby also, and Harrogate too. Richie must make good any errors for whoever hunts him will be closing in once more.

He walks up the stone steps of a house that he did not expect to visit again and the front door opens as he does. There is Miss Ploughman with her face pale and her hand on her cheek in worry. Something is wrong. Richie's hand goes between the shiny buttons of his jacket to touch the pistol that is hidden there, but he does not draw it.

"A terrible thing has happened, Mr Underhill," she says as she steps backwards into the hall of the house. "It's the livery girl." As she says the next few words, Richie feels sickness begin in his stomach and windpipe, his legs weaken and his throat is dry. He follows Miss Ploughman along the hall, past the staircase and then down the few steps to the kitchen. There are four others in the room as he enters, two coachman without their hats, the serving girl and the cook. They wear grimaces as they look down at something laid on the kitchen table, a body.

"We must inform the constable, at once," says Miss Ploughman as she turns back to look at Richie. "The coachman found her in the stable not ten minutes back, and he brought her up to revive her." A young looking man with his cloth cap clutched in both hands does not take his eyes off the body on the wooden table.

"She's dead," he whispers.

It is Kat but somehow, no longer her. She's on her back with her mouth open. There is no noise to her, and her eyes look up to the ceiling, like a doll without emotion. Richie feels his stomach tighten, his throat is wooly and he struggles to breathe. His hand reaches out to rest on the dead woman's shoulder, with reverence. Here is a thing of real value, lost. In the satchel over his shoulder, he has four or more pouches of fresh minted guineas, rings and necklaces that are worth a tidy penny. Richie Turpin could buy a hundred horses and servants to ride them too, new boots and freshly stitched hats from Atkinson's down the road, but these things are not worth anything at all, not compared to the woman who lays dead on the table before him.

"Mr Underhill?" asks Miss Ploughman. "You seem to have taken on a pale countenance. We believe she may have been kicked by a horse or squashed somehow." Richie puts his hand to his face. He has killed men without a single thought before, and yet here, looking down on his lifeless friend, he is consumed. His hand goes to the scarf around Kat's neck and moves it upwards to show the bruising.

"She's been strangled," he says. Miss Ploughman draws in breath sharply.

"Strangled?" she repeats.

Kat would not have gone down without a fight. He picks up one of her limp hands and examines the fingers. One of her short nails is broken and there's blood underneath the others, the knuckles are red from striking something.

"Best get the constable quickly," says Richie. "Do you have a gun in the house, Miss Ploughman?" She looks back at him with flared nostrils and wide eyes.

"The coachman has a pistol, yes. What on earth are you suggesting?"

"Whoever did this will be back," he answers.

"Whatever for? We have nothing of value."

"It's not money they are after, Miss Ploughman."

"Then what do they want?"

"Me."

"Mr Underhill?" she asks.

He looks down at the dead body on the table one last time and there is a lump in his throat. There is a part of Richie that wants to tell Miss Ploughman what is waiting for her in the future, that there will be someone who will ask questions about him, that she may be slapped and kicked and her house ransacked. Her clear blue grey eyes look back at him. It will not take them long to realise that Miss Ploughman here knows nothing about Dick Turpin at all.

"Hide everything that is of value and tell them anything they ask." She cocks her head. "That goes for all of you," says Richie to the room around him.

"Are you quite mad, Mr Underhill?" she asks. "A woman is dead here?"

"Good day, Miss Ploughman," he says. In a few steps, Richie is down the hall and at the front door.

In an hour he will be on the edge of York.

CHAPTER TWO

At Four Ends Lane near Dunnington there's a coaching inn called the Twine and Barrel; Richie pays a man 3 guineas for his horse - it's well over what the animal is worth. He rides southeast across the flatlands towards Market Weighton and the East Yorkshire Wolds where the chalk hills roll and the horizon is green with well-tilled fields. This is a way that Richie has not ridden for a long time indeed, more than twenty years almost. At midday, he sits atop the horse on Weighton Hill, looking down on the valley behind him, with the blue sky above and the clouds delicate white lines therein. He feels nerves in his stomach. The past is on him. Fears that were real then, and that he has buried deep are coming to the surface like worms in the rain. He turns the horse and rides southeast once more, closer than he has ever been in twenty-three years to a place he once called home – North Burton.

There was always a reason not to come back near here. There would be someone that knew him, he had family in this village once upon a time, and did not want to put anyone in danger. So he held the fast rule that he would never venture past Market Weighton. Richie is still wanted as far as he knows, for the murder of two men at the Pennyman Estate in North Burton and, more pressingly for the murder of the magistrate, a man named Stephen Middleton who he shot just north of Bridlington. All those years ago, they chased him and his dog, Bess, as far as Malton and north too, right up to Middlesborough and beyond to Durham. Richie told himself that he would never be back again and yet, all this time later, with all that he has done behind him, he is here again, at the fork in the road, one way to Beverley and another that will take him back to North Burton where this all started. He is not the same man and yet, there are the same feelings. He wonders about his Nana, and his mother, Meg over in Etton and the lass that he saved and loved, though he only kissed her once.

Her name was Elizabeth Pike, but Richie imagines, she will be a mother with grandchildren now, married off to some man of wealth and grace. The last time he saw her, he saved her life and she in turn saved his.

The sky is a pale blue above the wide and open rolling hills. When he was seventeen, this was the furthest he had ever been from North Burton. He looks down the little track that leads off to his old home and there's a stirring in his stomach, his brow frowns, an autumn fly buzzes in front of his face, the horse's tail swishes. There is only danger for him down that path, and the pale ghosts of what could have been. Richie takes a deep breath through his nose. Had he made different decisions, he could be a father and a husband somewhere with a roof to fix and mouths to feed. Instead, all he has is this black pistol under his cloak. It's time to get this over with. He has to go home because there is nowhere else for him to go.

It's late under a silvery moon when he pulls up his horse a mile or so away from the village. He gets off and ties the reins loose to the fence inside an open field, the horse whinnies a little and so Richie puts his hand to her face and whispers. There was a time when he was terrified of these animals, not so anymore. A man learns to change. He undoes the straps to the saddle and gently pulls the seat from the horse's back, then dumps it. This will be a good find for someone, he hopes as he sets the animal free - he no longer needs it.

Richie walks through the silent village he once knew with the night around him. It's too late for there to be any lights. His boots are noiseless on the hard mud road below and the only sound he makes is the slight clink of the satchel over his shoulder. This is where Richie grew up. At the end of Highgate, he stands for a moment, looking off down Etton Road and at the white sign in the moonlight. He thinks of the woman who served as his mother all those years ago, Meg, the once wisewoman of Etton.

Richie continues on down the village, past open fields and the big Manor house that he knew as the Thorne Farm. There are no lights again but it looks well-kept in the glow from the moon in the black sky. In another two minutes he is outside the pub, the Bay Horse, and the same sign he always knew swings on a metal pole above his head. The windows are dark too – it is late. Across the road, there's the front door of the cottage where he grew up, melancholy surges into his legs and up into his chest. He remembers his Nana sat in front of the fire in that big old chair telling stories, and his fingers go to the bird scar on his chest that he got from falling into the fireplace. There are ghosts all around him in the darkness, old folks who walked these streets and stories that buzz like clouds of insects on spring days, but all is silent. It's as if the sleeping dogs inside these little cottages cannot hear Richie as he steps past the pump and the pond, up the hill in front of the Pennyman House and then up the steps to the church. As if he is a ghost already. He pauses below the squat tower in the moonlight.

At the big church door, he takes the satchel from over his shoulder and sets it on the ground in front of the foot scraper - there's a clink as it hits the stone. Richie hopes the rector is still Mr Page from twenty years ago, he was at least honest back in the day. He turns and adjusts his jacket. There's a figure standing in the moonlight behind him, with his face covered by the wide brim of a hat and a long dark coat down to his ankles. Instinct makes Richie reach into his cloak for the blackwood pistol he carries there and his fingers go around the handle, but he does not draw it – what would be the point? There is nothing left to fight for, not even himself.

"Are you a robber?" asks the figure. His voice is pebble smooth although just a whisper. He has his arms behind his back as if he is examining Richie, without a trace of fear or threat. Richie swallows.

"The opposite," he answers. The man nods and then approaches. They regard each other, these two, in the moonlight outside St Michael's church at past one in the morning. This is the man Richie hopes he would see.

"Rector Page?" he asks.

"Aye. Who are you, Sir, to come a knocking so late?"

"My name is Turpin," he answers. "I'm not knocking, but leaving all I have here at the church door for I do not know what to do with it." There is no hurry from Rector Page.

"You are a man lost, Mr Turpin," he whispers. There is no point trying to deny what is true. Richie takes a deep breath and feelings that have not come out for so many years wriggle to the surface.

"I am," he answers.

"Then you are like everyone else, Mr Turpin. Would you step inside and allow me a little of your time?"

As if Richie has anywhere else to go.

Inside St Michael's is a room at the back with a curtain drawn across the doorway to the main chapel. There's a simple table and four chairs with a candle stick in the middle. Mr Page lights the wick with a match and the room flickers into life. There is no grandeur here, no stained-glass window or golden cross or carpet, no pictures or lectern and yet, this is where Mr Page conducts his most important business. He sits down opposite Richie in the candlelight. Here he talks to those who need his help, offers advice and counsel, listens to grief and concern, it's what makes Mr Page wiser than some.

"Do you often walk at night, Mr Turpin?" he asks.

"When I have an errand, aye. I might ask the same of you."

"I watch the stars on clear evenings like this. I saw you coming up the road from the tower. You have a strange quality in your movement, like a mouse almost between the shadows. I was not certain there was anyone there."

"More like a rat," adds Richie.

"Are you the same Turpin who, legend has it, was born in a cowshed behind the Pennyman Estate here?"

"Aye."

"You were hung up at York."

"Someone was. Not I."

"Then you are Richie Jackson." The man who said his name was Mr Turpin takes off his hat and sets it on the table in front of him. His eyes are deep.

"I was he, aye."

"Are you not him now?"

"People change. I have changed. Young Richie Jackson is now Richie Turpin, the name of my mother."

"I forget my manners, Mr Turpin. Can I offer you a drink? I have a bottle of something here in the cupboard." Richie shakes his head, and for a moment the two of them sit facing each other. Richie with his expensive jacket and the collars turned up and Mr Page wearing a simple waistcoat over a white shirt, his thin beard is grey along his jawline.

"Why are you here, Mr Turpin?"

"To make my offering," he nods to the satchel on the table that he has brought in from outside.

"That's not really why you're here."

"No." He must be honest. There is nothing else. "I have nowhere else to go."

"I see. You are a wanted man in many places, I hear for many crimes, yet, I do not feel there's danger in you, Mr Turpin."

"People tell stories. Some of them are true."

"Are you here to confess?"

"No."

"Good. Anything you have to set straight is between you and God, nobody else, but, if you should want a friend to listen to you for a moment, young man, then this church is here for you, and God is here for you, and more than that, I am also here for you."

"Do you believe that God can forgive?" asks Richie.

"Yes, but it's not as you might think. The hard work comes

first, a person must forgive themselves and make a promise that they will be better than they were. Nobody can bestow forgiveness on a soul that has not found peace with itself first. Do you believe that, Mr Turpin?"

"I don't know. I have done things, that, at the time, I believed were just. If they are not so now, does that make me evil to God?

"The answer lies, not in what God judges first, but how you judge those actions. He gave you the capacity to know within you if your actions are good or wicked."

"You sound like any other rector I've heard, full of riddles to confound poor and hopeless minds." Mr Page smiles. He's not like this at all. The men who tend these churches are not corrupt nor are they fools. "Would you see that the poor of this parish get the money I leave? It is for them, not for rich Charlotte Pennyman across the road to glug down in French Brandy."

"I'll see they get it, in one way or another." Richie examines the rector's calm eyes. He sees truth here. "Is it redemption that you are after, Mr Turpin?" Richie looks at the face of the man opposite. The truth is not easy.

"Perhaps, but not for what you may think. Not for the people I have killed, nor those that I have robbed or struck, I stand by the man who did those things, he did them in the name of justice in some way."

"Then what are you sorry for?"

"The way I treated some. That I wasn't better for them, that I couldn't help them as much as I hoped, and perhaps that in crossing my path, some may have followed a road that made their lives worse."

"The regrets are numerous."

"Aye." Mr Page rubs his eyes with his finger and thumb. He looks tired.

"I think anyone with imagination can have such thoughts, Mr Turpin. The only thing we can control is the present moment, all that goes before is already written. You said that you have nowhere else to go."

"Aye." There is no emotion in his voice at all as he says the cold truth.

"You and I are both men of deeds, I sense. We may talk like this, in riddles as you say for some time and not get any further than we are. It is late also." Richie smiles at this.

"You are looking at a man who has nothing to do but die, rector."

"To speak plainly, that is what I suspected. What if I told you of something that may assist you?"

"Go on."

"It will take a few moments to tell. Will you not take a drink with me?" The rector does not wait for an answer as he gets to his feet and turns to the cupboard behind. He opens the door and reaches down a bottle from within, sets this on the table then returns to the shelf for two chipped china cups. He pops the cork and fills one halfway.

"Not for me, Mr Page," says Richie. "I've drank enough for two lifetimes thus far." The rector puts the top back on and sits down.

"Drinking is not a crime, Mr Turpin."

"Not all things that are wrong are crimes. The drink is a cover story, Mr Page, it dulls the real problems we face."

The rector nods and takes a delicate sip on his teacup then sets it down. He places his two hands level on the table as he begins his story.

"There were two shepherds in the mountains with their sheep, one, the old father with his grey beard and missing teeth, the other, his strong and healthy son. They had spent many days driving their sheep high up to the mountain pastures where the grass was sweet. On the third night both the men were tired of the march and they set themselves down under the stars to rest. The old father spoke: 'Son, I wish to tell you something.' The lad replied with a little anger, 'Father it is so late, I have a headache and I am weary, we will speak in the morning.' The old man asked again if he could talk to his son. The young man replied once more: 'I am weary from the climb, whatever you have to tell me can wait till first light.' The father sighed, and, when the young man woke the next morning, he found his father was dead."

"What am I to make of that?" asks Richie.

"I'm not sure," says Rector Page. "What would you have done if you were the young man?"

"I would have felt very bad indeed," answers Richie. Rector Page nods.

"How would that have helped?"

"I guess it would not."

"The young man still has the sheep to look after and it was not he who was the reason for his father's death. Unless he wishes to spend many of his days in anguish, he will have to forgive himself for not listening to his father. I think, Mr Jackson, we must all forgive ourselves in the end." Richie looks at the earnest face of the rector. There's a sense that these village men of God are unjust and stupid, greedy even, but this is not the case. In many ways they hold the community together. Mr Page means well, Richie cannot be angry with him, even if the story makes his head spin.

"It's not so easy for me to forgive myself, Mr Page."

"Perhaps not, but until you do, God cannot help you." The rector finishes his drink and sets the teacup that was previous full of port back on the table. "It is late, Richie Jackson, I must get some sleep. You are free to camp down here for the night. When will you be gone?"

"In the morning, at first light," says Richie.

"See that you are," says the rector as he stands up. Richie watches him walk out through the curtain and into the main hall. His feet are noiseless as he moves across the stone floor.

Mr Page closes the side door of the church without a sound. He takes the long key out of his pocket and fits it in the lock. The man inside must have known this was going to happen. Mr Page walks the path to the steps leading downwards towards the village and his mind races though his legs do not carry him as fast as his thoughts whizz. There are those who would very much like to find Richie Jackson who sits in the back room of the church, folk who would pay dearly for the information too. Mr Page is not a cruel man, but nor is he stupid. Like any village lad of the cloth or not, if he finds a hen trapped in a thorn bush, he will wring its neck and take it home for the pot. This is not mischief or greed, it is simply the way life is. He opens the door to his little cottage and walks inside, the fire in the hearth is just embers and there's a figure on the wooden bench asleep covered in blankets. It is the young lad who helps the rector with his duties around the church, a good and dependable boy, if a little too green. Mr Page shakes the lad awake and sees his eyes open in the darkness.

"I need you to get to Beverley, young Jim, as fast as those legs will take you. I've a message for you to deliver."

CHAPTER THREE

It's just after six in the morning. On a normal day, Mr Page's lad, Jim, would be inside the church ringing the bells, but not this Monday morning. After he delivered his message in the early hours, two men accompanied him from Beverley. Mr Page turns the key in the lock on the wooden door to the church, the same one he closed last night, and steps backwards, then to the side. A man with a moustache under curly dark hair opens the door wide, and he too steps back so a much larger body carrying a loaded musket with a bald head can aim inside the darkness of the church. These are the only two men who were available from the Sullivan household where Jim took the message. The serious man with dark hair is known as the Frenchman, and the big doughy one with the musket is Binx. Their faces are stern and cold as they advance for they already know a dangerous man is inside.

"He's not to be injured," says the Frenchman. He has earnest blue eyes and aims a flintlock pistol in one of his worn gloves. Binx grunts back at him with his fat, pock marked face. There should really be more than just the two of them if they are to catch Dick Turpin alive but there was no time to prepare, indeed, the Frenchman could not be sure the information was correct, he still can't. The two men move on into the room.

It takes a few moments for their eyes to adjust to the darkness. There, standing in a long dark cloak and without his hat is the man who Mr Page informed them was Dick Turpin. It appears this gentleman has been waiting. The Frenchman levels his gun at the tall figure standing behind the table.

"What do you call yourself?" he asks. His accent is educated and smooth – not at all French.

"Depends on who's asking," answers the man. He is tall, much more than six foot with wide shoulders and dark hair.

"The rector here says you're Dick Turpin. Is this so?"

"Aye," answers Richie. His voice has a faraway quality, and he fixes his gaze upon the man with curly black hair.

"You do know that Dick Turpin was hanged up in York some five years since," says Binx. Richie tries to give him a wide smile, but Binx is ugly and ignorant.

"I know that," he says.

"Would you please hold out your hands together in front of you," asks the Frenchman. This is not really a question.

"So you can put me in irons?"

"Yes." Richie holds his hands out together. To think it has come to this, of all the time he spent running away, to just give himself up. There's the clink of metal as the Frenchman steps forward and fixes one, then another metal cuff to Richie's wrists. He keeps his eyes on the man as he does so, worried somehow that this is a trap. When the key is removed Binx lowers his musket, his arms were getting tired. The Frenchman steps back.

"How can I believe that you are Turpin?" he asks. Richie, moves his hands in the chains to his chest and pulls down the neckline of his shirt to reveal the bird scar next to his nipple - the one he got from nearly falling into the fire here all those years ago. The Frenchman does not grin. "I'll need more than that," he says. Mr Page enters the room with his lad Jim behind. His eyes fall upon Richie, now in irons and there are creases of worry on his face.

"I'm sorry," says the rector.

"I knew you would, Mr Page. It was the best night's sleep I have ever had, here on this floor, knowing that the next person to come through that door would be here to arrest me, and knowing too that I'll be hanged, and this can finally be at an end." The rector swallows at how earnest his voice is. Last night, Mr Page felt guilty about what he had done, now he feels duped.

"I will be there for your last rites, should you wish it, Richie." Rector Page means this.

"No need. I've made my own peace with God, Rector. I'm ready to face his judgement also."

"Where will you take him?" asks Mr Page. The Frenchman fishes a cloth bag from his satchel and fans it out with his hand. This will go on Richie's head.

"We'll deliver him to the magistrate," he answers. "You'll get your rewards, Mr Page. I'll see to it."

"I did not do it for the reward, Frenchman," he says. Everyone knows this is not true, even Jim.

Richie is not in control of himself for the first time in so long. With the bag on his head and his hands in the stiff irons, he is bound and blinded. They march him from the church of St Michaels into a trap pulled by two horses, and he sits between the men as they bump on unsteady wheels towards Beverley he guesses, but it does not matter now. He has given up, knowing where he is going is not his concern any longer, nor is knowing who is hunting him or if he is going to stand trial or when they will hang him. This is all out of his hands, and all he has to do is sit down and depend on the decisions of others. It's like being free. The horses slow in front of him, he hears the one they call the Frenchman tell the other man to make sure the prisoner has a drink. The sack goes up and the end of a bottle with flat beer is poured into his mouth, before the material comes back down. These men are not rough with him, more perfunctory, as one would be with a bull or a pig; there's no need to hurt him unnecessarily.

It does not take long for the sounds around them to change from autumn birds to voices, there's the clatter of hooves on cobblestones and early morning chatting, the call of some lad up the street to another, the heavy creaking of a gate opening and the feeling of the wheels stopping. The men beside him clamber down and he is guided by his hands in irons from the trap and onto the ground below, he smells onions cooking and lavender, horses and leather polish. This is no jail, he thinks.

He is led into a house, up a few steps and round into another room, the men's voices bounce off the high roof and his big boots squeak on a polished floor below.

"Please sit down," whispers the Frenchman in his ear, he presses lightly on Richie's shoulders. As his bottom hits the seat, someone removes the sack and he winces at the light temporarily. Richie blinks a few times and sees that he is in a bright and large room with an open fire burning opposite, behind him is Binx and standing beside is the Frenchman.

In front of Richie, sitting in a plush chair by the fire, is a well-presented gentleman with long thin black hair and a foxlike goatee beard. This man is Mr Sullivan, a rich and influential figure in Beverley town with his white knee socks and pure white shirt. He is someone Richie would happily rob. He sits forward and has a pious look to his smooth features as he examines Richie for the first time.

"Could you tell me your name?" he asks. Richie takes a breath in and considers his surroundings, the big rug next to the unnecessary fire on a warm day, the paintings hanging on the wall behind, the smell of perfume from this gentleman, and his shoes that seem so shiny they may be brand new. Richie is not going to lie anymore.

"My name is Richie Jackson of North Burton. I am also known by my mother's name of Turpin and in certain places, I am referred to as Dick Turpin."

"We are familiar with these details, Mr Turpin, but why North Burton? You haven't been seen around this part of the East Riding since I was a lad."

"I have come back here to face judgement and since North Burton was where it all began, that's where I decided to go." This is a lie also, Richie has been telling lies for so long that they drip off his tongue and into the air. He corrects himself, "I had nowhere else to go."

"Do you know who I am?" asks the well-dressed man.

"I do not," answers Richie.

"My name is Mr Sullivan, I am a merchant and a man of wealth here, this young man is my ward, he is Marcel Pike, of French descent. I have been up all night, waiting to meet you, Mr Turpin, you have quite a history."

"If you knew a quarter of what I have done, I would be surprised," says Richie.

"I know that you are a brawler, a horseman, a poacher, a murderer, and above all a thief. You are a thief are you not, Mr Turpin?" Richie is not at all afraid of this gentleman with a silk neck scarf loose around his throat, as a young man he would have been terrified of him, later, he would have robbed him, now, he doesn't have any feeling left.

"I stole from those who deserved it," he says. "Some men have much more than they could ever need, and it makes me sick yet to think on it."

"You know you will be hanged for your crimes, for the murder of Stephen Middleton primarily, though it was many years since."

"Another has already hanged for these crimes, Mr Sullivan." He refers to the poor fool named John Palmer who swung up in York in 1739. "Am I to be taken to jail?"

"Not yet. I have something I would ask of you."

"What?" Sullivan wants him to do his bidding, and perhaps with the threat of the gallows hanging over his head, he expects Richie to accept.

"I need you to obtain something for me."

"Why don't you steal it yourself?"

"I cannot. I am too well known to complete the task, and I do not have the necessary skills. I am more a scholar than a gentleman of the road, you see, Mr Turpin. Should you complete this deed for me, I would spare your life. I have wit enough in the courts to arrange that."

"I will not do it," says Richie. The words come out without thinking.

"You have not heard the task."

"It does not matter, I will not fulfil it."

"Then your life will be forfeit. If I do not assist you in your case, Mr Turpin or Jackson, you most certainly will be found guilty of murder and be hanged."

"Your men did not so much as catch me, Mr Sullivan, rather I allowed them to take me. The game is over. I will murder and fight no more."

"You will hear the proposal before you decide."

"I am unable to go anywhere." Richie's voice is dark in the grand house. His big hands grip the arms of the chair he sits in and the knuckles are huge, the Frenchman glances uneasy at his master, he has a bad taste in his mouth about this.

"Some weeks ago, Mr Turpin, I was visited by my cousin, here in Beverley. He is a man from north of the border, a remnant from another side of the family of Edinburgh. If you are aware of events of late, there is some bad blood brewing up there in Scotland, Jacobites have threatened to return their Catholic king to the throne and there is appetite for war in the north."

"You may dress your story up in whatever fancy ribbons you wish," says Richie, "but it would serve us both well if you got to the heart of your proposal forthwith, and then I may find myself quicker to the gallows." People do not speak to Mr Sullivan in such a way – they would not dare.,

"I was hoping to allow context, Mr Turpin. I am not a criminal. My cousin came to ask for my support in monetary terms, and I refused and so, in the morning of September 19th, he took my daughter." As this last sentence leaves Mr Sullivan's mouth, Richie can see the man behind it, at once, he can see the eyes that have lain awake and the cracked lips, the hand shaking slightly and the pale skin. His eyes blink in worry. "She is sixteen years old, Sir, and my only child. He has ransomed her for a thousand pounds, a sum which I would happily pay if I had it."

This changes things somewhat. Richie frowns as he thinks

and he leans forward.

"What about the constable of the peace here at Beverley, could he not be asked to hunt for her?"

"My cousin has explained to me that he will do away with her if I call upon such help. Mr Ryder, the constable, is a capable man, but this must be handled delicately." Richie is intrigued. He has also heard of the constable of the peace here called Mr Ryder, a formidable man that your average thief would try hard to avoid.

"Has he taken her already to Scotland?"

"Not yet, I received a letter from him that he is close by, far enough to return her yet for the payment he requires."

"How long do you have to come up with the money?"

"Sunday. The end of the week." Richie sits back on his chair and takes a breath.

"What makes you think I can get her back for you?"

"Isn't that the sort of thing you do?"

"I'm a robber."

"That's not what poor folk call you Mr Turpin. It may have gone unnoticed on the ears of other, richer men, but I have heard that your profit falls through your fingers for beggars to pick up." This Mr Sullivan is unusually sharp. Richie never wanted the money he stole anyway, there was the buzz of stealing it and then the buzz of giving it away.

"I may have offered alms to the poor, Mr Sullivan, but that did not include rescuing kidnapped girls. You best look for a handsome prince to assist you." Mr Sullivan stands up and paces to the fireplace, he looks down into the flames with his hands on his hips.

"Do you believe in fate, Mr Turpin?" he asks.

"Not at all."

"Do you not think it is fate that you happened to give yourself up in the church at North Burton, at exactly the time when you were needed? That you are out of chances as you sit in that chair facing the gallows? This is the way God works,

Sir. Would you not agree?"

"I have not accepted your task, and I will not accept it. I'm not the hero you seek, Mr Sullivan."

"I could pay also, for your services and promise you a free passage, out of England, to somewhere you could make a new life." Richie's voice takes on a hint of iron.

"You are not listening to me, Sir. I will not take your employment. I have given myself up, and, what is more, you have misjudged me, so wholly, that I feel my heart burning in shame. If there were a kidnapped young lass of a penniless shepherd, then I would freely offer my life for his daughter. The state that my soul is in right now, I believe, in punishment God would not let one hair on my head be harmed. If it were a whore, or a beggar in the streets I would gladly take up arms, for nothing, but your kind, Mr Sullivan, you of the better classes have been the ruin of me my whole life." It is more than Richie has said in many months in one go, and he does not know where the venom comes from, his Nana perhaps. Mr Sullivan turns to look down on Richie and his face is creased with worry.

"I'm a good man, Mr Turpin. My beginnings are not humble, but wealth does not make me evil. I need your help. My daughter's life should not be forfeit."

"It's been my experience, Sir, that men who say they are good, are seldom true to their word and that the pious are rotten. I will not help you."

"Then there is another who you may help," he says.

From the darkness in the corner of the room, a figure moves into the light. If he had his wits about him, Richie would have seen the woman as soon as the bag was removed from his head. She wears a wide dress and a shawl over her shoulders, her red hair is done up in a bun on top of her head. There's something familiar about her to Richie as her face comes into view, she has high, proud cheekbones and hazel eyes. She is twenty years and a lifetime older than the last time he saw her. Richie gets to his feet immediately. His nostrils flare. His heart beats into life and the hands in the iron cuffs close into fists. This is the reason he has never been anywhere near Beverley in the last twenty years, it is the woman whose life he saved, and who in turn saved his. Here is the first woman he ever kissed, and the feelings that he buried all those years ago surface in him once more, raw and real and profound. She is Miss Elizabeth Pike. Richie is afraid of her because she is all he has dreamed of all these years.

"This is my wife, Mr Turpin. Elizabeth Sullivan, she knew you well once upon a time. It is she who has faith in you."

"It is good to see you once again, Richie," she says. She uses his name because she knows it. "You have aged well." He sees that her face is no longer as smooth as it was, and her eyes no longer shine, but the air of bravery and dignity, she still carries. In the years since he knew her, Richie has learned that sometimes to say nothing is better than words you are not sure of. Elizabeth moves closer to him and stands in the space before her husband. She regards Richie and her eyes are worn.

"She is my daughter. We helped each other once before. We can do so again." As Richie recalls, it was he who took the risk to save her life first and in doing so, he was driven from his home and his family. As always, Richie resists saying the first thing that comes into his mind. "I have often visited your mother, Meg, she is out at Goodmanham, behind the church, and yet the wise lass there who heals wounds and sets bones. She will be happy when I tell her I saw you." Elizabeth moves a little closer towards the man in irons, and there's a sense of uneasiness in the Frenchman and Binx, the beast has not been awoken in this man but they would not like to face it.

"Please look at me, Richie," she asks, and for a moment, the highwayman wishes the patterns of the mat he stares at under his feet would swallow him up. If he looks into her eyes she will have him, just like all those years ago. Richie lifts his head and meets her gaze, at once, there are the calm and smooth hazel eyes above slender lips and the curve of her jawline and neck. This is Miss Elizabeth, not as he remembers her, but better, now a woman of real substance and demeanour, with flared nostrils and a steel expression. She is breathtaking.

"I need you to bring her back to me, Richie. They will not be far. They are south of here towards Kingston Upon Hull, they have promised to have her on a boat to Holland of we do not hand over the money."

There is electricity between the cool blue eyes of tall Mr Turpin and the hazel of Mrs Elizabeth Sullivan.

"God has brought you here, Richie, do you understand that?" she asks. He steps forward, and though he is in irons, the Frenchman is nervous of such movements. Richie meets Elizabeth's stare with his own, and a life that has made him a different man from the wide-eyed, brave lad she once knew. He is better now than he once was just as she is.

"I would ask a favour, Elizabeth," he says. It is rude for him to use her name in such a way.

"Say it," she answers. "She is my only child. I will do anything for her safe return."

"When I bring her back," he says, "you will take a pistol and put a bullet through my heart." She swallows, looks down and then back up to him. Her hazel eyes narrow and her brow frowns, the voice is just a husky whisper.

"I will do that for you, Richie Jackson, if that is what you wish."

CHAPTER FOUR

Richie washes from a bucket in one of the stables while the Frenchman stands at the open door with a freshly laundered shirt in his hands. The cold water feels good on Richie's head and neck and he scrubs under his arm pits and down his chest. This is the old Pike residence, where Elizabeth once lived with her father, and where, as a young man, Richie was told that if he thought anything of her, he would leave her alone and never see her again. It seems that this place has passed through Elizabeth and to the man she calls her husband, Mr Sullivan. He has thought of her many times since and wondered about the path their lives may have taken together, if they could have been man and wife. The Frenchman passes Richie the shirt and he slips it on over his head as his arms find the sleeves.

"I am the Frenchman. You're to have anything you need," he says.

"Did you bring my effects with me from the church?"

"Aye, your coat, and a hat. They are here."

"There was no satchel?"

"Not that I saw." Mr Page will have it somewhere. Richie goes to the dark frock coat and picks it up, there's a belt and holster too. He fits it around his chest and adjusts the buckle with a creak.

"My pistol?" he asks. The Frenchman gives a weak nod. It does not seem a wise idea to give this man a gun somehow, only a few hours earlier he had him in irons. The Frenchman passes Richie the heavy dark wood by the barrel. "Are you really a Frenchman?" he asks.

"My mother was from Marseille, they call me the name because of my looks." Richie fits the gun into place at his chest.

"Is there another name I should call you?" asks Richie.

"It is what I have become known as, Mr Turpin, I cannot change what I am," he answers. After this response, Richie examines the man as he stands in the door of the stable with his black leather waistcoat and shoulder length curly hair.

"A man may change, Frenchman, do you know that?"

"Not here in Beverley, Mr Turpin. We are just as we are meant to be." Richie sees his serious face and the creases of worry there.

"I shall need a steady mount, nothing flashy, powder as well as lead for this pistol."

"Mr Sullivan has offered my services to you, Mr Turpin, in your endeavor to return his daughter. Hear me through before you reject my offer. I'm a fine shot and an excellent horseman, I know the East Riding as well as any and I'm known in these parts also, with good will, my assistance could prove helpful. The girl in question is also my niece, Sir and honour demands that I cannot stand aside." Richie examines this man once more with his earnest eyes and curly hair.

"Who was your father?"

"Captain Pike, this was his house."

"You are Elizabeth's brother then?"

"Aye, half-brother." Richie now understands why he is known as the Frenchman, perhaps they cannot call him any other name.

"Where is your mother now?"

"She passed on, Sir."

"Was she a lowly lass, Frenchman?"

"Aye, she was housemaid here for many years."

"You are as I, a bastard, then."

"Aye, but not ashamed of it as others may be. It was not my doing, after all." Richie looks down at him again and sees the hurt just behind this man's dark eyes, however hard he tries, he will never be the same as the folk in this little market town.

"I see you, Frenchman," says Richie. "I see that your hands are rough from working and you have legs a little buckled from too much riding. I see your boots are polished as is the leather buckle on your belt. I have known men such as you who have to work hard to prove their worth, but, I cannot take you with me. I know you would help but I will tell you this as true as I may, no other man shall die because he rides with me, never again." The words ignite the Frenchman's curiosity.

"It would be my choice to ride with you."

"There's a curse on me, I can feel it in my chest, perhaps for the things I have done, I know not. Fate will see to it that you are killed and not I, of this I can promise you, and I will not see a good man as you wasted."

Miss Elizabeth warned the Frenchman that he would like Turpin, and he did not realise just how much. He has heard the stories of this man of six foot four, how he bested robbers in North Burton, how he outran a whole battalion of Beverley garrison soldiers, on foot, how he has robbed the roadways of England for over twenty years. The Frenchman has also heard tales of him from the White Horse pub and up at the Kings Arms, how he gives away as much as he robs, how he owns the river that runs through York and a street of pubs in Scarborough with a fleet of ships that run rum from the West Indies. With one stout punch, he has heard that Turpin can smash a man's jaw from its socket and that he can shoot the wings from a dragon fly. The Frenchman thought it was all lies, but now he sees the man, and has spoken to him, his mind is changed, some of the stories will be true. He can see why his sister has faith in him.

Mr Sullivan does not have much evidence to go on. In the big room of the house on Toll Gavel, Beverley, he explains the events that led to his daughter's abduction. He tells Richie of his cousin, the big Scotsman with a wide and white paint brush style moustache, and his squad of five soldiers at arms. He details how the game has been played, that the Scotsman asked for money and he refused, then refused again, and again a third time and all was smiles until the same evening when the five men at arms broke down the front door, their boots rumbled up the stairs and they dragged Nicola out from the big, resplendent house on Toll Gavel, and into the night they clattered off into the darkness with their horses hooves loud on Beverley cobbles.

The next day there was a note and a meeting point on the river Hull to which Mr Sullivan did not attend for fear and worry, and that was the day before yesterday. Richie has examined the note and sniffed the envelope, though he cannot read the words well enough, he knows the smell of corn about to turn rotten. There is only one place where there is a great deal of this, in the port of Kingston Upon Hull where the grain of the East Riding of Yorkshire is delivered to London, and at times stands so long in the warehouses that there's the musty smell of it going off. The easterly wind blows the smell a street away to Blanket Row where the whore houses and pubs are full. Richie knows this because he has been there, and anyway, the best place to hide a person is among many other people. He reasons that Nicola Sullivan will be there, in Hull, somewhere along that street.

The afternoon is just beginning as Richie rides alone along the riverbank, south, towards Hull. He has that old horse he asked the Frenchman to find him, it's a steady cob with feathered feet. He wears his black tricorn hat, and his pistol is well covered up under the buttons at his chest. Richie does not want to think about seeing Elizabeth again after all this time or how her eyes affected him. The path he was on, where he was to be hanged and to have all his business put to an end finally, has been altered - he has taken a fork in the road and it will take him more time to reach his destination. He is only happy that he did not have to see Elizabeth again before he left.

Richie passes the Ship Inn at Dunswell late afternoon and in another hour and a half, he is outside the north walls of Kingston upon Hull as the autumn sun is going down over the river water ahead. This is the north gate to the city and there are two big towers that hold heavy wooden and metal doors. The wall snakes south and is uneven in places but rock solid to protect the city inside. Richie pays the watchman three pennies to let him in just before the man shuts up for the night.

He knows this city better than most.

Those who are not from here might call it Kingston Upon Hull, but nobody in this city calls it such. It's not a king's town despite the name – there's more irony in it than truth. It was here, after all, that the folk refused to let King Charles enter a hundred years ago, and thus began the civil war. Some pretend allegiance to the crown, but only those with money. The rank and file of this walled city look after themselves and each other, the king in his castles in London can hang for all they care.

Hull has the stink of people living too close together, of their bodies and cooking, there's the smell of gun powder too, the river, animals, tar that they paint on the side of their boats, beer brewing somewhere, the odour of corn going rotten, fish as well. Richie leads the horse unsteady on the cobbles, he turns right down Salter's Lane and a big rat waddles across the street in front of him in the half darkness. There are worse things than rats down these city streets. At the bottom of Bowl Alley Lane, there's a coaching Inn called the George that Richie has used before, it's not cheap but they don't ask questions. He leaves the horse with a lad and pays up a few pennies from his pouch, Richie recalls him from the last time he was here.

"Want to make a penny more?" asks Richie. The lad looks up and his face is grey flat. Of course he wants to make a penny, it just depends on how he has to do it.

"What do you want?"

"There's a group of Scotsmen in town, perhaps five or more of them. Have you heard anything?"

"I'll need that penny first," says the lad. Richie fishes out another and hands it to him.

"The Old Mare," says the lad. "There's talk that they're Jacobite." This is a pub on Dagger Lane, not the nicest one either.

"I'll need that horse ready again by the stroke of midnight, lad. You'll see that it's fit to ride." This is an order. The boy narrows one of his eyes as he looks up at this tall man with his tatty tricorn hat and steady gaze.

"You'll not get far at that time, Mister, all the city gates will be closed, best wait till morning."

"There'll be a guinea in it for you, if you have the horse ready." This is a lot of money.

"Are you a Jacobite too?" he asks.

"Not I, young lad, just a man who pays well for a job to be done." The boy is not so sure, but this fellow has already paid him for information and, there's a steady feel to him.

"I'll have your horse ready," says the boy. Richie smiles and tips his battered hat.

"Just one more thing. What's a Jacobite to you, lad?" asks Richie.

"Someone who we don't like."

That about explains it. The lad will have no idea that far north in Scotland and West in Manchester, there are men who want to turn back the clock and put a Catholic on the throne. Richie watches him lead the horse off to the livery yard behind the pub.

He'll have to have this all done by the strike of twelve.

There are more rats on the corner of Trinity Lane, they scatter as Richie approaches and there's a lass with a long frilly red dress down to her ankles and white make up with a black dot on each cheek. She looks dreadful.

"Evening, Miss," he says as he walks past. She grins at him with black gums. Richie's pace is too quick and certain to be in need of anything she can offer him, so the smile is all he'll get. It takes Richie another few minutes to reach Dagger Lane and the wooden building that stands in the middle of a row of rickety, jerry built houses. There's a sign swinging in the fading light above the green wooden facade with a tatty looking painting of a donkey. This is the Old Grey Mare, a bawdy house, a sporting house, a disorderly house and well known in the city.

Richie pushes open the door, and the smell of beer, incense, and perfume wafts into his face, covering the other odours that lie somewhere underneath. The pub is just busy enough for nobody to bother looking at him as he walks in and makes his way to the long oak bar at the far end. Richie has been here before under more exciting circumstances. Today, he doesn't feel like a drink but orders one anyway and it comes in a metal tankard with a lid from a woman with curly black hair and dirty fingernails. He takes a sip and winces at the ale inside. Drunks on the verge of fighting natter in the far corner and there's the high cackle of laughter from some lass he can't see. A group of lads are playing cards behind him and the fire at the side of the big room is lit. Next to it, leaning on the wall with his arms folded is a large man with a moustache and a short-brimmed hat pulled over his eyes. This will be the watchman and if the drunks get too rowdy, he'll use the heavy metal walking stick leaning on the wall next to him to get rid of them. Richie notices the stairs leading to the bedrooms above. He takes another sip on the drink and rests over it on the bar on his elbows.

The Scotsmen will be here.

There is nowhere else that would have them, for sure. Richie has many advantages in this situation, he has time, and they will not know that he is coming. Back in the day, he would have considered meeting the situation head on, but the years have made Richie wise, if you can do a thing without cracking your knuckles then so much the better. He'll have to find out where they are before he makes any move and, if the Scotsman with the white moustache really is the kind of man Mr Sullivan explained he was, it won't be long before Richie hears something. Hunting does not work quickly, the more you want the job done, the longer and harder it will be, and the more chance you'll give up and go home. Like always, Richie will do it properly and see it through to the end. He takes another tiny sip of the bitter ale and then looks down to his boots and back to the bar, and the reflection of himself on the thin sheet of metal behind the bottles, his face is drawn over a thin black beard.

In all honesty, Richie does not have anywhere else to go. He might as well make this last.

A figure appears at the bar next to him, six foot perhaps, well short of Richie's height but the man is wider somehow. He turns his head and their eyes meet, only for a fraction of a second. Richie takes in all he needs to know straight away, there's a white moustache and the red face, the piggy eyes and some sort of round hat perched on his head with two manky feathers pointing up at one side out of the rim.

If you don't look too hard, you can find what you want. Here he is. This is Mr Sullivan's Scot. The man moves off after he collects his drink. There's a room through a swing door to the side where lads can play card games and discuss things that they don't want others to hear, Richie sees it swinging open and through the gap he spots the Scot with a white moustache sitting down at the big round table with others. The door closes fully, and Richie picks up his tankard and takes a glug. It has been some time since he has taken a drink and he does not miss it. He did not have to wait nearly as long as he thought he would.

The last time Richie was at the Old Grey Mare, he was a little more reckless, he and Kat played cards in that same swinging door room and took a pile from some smart arsed merchant with a pointed nose, Richie was drunk and bawdy and not like himself. They rented a room on the top floor with a double bed that they both slept in, fully clothed for a few short hours till the landlord turfed them out into the ringing bells of Sunday morning. Richie glances over and sees that the watchman is nattering to some lass with a long dress and her shoulders showing. Just because he is not looking, it doesn't mean he won't notice Richie leaving the bar and walking towards the stairs, but, this is a chance that he must take if he is to do what he is about to. The smoother his movements, the less obvious he will be. In a few steps he has disappeared behind the bar and is moving up the stairs, one at a time, nice and steady as his hand goes under the buttoned up jacket to the handle of the blackwood pistol in the holster at his chest. There's no need to draw it, not if he doesn't have to. He manages to get upstairs unnoticed.

The red carpet is threadbare on the landing as he turns to the corridor. There are a line of doors stretching downwards on one side and one at the far end. Richie thinks about last time he was here and that Kat wanted the largest room there was but it was already taken by some gentleman and his party who had better money than they did. This is where they will be, reasons Richie, at the far end. Sullivan mentioned that there were five or more of them and they will need a place big enough for that many and the girl too. If he knew more about the Scot with the white moustache, then Richie could make a more educated guess about who will be behind the door. All he knows is that the man is a Catholic in a Protestant city, and that he wants to put a Catholic king back on the throne. Either he's as dull as a rainy day or he's a nutter. It's quite possible to be both.

Richie makes his way down the corridor slowly, aware of the sounds around him, the creaking of his feet on the floorboard under the thin carpet, the squeak from the bed behind one of the oak door and the chatting drifting up from the pub below. If it were Richie's gang who had captured the girl, none of them would be down in the bar below at the ale – that would come after, not until the job was done, Richie and whoever he was with would be with her. He approaches the door, and, like old times, he produces the curtain mortice lock pick, looks back over his shoulder to make sure there is nobody there and then back to the door handle. He slips the bent metal bar into the hole like it is the real key, gently jiggles it till he finds the bite in the mechanism, and the bar that keeps the door in place moves back. Bawdy houses have bad locks by design, the landlord needs to get into the rooms sometimes, if it's clear there's something unpleasant happening behind one of them.

He turns the handle and slips into the darkened room. The window is open and one of the curtains flaps in the light breeze, there's a chair facing it with a thin figure dressed in white therein. He approaches with silent steps, expecting that the Scots party would have left someone there to guard her. He pauses a few seconds as his eyes adjust to the light, searching the four beds and the chairs for movement, the table and the leather horse bags left piled on the floor. There is nobody here except the thin figure, immobile on the chair facing the window. There's a white gag fitted around her face and when Richie moves into view, she jumps in her skin but does not move from the chair – a ripped up bedsheet holds her around her arms and body. Richie puts one of his fingers vertical to his lips to quieten her. It is important he gets this bit right, for he will need this girl's help if they are both to get out alive. If she has anything of her mother in her, she will be brave and perhaps fierce too. He draws his face close to hers and sees her frightened pale eyes and red hair, the freckles across her nose and cheeks and the flared nostrils. He puts one of his hands very gently on her shoulder. He whispers calm and smooth:

"My name is Mr Turpin. Your mother sent me here to get you. I'll use my knife to cut off these bonds, but you must make no sound when I do so. Do you understand?"

She nods frantically. Richie draws his knife from his belt and cuts free the cloth from the back of her head. He hears her gasp in air as he does, next, he works on the rolled up bedsheet that is tied too tight around her arms and body as well as the chair. He senses her pain when the bond is cut, she lifts her arms and winces as the feeling comes back to them. She is dressed in a long nightie without socks and, although it is September, she will be cold.

"Do you have clothes?" he whispers.

"No, Sir," she whispers back. Her voice is steady but her eyes are frightened in the darkness. Richie casts around the big bedroom floor for what he can see, there's a black cloak on one of the beds next to a battered flat cap, it's brown and well-worn. He hands it to her as he picks up the cloak.

"Put this on," he says. "Hide your hair if you can." She looks weak as she scrapes back her ginger curls and fits the cap over them. Richie thinks about the steps leading downwards and the not so busy bar room of the Old Grey Mare, he thinks of the Scotsmen in the swinging door room and the night watchman. It would be too risky to just walk her out through the front door. It was risky enough for him to just walk up here. Richie has not thought this through. He looks at the girl with the oversized cloak around her shoulders and the cap on her head, now she is in his care, he worries somehow. Her bare feet point outwards. How will this look walking down a cobbled street?

"We will have to leave by this window here," he says. There really is no other choice. The girl steps forward.

"Are you Dick Turpin?" she asks in a tiny voice.

"Aye," he answers.

"You were hanged out at York. My mother said."

"Not this neck, Miss. Not yet." It's his standard line. They do not have time for this exchange. Richie steps over to the window. It is just big enough for him to climb through.

"We are high up," she whispers.

"Not so high, lass," he answers as he bobs down and through the window. Outside the smell of the town is rotten, there's the brewery must and the stench of the docks in his nostrils. He climbs out onto a sloped roof, the tower from Holy Trinity Church looks down on him in the moonlight. He tests his footings on the heavy thatching. It's safe enough. Richie puts his head back into the room and holds out his hand for her to follow. She is unsure of herself, this ginger lass, careful with her bare feet as she steps through the window, her hand is light on his and her eyes wide with fear. Richie guesses she will be a well-kept girl, not used to mucking out horses or handling a spade, kept out of the hot summer sun and cold winter wind. There's a sweetness to her, it's honest fear as she walks out onto the roof. In a few careful steps they are at a straight six-foot drop to an alley below. Richie looks over the side, then crouches and jumps down onto the cobbles below, he lands on his powerful bent legs and there's the jangle of his gun and his knife at his belt. You can do this kind of thing when you are six foot four. He looks up and the girl sits on the side of the roof, he nods. This lass is too afraid to hesitate. She slips off and he catches her before her bare feet hit the stones. There is more weight to her than you'd imagine.

"We must keep to the shadows," he says. "It'll not take them long to find out you are gone." She nods with her ginger hair falling over her face from beneath the cap. He can sense the fear on her.

They pass behind the back of the Old Grey Mare to the livery yard. There's a breeze that brings the smell from the animals inside. As soon as the Scotsmen find out she is missing, they will come here. There's nothing more indignant than a thief who has had something stolen from him. Richie knows the way round this town, he has been drunk here in days gone by, he and Kat and the others used these alleyways to get through the city. He squeezes through a gap in the livery yard fence and they walk quickly down another alley, away from Dagger Lane and back to the Inn where Richie put his horse with the lad. He glances back at her as they move between the buildings in the darkness, she is slight but matches his pace easily, even without any shoes on and she stays close to him. This is good. She's not as wet as a fish. There must be some of her mother in her.

They cross into White Friar Gate and move north towards the George where Richie left his horse. He keeps to the shadows. She does too. The whore on the corner is now gone. It's late. At Bowl Alley Lane they turn, and the coaching inn is right next to them, there are the big double doors to the stable. Richie turns the handle and steps inside, the girl follows. It feels safer already as he shuts the door, the stable lad appears when he hears someone. He is much the same as he was an hour earlier, with his face smooth and impassive. He sees the girl behind Richie and his eyes narrow in mistrust.

"You said you'd come for your horse at twelve," says the lad.

"My business concluded earlier than I anticipated," he answers. Over the years Richie has learned to use more words than are needed.

"I'll get her ready," he answers and disappears. There's light from a lamp hanging from the rafters of the stable and the smell of horses, the lad has a little bed in the corner. From somewhere further back he leads Richie's horse through. It's still fitted with the saddle and the bridle as Richie requested.

"You can lead him out the doors," says the stable lad. He tries not to notice that there is a pale faced girl with ginger hair under a cap standing so close to Richie that she might be his shadow.

"One more thing," says Richie. "How much do you want for your shoes?" The lad gives a strange grin as he hands the reins to this tall man.

"I've just the one pair."

"A penny for the shoes."

"They're not for sale," says the lad.

"We have a long way to travel and she needs your shoes." He looks at her pale face.

"They're not for sale," he repeats. The lad is nervous also. He does not like this at all. He should be asleep already.

"Two pennies." The lad shakes his head again as Richie takes the reins and hands them over to the girl. He reaches under his cloak and draws out the blackwood pistol then levels it down at the lad.

"Two pennies," he repeats. "Take off the shoes, as quick as you like, the pants too and the shirt and the waistcoat." The lad goes paler yet.

"I only have to shout and the landlord will come running,"

"Do you think he'd be able to deal with me?" whispers Richie. It's rhetorical. "I've been as pleasant as I can be, lad, and you'll get your money anyway. You'll be able to buy a whole new set of clothes."

"Just who are you?" asks the lad.

"He's Dick Turpin," says the ginger haired lass.

Richie leads the horse out into the deserted cobbled streets in front of the coaching inn, he gives it a slap on the back so that it bolts off into the darkness and they hear it clatter into the city. It's a decoy.

A few minutes later, they are in another alley much nearer the dock. The lass is wearing the dull leather shoes of the stable lad and has tucked most of her hair into the cap. She wears his sackcloth waistcoat over a black shirt and his pants are too big on her. She seems calmer. Richie leads the way onto the jetty. There are boats of all sizes moored alongside each other in the silence, from huge frigates to fishing boats. The river is high and the moon plays on the calm water as they walk along the wooden boards, there are the creaks from ships and the jangling of rigging in the light breeze. Across the river, behind big walls is the garrison. There's a figure standing at the far end of the jetty, a man with a wide hat and a glowing yellow lamp on a staff - a watchman. Richie stops and turns back to the lass.

"Be confident," he whispers. They walk on. Richie in front with the lass behind in her flat cap and oversized cloak. From behind them in the city, they can hear shouting and commotion. It could be the Scotsmen or just drunks railing against the night sky. The horse will have thrown them off somewhat. Richie approaches the man with the wide hat and the lamp.

"Evening," he says.

"What's your business?" asks the watchman.

"Me and my lad are off fishing," replies Richie as he walks past. The lass follows and looks the watchman dead in the eye as she does.

"Where's your boat?"

"Down here on the left," says Richie. He could pay this man off like he did the lad, but that would raise suspicion, best play this one straight.

"Right you are," says the watchman. "Sounds like there's some bloody idiots in town tonight," he offers.

"I heard they're Scotsman," calls Richie.

"Aye," says the watchman with a half snarl. Richie walks down some steps and to a line of rowing boats that are tethered to the jetty. He picks one which he can see has oars and doesn't look too pretty. There's the sound of gunshot from the streets close by and Richie turns to see the watchman move towards the town centre with his lamp on his big stick.

"Get on board," says Richie. She clambers on and sits down as he follows. He pulls up one of the oars from the bottom of the boat and uses it to push them off into the river.

It takes Richie another few minutes to row them out into the muddy waters, they pass by huge whaling ships and wide three mast schooners with their sails wrapped up tight. Richie rows steady. There are more shots fired from behind them in the town but out here on the river in the moonlight, it's quiet. There's a great chain across the entrance to the river that's high enough for Richie to row right under. It's here to stop any old ship sailing in or out the port town without paying duties.

"We'll get out onto the Humber," says Richie. "Past the garrison and on toward Paull, there's an inn there I know called the Oak." He didn't expect to rescue the girl as quickly as he did. The lass looks at him with her wide hazel eyes and nods in the moonlight. There's the smell of rotten wood and a light mist drifting over the river towards them, the water slaps at the side of the rowboat as Richie pulls the oars in a slow rhythm.

"Did my mother really send you?" she asks from opposite him. The flat cap makes her look like a lad.

"Aye," he answers.

"She told me she knew Dick Turpin, many years past."

"She did. She saved my life."

"In the story I have heard, Sir, you saved hers." Richie keeps up the rowing. He can see she has hold of one side of the boat and that her knuckles are white. There is steel in this slight, ginger girl. He likes her.

"She told me of you, of what kind of man you are, and she was bitter when she heard you'd been hanged."

"Best keep quiet lass, there are ears everywhere on this river." She nods and sits back, clasps the cloak in front of her with her free hand and turns to look out in front towards the darkness. Mist envelops them. This is where the river Hull meets the mighty Humber. She turns back again to him, and manages a weak, honest smile.

There is a lot of her mother in her.

CHAPTER FIVE

It's just morning. The birds start up first with their fine dawn song, as orange sunlight breaks over the waters of the Humber to the east. A heron flaps low over the silty water. From the reeds where Richie moored the rowing boat the night previous, the ginger haired lass watches the river. She sits inside with her knees up to her chest all covered by the oversized cloak. She has not been awake long. Her ordeal so far has made her timid. Richie stirs from under his cloak in the warm orange light and sits up. She looks back at him and still wears the dark brown flat cap. They are far from the town and deep in a patch of reeds on the north bank, Richie thinks they maybe near the village of Salt End. They were lucky to get away this easily.

"Are you hungry, lass?" he asks.

"My name is Nicola, Mr Turpin." She seems to have regained some composure. "I am in your debt, it seems. I am hungry, yes." Richie fishes around in the inside pocket of his cloak and pulls out a cloth, he passes it over to her and she unwraps a piece of pork, it does not look very appetizing, but she takes a bite. There's a little more to this lass - Richie sees that her hands are strong from work and her jawline is straight above a slender neck. She is not quite the frail creature he thought she was last night.

"I'll call you Nik," he says. "If anyone chances on us, you'll pretend you're my lad, till I get you back to Beverley. The cap suits you, keep it on." She takes another tiny bite on the pork chunk and attempts to chew as she looks off through the reeds that hide them, and then back to Richie.

"Will the men who took me follow us?" her eyes are frightened.

"They won't think we came this way, young Nik. That horse that I set free in the town streets might put them off a bit, and I'm not so sure they know this area well enough."

"How will we proceed back to Beverley?" Richie picks up his tatty tricorn hat from the floor of the little rowboat and sets it on his head over his brown hair.

"No doubt your mother and father want you back as soon as is reasonable, and you wish to return also, but, to my mind, we should take a longer journey back, on safe roads. There is a lad I know at the Oak Inn at Paull who will take us round the tip of Spurn Point and up to Withernsea. From there, we will ride up to Hornsea and cut across to Beverley on the east road, nobody will expect us from that side." She blinks back at him. He is much more lucid than she imagined. Her mother described a lad with wide blue eyes and the whole world before him. This man is worn, bathed in the orange of the morning sun, has rough skin from the elements and his plans are made from experience.

"How long?"

"Three or four days, maybe more." She puts her hands to her forehead under the cap in stress.

"Can you not take me back now? My father has men and horses, he is a merchant at Beverley, a man of substance."

"If we take the straight road back to Beverley now, then we'll meet your Scotsmen. They already captured you when you had your father's protection, how will we fare with just me at your side. The best way to win a fight is to avoid it altogether." She takes a deep breath.

"I do not think I can survive that long, Mr Turpin. I could not close my eyes last night for thinking of those men." Richie knows the feeling of dread she has, it's common when experience has brought you close to death. There's the rush of adrenaline and the fear and the crash afterwards.

"Were they rough? You were valuable to them, they would have been foolish to hurt you."

"They bound me to a chair and told me they would cut my throat if I made a noise. They took a chunk of my hair too, from the back, a big piece right down to my scalp." He can see the tears welling in her eyes and her chin beginning to wobble. "If I were a man," she continues, "I tell you, I'd sail back there and rip open their throats." There's the mixture of fear and hatred in her.

"Can you use a pistol?" asks Richie. She frowns.

"I have fired a musket previous, Mr Turpin, aye."

"Then here," Richie reaches inside his jacket and removes the blackwood pistol from the holster. He is gentle with it as he holds it out to her by the handle. "It's loaded. You only need cock the flintlock at the back and pull the trigger to use it." She seems confused. "If I'm ever afraid it gives me a little comfort to know I have it, perhaps you could keep it on your knee while we row." She takes the pistol and it is heavier than she thought it would be.

"And you would trust me with this?" she asks as she looks down on it.

"Aye," he answers. Richie is not sure why he would trust her, but the words come off his lips. "That pistol will stop a bull if you hit it in the right place. You may feel comfort knowing you are safe." She holds it up in one of her hands and examines the mechanism, the flintlock and the pan, the heavy handle, and the black iron trigger. She rests it on her knee and her eyes find his. She looks better.

Richie draws up one of the oars and fits it through the crutch that holds it in place.

"Who did they hang in York?" she asks.

"A man called John Palmer who they thought was me, but, John Palmer did a great deal more wrong than I ever did."

"How did my father find you?"

"By chance." Richie does not want to explain further.

"So you are in my father's employ?"

"Not really, I said I would do this for your mother, because I knew her many years ago."

"What are you to be paid?" asks Nik. Richie draws up the other oar and fits it into the crutch on the right side. He remembers what he asked Elizabeth Pike now Sullivan to do and she promised she would put a bullet through his heart when the job was done. There's no need to burden this lass with that.

"She'll pay me what the job's worth," he answers. He pulls on the left oar to get them straight and then both to move the boat through the thick reeds that grow out of the water. Richie must lighten the mood. That's how he's been taught.

"I'll row first and when I'm tired you take over."

The tide is coming in on the river Humber and the going is not easy in the swell, the flow of the water and the waves battle against each other. Somewhere off into the distance, in the flat orange glow of the autumn morning, a sailing ship catches the wind as it draws nearer the port of Hull. When Richie looks at this wide and big landscape, he feels small and lost and breathless almost. In his younger days he thought the river might one day take him far away, for some fifteen miles to the east is the open ocean of the North Sea and from there lies the whole of the wide, rich world.

The waters of the Humber are fickle and troublesome, there are sandbanks that move with the seasons and tides, and the brown waters deserve respect. The ginger girl, Nik, is silent as she too watches the schooner in the distance with the huge sails flapping in the strong wind and little figures on the deck. He considers her neck and the hair spilling out from under her cap, the pale skin, and the way her hands rest on the blackwood pistol he has loaned her. He does not want to have to care for her, and the sooner he can get her back to her father in Beverley, the better. Richie has tried to look after people before and it does not end well. He remembers the dead body of Kat on the kitchen table back in York, her mouth open and her eyes wide and cold. He remembers too that whoever did this to her is still out there somewhere, although, Richie reasons, he will not have been able to track him out here. The more times they change direction the harder it will be for them to be followed.

Richie turns the little boat towards the shore where there's a mud bank between the tall reeds. A huge flock of wader birds take to the sky as they approach, there's the sound of their little wings and they fly behind the rowboat and across the orange sun. Richie rows as far as he can into the reeds until they are too thick to go any further, he clambers out and sinks in the soft mud up to his shins.

"Would it not be easier to row?" asks Nik.

"I didn't see you doing any of the rowing," he answers. This is not malicious.

"If you had asked me, I would have taken my fair turn, Sir," she says. Richie looks back at her as she clambers out of the boat towards him, he must be careful to realise this lass has grown up in a life of relative ease, perhaps the cut and thrust of working folk and the way they talk is not what she is used to.

"I was pulling your leg, lass."

"I think you should stick to calling me Nik, Mr Turpin. If anyone is to hear us talking, it will make it seem that I am your lad." He nods and smiles. She's earnest.

"Aye, lad," he says. "Careful with that pistol mind."

"I have it, Sir," she says as she steps over the side and into the mud of the reeds. "My question stands, however. Would it not be easier to row on the river towards Paull?" She is quick, he notes. It would be better if he explained his reasoning.

"We are easy to see on the river. That sailing ship passing will have seen us. The waters are dangerous too, even those who've lived a life on the Humber don't know what she'll do. We can cross into the fields here through the marshland and approach the Oak, it's on the edge of the village and when we arrive on foot we will not be noticed." She nods at this.

"Then what?"

"Years ago, I hunted here, out at Burstwick Woods, deer

mostly but there are boar there too. I sold the meat to the lads on the ships at Paull, they'd trade it with the smugglers. The big Dutch fluyts or flutes come as near as they dare to land and the cobles sail out to meet them."

"My mother said you were a highwayman."

"There's not always folk to rob, Nik. Sometimes a fellow has to steal game as well." She examines him as he speaks, watching his eyes and studying his features.

"Do you not worry, Mr Turpin, that we may have cost a family their livelihood by stealing their boat from the docks in Kingston Upon Hull?" He begins forward through the reeds.

"That is a good question, Nik. A thoughtful one too. I will endeavor to show you as we progress through our journey that we can balance our actions. Sometimes we take and sometimes we are able to give."

"Is that how a highwayman works?" She struggles on towards him with the mud going over the sides of the shoes they got from the stable lad back in Hull. Her ears have probably been filled with stories of gallant men and fine deeds, of Robin Hood and knights of the round table.

"That is how it works in my gang, aye. I paid two pennies for the shoes you wear," he says. "That's as much as that lad will make in a good while." This is the truth. Richie smiles as he feels the ground getting firmer under his feet. It is nice to have someone to talk to, but as soon as he realises this, he understands that it is a feeling he should not be allowed - he does not deserve it, not after what he has been responsible for. Any communication with this girl should be kept to a minimum with no stories or friendly comments. It's easy for Richie to make friends, too easy, he feels the pull of folk and likes to see them smile. He cannot let himself be a friend to this lass, not at all - for her sake. Being Richie Turpin's friend will only mean sorrow. Even now, there's a trap forming around him, how quickly it will on him, only the Lord knows.

Richie draws in a sharp breath as he senses a flash of

movement up ahead between the reeds. There's the immediate sensation of worry in his stomach, and the hairs on the back of his neck stand up in fear.

The moment is already here.

Through the undergrowth to the left of him, coming at speed on swift legs, is a figure. Richie's fingers go to the handle of the blackwood pistol under his coat. It's not there. That pistol swings even now from the hand of the ginger haired lass walking behind him through the reeds. He is undone. In going for the gun first, Richie does not have enough time to draw his knife either.

The figure crashes through the reeds and Richie manages to turn in time to meet him. He sees the face and wrinkles of an older man under silver hair, his eyes narrow in hatred as he gets closer. How could Richie not have heard him approach? Either the silver haired man is very good at this sort of thing, or else, Richie was distracted. The figure feigns a right hook and then brings a baton in his left hand up to connect with Richie's neck. The move is swift and precise. He has done this kind of thing before. Richie crumples forward, his chest gasping for air and the figure moves swiftly, there is suddenly a length of chord in his leather gloves. He steps over Richie as he falls and slips this around his neck, pulling it tight so that his head does not hit the mud below. It's a practiced manoeuvre and Richie is not an untrained fighter, but, next to this figure with silver hair falling over his face and his teeth barred, he looks like a child.

"You're quite a man to find, Turpin," he whispers at Richie below him whose face is already reddening up. "Quite a man, who moves as quick as you like, but I got you in the end, I said I would as well. That girl in York, she wouldn't say a word. She was a tough one." The silver haired man could pull the chord tighter if he wanted to, but there is something about this meeting that he savours. Richie grunts as his hand comes up to the thin rope cutting off the blood to his head and stopping him breathing, he is powerless and his eyes bulge. "I said I'd get you, you bastard, and I have. I've to return you where you came from."

There's the click of the flintlock on the blackwood pistol drawing back some six feet away. The silver haired man looks up and he smiles, his teeth are straight and white, well-kept and his beard trim. He grins at Nik as she stands with the pistol trained on him in unprofessional hands, her arms are shaking at the weight of it:

"I have a penny for you, son, if you're no friend to this man." Nik flares her nostrils. "Seems to me," the man adds, "that a lad would have pulled the trigger already if he was going to, or if the gun was loaded." Nik has already calculated that she does not like him.

She pulls the trigger.

The powder in the pan ignites with a flash and the silver haired man moves backwards. He knows that there could be a few seconds between the strike of the flint and the ball leaving the barrel. It could save his life. However, Richie Turpin keeps his pistol well-oiled and in order, so that it will respond when he needs it to. Couple this with Nik's inexperienced hand jerking backwards as the ball leaves the chamber and, there is an unpleasant accident for the silver haired man. The ball travels the six feet at speed and strikes the soft part of the man's neck, just above his black scarf. It takes a good chunk of his throat with it as it continues through into the reeds behind with a whizz. He collapses backward and his black gloves go to the gap in his throat, he draws in breath through a mouth that is no longer connected properly to anything, his eyes are wide when he falls.

Richie's head swims as the pressure releases from the chord around his throat. The darkness that crowded his eyesight begins to lift, he pulls the thin rope away from his neck and gasps in air then looks up to see the smoking pistol and Nik behind, her face pale in fear as she steps backwards.

Richie cannot act as quickly as he should, he staggers to his feet and draws the dagger from his belt. The silver haired man beside him fumbles under his own jacket for something. Before this hunter can draw his pistol from his chest, Richie falls upon him, the blade hammers into the soft flesh under his chest bone, just above his stomach. Richie sinks the knife in, up to his knuckles and twists, takes it out and stabs again into the stomach as he pushes down on the man with his big hand over his face, holding him as he struggles. The body bucks and kicks, twitches, and shivers. Richie keeps tight on him while he dies, and even when he stops moving, he does not get off, experience tells him to make sure the heart has stopped beating.

The reeds and the riverbank around them fall back to silence. Richie stays on top of the silver-haired man who attacked him, there's the sound of the birds above and around them, the smell of the mud and the rising heat of the autumn morning. Richie pulls himself from the dead man and slips on unsteady feet as he stands. He is muddied all up his body and there's blood on his face, he's lost his hat and his eyes are misty from the pain of being strangled so effectively. He steps forward still carrying the knife in his hand, wet with the man's blood and takes a deep breath as he examines the girl. She has dropped the pistol in front of her.

"I am sorry I brought this upon you," he whispers. This is Richie's first thought.

"Who was he?" Richie looks back at the body.

"I do not know, in truth," his voice is husky. "I have wronged many men, especially wealthy men. Seems this is the hunter who's been tracking me." He turns back to Nik.

"I killed a man," she says. "I have done a great wrong." She is a lass of conscience.

"Not so. He would have lived from that wound. I've seen men shot in the neck before and they've survived. It was me that finished him, Nik, and you saved me rather than killed him." Her face is pale and white. One of the strands of her ginger hair has come loose from the cap and falls over her face. Richie knew this little trip had been too easy so far.

"What am I to do?" she asks.

"This changes nothing, young Nik. We leave the body in the rowing boat back there, then we find his horse and we go on to the Oak Inn at Paull."

"The man needs to be buried. What of his family?"

Richie moves forward so that he blocks her way and she cannot see the body that lays half buried in the soft, watery mud behind him.

"There may be more than just him," he says. "We must keep moving." This has the desired effect. Nik leans down and picks up the blackwood pistol, then gives it to Richie by the handle. He nods in thanks.

"You just saved my life Nik Sullivan," he says with his eyes on her, "now it seems that I am in your debt."

CHAPTER SIX

The hunter with silver hair was something special. Mark Willow back in York said he was. Richie has removed the man's jacket, checked the pockets inside and taken the chain with the locket on it – there's a portrait of a lady, done in colours that are faded, meaning that it's old. There's a silver pocket watch, a pouch with a few coins and a knife with an ivory handle. Around his neck is a bone on a cat-gut necklace – this must be the monkey's finger that Mark Willow spoke of. All these are of value. His boots are well made, not new but built by someone of skill, just like the pistol that he did not have time to draw and shoot - it's hazelwood with a golden brass stock, well-polished and oiled. He was a man of something, possibly wealth, certainly wisdom, to have tracked Richie so far and in such complicated circumstances. He must have followed him to Hull somehow, inside the city, and also, seen him leave via the rowboat. Richie is sorry that he had to die, for he would have spent a lifetime honing the very skills that brought him to his death. In another moment he sees the dead body of his friend Kat on the kitchen table in the big house at York and is glad that Nik shot him, and through the neck, so Richie could stab him.

Nik carries the man's legs while Richie takes the shoulders and they dump his body in the rowboat with two wet sacks over him. Richie has the man's things in a satchel over his shoulder and where Nik seemed pale with fear before, she now just looks weak. They move on through the reeds, Richie follows the way that the silver haired man must have walked. It does not take them long to find a half-grown willow on firmer ground with a black horse tied to one of the lower branches. Like the man, the horse is well-kept. Richie approaches and runs his hand down the sleek well-clipped neckline of the beast, he sees the water skin hanging from it. This he unhooks and passes to Nik behind him. It's a fine animal, with tidy saddle bags over the rear end and well-made tack, the leather smells like it has been freshly oiled. This man was careful. Richie sees Nik is holding the water skin in her hands like she does not know what to do with it.

"Take a drink," he says.

"I don't want to," she whispers. There's a dirt path snaking back along the edge of the river, he must have followed them here and made a guess as to where they would be. If Richie had been thinking straight, he might have heard him coming.

"If he does not get the proper burial, Mr Turpin, the man may go to hell. I do not want that on my soul." Richie undoes the reins from the lower branches, even the knot the man made is professionally done.

"He has killed many, this one. He killed my friend back in York. She was a lass smaller than you, and she was unarmed as well. He strangled her because she would not tell him where I was. How many more do you think he's done for? Fifty? A hundred? If God is in his heaven at all, he would think you did a fine job this day, even though you did not kill him."

"What wrong did you do to him?" Richie looks back at her.

"I do not know," he answers. It is the truth. "I have never seen him before and I do not know how I wronged him. I think he may have been paid to hunt me down."

"You must have done a great many bad deeds."

"Aye, but I never killed a man in cold blood."

"You'll be judged for your sins," these are not Nik's words, but some rector or school master's attempt at a sermon.

"We judge ourselves in the end, Nik, and conversations such as these are for summer nights in front of the campfire or a snowy day with a warm hearth, not for mornings where we are to make good our plan to get you back to your family. Conscience is not swift, Nik, it takes time and money to develop and before your mind and your sermons run away with you, consider that you saw a man being strangled to death back there, and you saved him." Richie is delivering a sermon himself. His voice sounds unnatural to him, but not unpleasant.

"We at least have a horse to ride," she says.

"Not so," says Richie. "It's better for us to arrive on foot. This animal belongs to whoever finds it and needs it." He goes to the satchel by his side and fishes out the effects he took from the body of the silver haired man, the locket and the ring, the wallet which he has emptied of coins and he slips these into the saddle bags of the black mare. He turns the horse and tucks the reins into the saddle then slaps the backside to make it trot off down the path from where it came. "Not everything you steal belongs to you," he says as if talking to himself.

They walk the thin path that follows the reeds along the Humber River, off to the left are wide and open fields under a pale blue sky, clouds stretch out as woolen threads on a farmhouse spinning wheel. Richie makes Nik walk in front so he can keep her moving. He should feel better now that he knows the person who has followed him all this time is gone, but he is not calmed, more worried for Nik who walks a few yards ahead of him in shoes that are slightly too big. She looks back at him often and is watchful but he does not dare pass her the gun as he did previously. The little path comes closer to the bank and there's the sound of voices on the wind from way over the shelter of the high reeds, the village is closer than Richie thought. She stops and turns back to him. A big piece of her ginger hair has come loose from under her flat cap, again, and it falls to her shoulder and over her face. Richie stops in front of her.

"You'll have to hide that hair if you're to pass as a lad," he says. Nik takes off her cap and what's left of her thick ginger mop falls. There's a large chunk missing from the right-hand side down to her scalp, her fingers go to it.

"I am not ready for this, Mr Turpin. I'm a young woman. I'm not ready to face such things as I have seen, to be captured by those rough Scotsmen, to shoot a man's neck out from under his head or to travel in such a way."

"Draw your hair up in a ponytail, Nik, and hold it tight behind your head." He takes his knife. "It will have to be cut off anyway when you get home." She gathers her hair and holds it in one of her hands as Richie leans around and slips his knife through the ginger strands. Her hair blows away in the light breeze.

"Nicola Sullivan may not be ready for this," explains Richie, "but Nik is. She's shot a man in the neck, escaped from a bawdy house window, and stole a boy's shoes too." She places the cap on her head and it fits snug. Apart from her well-kept and white teeth, she could be any poor Yorkshire lad from here to Wetwang. He turns her around by the shoulder.

"Now, on you go. I'll buy you a half pint of ale once we get to the Oak."

They walk side by side down the deserted Main Street at Paull under dull skies. Along the left are East Riding mud and daub cottages that look like a strong wind would blow them over, roofs have fallen in and the walls look bent and poorly made. On the right is a sloping gravel and mud beach with a jetty. Three mid-sized cobles lay on low water that will get higher as the tide comes in. These boats are flat-bottomed, chiefly propelled by oars but have a sail too, the locals here use them for fishing, or smuggling, they're different from the big barges that Nik's father runs along the river Hull. Further down, there are row boats, some pulled right up onto the grass and others upside down and rotten with weeds growing through the planks. Nik looks up to Richie from under the peak of the cap with weary hazel eyes.

"Now you just keep your chin up," says Richie. "We're here to catch one of them cobles when the tide comes in."

At the end of the street, set back from the mud beach is a long and low building with a well-maintained thatched roof and a squat, smoking chimney. The smell of cooking and burning wood come from within. There's no sign, but this must be the pub, the Oak, that Richie spoke of. At the door, he takes off his hat as he dips his head to enter, Nik follows but does not take off hers.

It's warm inside with a big fire for cooking at one end and low beams vertical across the ceiling. Here hang tin mugs and old horse buckles for decoration, it's too early to be busy. There's a man with a dirty apron scrubbing the floor next to the bar and in the far corner someone asleep in a chair with his head leaning back against the wall. The lad doing the scrubbing looks up as Richie walks across the pub, he nods and then goes back to his work. He can't be bothered to serve.

Richie's been here plenty of times before. At the far corner, the sound of the man's snoring is loud, he has a bald head and a fat smooth face, a white shirt open to his flabby chest and his sleeves rolled up. Richie stands over him.

"Pollard," he says. The man slaps his lips together as he hears the voice. "Pollard," repeats Richie. "You'll have to wake up, it's closing time." This is not true, but it has an effect on the man. He doesn't open his eyes.

"This is the Oak," he says. "It never closes. Can't you see I'm busy?" The man's voice has a breathless quality from his meaty throat.

"Pollard," repeats Richie. Pollard pulls his head from the wall behind, and his piggy eyes fall on the man standing before him. He is about to say something when he recognises the face and the blue eyes, the great height, and the brown mousey hair. He looks at Nik with her flat cap and then back to Richie's impassive stare. His nose screws up in confusion.

"They hanged you at York," he says

"Not I," Pollard gives a false smile. He has rotten blue teeth and a double chin. He's not a pleasant man - you can tell by his eyes and the way he smells.

"You've got old," he says.

"You've grown fat." There's no warmth of friendship

between these two.

"What are you selling? This lad?" Pollard nods to Nik.

"I was wondering, have you seen MacManus?" asks Richie.

"The Irishman?"

"Aye."

"He's been dead a long time, Mr Turpin. He fell overboard and got caught in a net."

"What about Gibson?"

"That lanky bastard has done one as well."

"Who sails the cobles now, Pollard? Not just you?"

"What's wrong with just me? I've come a long way since you were last here, son. Those cobles are mine now. The Two Brothers, Freedom, The Crown. They all belong to me."

"The Crown?" he asks. He's not heard of it before. The name is perhaps a joke for a smuggling vessel.

"Aye. Now what is it you and this lad want from me? Most folk here pay a bit more respect."

"I need a favour, Pollard," says Richie. The man gives a grin and his eyes close. His bald head rests back onto the wall behind him, and he locks his fingers over his medium sized gut to return to sleep.

"I can't help you. Go back to being dead." Richie does not have time for this. They have hidden a dead body in the reeds two miles away, not far enough for his liking. Perhaps half an hour's ride up the coast is the Paull garrison and there'll be as many as fifty soldiers on the big cannons pointing out over the Humber waters. They have to get out of here as soon as possible. Richie leans his hands on both the arms of the chair that Pollard sits in, and puts his head down so he is close to the man's face and closed eyes.

"I need one of your cobles, Pollard," he whispers. "I need you to sail it for me, right round to Withernsea. There's a guinea in it for you." Pollard's eyes open.

"Twenty guineas."

"Ten."

"What are you running from? If I help you, I'll be in for it too. I'm not a bloody idiot. It's twenty guineas."

"If we leave now, I'll give you fifteen." Richie has to deliver the lass back to Beverley and they must not be stopped. He cannot get this wrong again, and his eyes are earnest as he looks dead ahead at Pollard. Richie is lucky, charmed even, for bullets have whizzed past his head previous, he has fallen from alehouse roofs to walk away, been thrown from horses, he's been clattered around the head with a rolling pin, punched, pushed and kicked more times than he could ever remember. Nothing happens to Richie Turpin - it's just the people that he cares about. This young lass with her wide hazel eyes and ginger hair is the last in a long line of those that Richie has sought to protect. He would rather die than fail again - he's going to die after this anyway and what will he need fifteen guineas for then?

Pollard sits forward and smiles, this makes him even uglier. Richie can see his eyes counting up the guineas.

"The tide is up Turpin, only a fool would set off now, we'd be run aground."

"Not a man like you Pollard, you know this river better than any bastard."

"If you're willing to take the chance then so am I," says Pollard as he forces a smile to show his rotten teeth.

Seafaring men don't take chances. Pollard may have pretended that it was a dangerous time to sail for effect only, he would never go out if he did not think there was a good chance that he would come back. They are out on the waters of the Humber with a blue sky above. The wind is good inside the grubby white canvas sail of Pollard's cobble boat. It's a simple affair. Wooden planks stretch vertical across the middle, there's a rudder at the back and a big sail on a sturdy boom. Pollard will use this boat to sail out to fluyts anchored way offshore, there, he'll pick up whatever they're smuggling, tobacco, spirits, sometimes people, guns, meat, cloth, anything. Pollard is not bothered.

Nik sits with a cloak around her shoulders and head down. Her short ginger hair no longer spills out from under her flat cap. Every time she looks up to the waters of the big river around her, she feels sick, so it's best she focuses on the slippery wooden planks of the bottom of the cobble. Richie sits at the back next to Pollard who has the rudder held lightly in one of his fat hands. They have already been on this huge river a good hour and travelled past Spurn Point – it's the slender tip of the East Riding coast. This is the sea proper now with nothing but a pale line on the horizon.

"Two hours with the wind like this, and then up to Withernsea in another two if we're lucky," says Pollard, he's telling the truth.

"If you get us there, I'll give you more than fifteen guineas, Pollard," says Richie. He has removed his hat so it doesn't get blown off and he is not looking at the cobble captain as he speaks. Pollard doesn't respond. He can sense this man is desperate. This is the way he likes them.

"I'm to make a stop, Turpin, out past the Dreadful, there's a fluyt, Dutch, I'll collect what's on offer and take you from there." The Dreadful is a sand bank off Spurn Point and a bastard bit of water to navigate if you don't know how to do it. It seems Pollard has a smuggling boat to meet. Richie looks at the fat skipper and grits his teeth in a snarl.

"You mean you were coming out anyway? And you let me beg?" Pollard shrugs his shoulders. "I've commissioned this boat, you'll sail straight to Withernsea, and no mistake. You can meet your Dutch mates another time."

"If I don't make eyes on them, Turpin, I'm a dead man. It's my job to bring the cargo ashore." Richie's lip curls up in anger. This is not what he thought the arrangement was, he's paid for the boat to take them to Withernsea and now, Pollard reveals he had to come out to the mouth of the Humber anyway to pick up whatever he's smuggling.

"You're a snake, Pollard," he whispers and his hand goes to the pistol in the holster on his chest.

"Before you think about doing anything unnatural to me, Turpin, you should consider where you are. It takes a skilled man to sail a cobble back to shore in these waters. I'm not sure that's you, nor your ginger haired lad neither."

"I could blow your foot off, Pollard, you can still sail without one." Pollard's piggy eyes glance uneasy at Richie. "I'll do a clean shot through your ankle, you'll lose a lot of blood, but if you make it back to shore in good enough time, you'd live. You'd never walk the same again though, if you'd walk at all." The words are cold. Richie has dealt with bigger and more evil scoundrels than Pollard here, and he will kill the fat sailor if it comes to it. The skipper looks past Richie to the thin mist clearing over the choppy waters, they must be way beyond the sandbank already, for there, melting out of the thin mist is the Dutch fluyt he referred to. It's huge.

The folk of East Yorkshire call them flutes sometimes, this one has three masts. They are faster than English naval ships, and they've got more guns too, which is why they operate this close to the English shore. It's like holding two fingers up at the crown.

The jibboom at the front is lined with sails flapping in the breeze and underneath is the figurehead, a woman with blonde hair painted in gaudy colours, the Humber water slaps at the keel as the ship banks, and along the side are the open gunports with cannons peeking out. There's a shout, it's the tuneful bellow of some sailor up above telling that the cobble has been spotted. There's another call and a whistle, the fore and main masts above are suddenly filled with figures climbing up into the rigging. Pollard pulls the sails on the cobble to turn it alongside the huge fluyt.

"You try any of your shite now, Turpin," he says through his barred teeth, "and you'll have a hundred Dutch guns on your arse." There aren't that many guns on the ship, but Pollard exaggerates.

"What would you care if you're already dead?" asks Richie. He realises that young Nik sits opposite, her face is aghast under the flat cap at the size of the ship slowing down as they turn. If Nik were not here, Turpin would shoot Pollard for sure, and hope either the waters of the Humber mouth or the Dutch muskets would send him to the bottom of the sea.

"You hold your bastard self, Turpin, you'll be where you need to be just as soon as I've got this done. Some of us work for a living, not like you bloody highwaymen who pull out their pistols and expect everyone to piss in their pants." Pollard is buoyed by the appearance of this big ship and he turns the cobble with the skills of an old sailor, the little boat moves broadside to the fluyt. Two ropes fall from the side of the vessel and, like spider monkeys crawling down a tree, a sailor descends each one. The first lands on the bow near Nik, he has a thick chin strap beard and no moustache, short black hair and a wide, nasty grin that shows missing teeth. The other lands beside Richie, he's thin with greasy blonde hair and narrow eyes. They have pantaloons on and no shoes because it's easier to climb without them.

"What've you got here, Pollard?" yells the one with a beard.

"Slaves to trade, lad, grab em while they're hot," booms the fat skipper. Richie tugs the pistol free of his holster, but before he can, the blonde sailor with greasy hair is on him. This is unfamiliar ground. The wood of the boat where he stands rocks on the waves underneath him, and the blond sailor leaps, pushing Richie backwards so they fall onto one of the benches of the cobble, smashing it as Richie hits the floorboards with the sailor on top. The dark haired one with the thick chin strap beard has already grabbed Nik by the shoulder, he's got her neck pulled back, and his knife at the pale, exposed throat.

"Tell the big lad to calm himself down, Pollard, or I'll spill

70

this one's insides all over the boat." His accent is thick Geordie. Any kind of robber can work these Dutch fluyts, English, Dutch, even French. Richie hears this well enough even though the blonde sailor has him pinned to the bottom of the cobble. He looks up and Nik's eyes are wide and scared under the flat cap. The sailor gets up off him with a grin. Richie looks at Pollard as the skipper ties one of the ropes to the side of his cobble to keep it level with the big ship.

"If you let this happen, Pollard," says Richie from below. "I'll come back and cut your bastard throat."

"You won't be coming back from this one, Turpin," he answers. "These lads will see you both sold or dead." There's the clank of metal on wood as something falls onto the cobble boat from above, it's a pair of iron handcuffs. The blonde sailor grabs them as Richie gets to his feet.

"Mr Strawberry is to put you in irons, fella," says the sailor who holds Nik, "unless you'd like me to slit this lad's throat, "ain't nobody out here to see." Richie considers Nik there, held tight by the rough hands of this sailor. What has he done? Where has he led this child and to what horror? "Quick about it then, laddo, give him your hands." Richie holds out his arms and the blonde man slips the metal handcuffs over both his wrists, pulls the chain tight and yanks out the key from the right side. He gives Richie a grin.

"Careful with that big one," says Pollard. "He's Dick Turpin." There's no trace of humour on his voice.

"They hanged him at York," calls the sailor with the chin strap moustache. Richie takes a breath in through his nose, and brings the front of his head down to the blonde sailor's face in a nasty butt. It's pure spite that makes him do it – and that's not like Richie at all. The blonde man staggers backwards, moaning, and his hands go to the blood streaming from his nose.

"He is nasty," says Pollard. "I did warn you."

CHAPTER SEVEN

The fluyt is too big to come into the rocky East Riding shore unless there's a port like Hull, so, they unload the rum, tobacco and whiskey into Pollard's cobble and he'll sail it to one of the villages on the east coast. It's a good business and there are men with boats, like Pollard, all the way up to Scarborough and beyond. The crown is greedy, it imposes heavy duty on imports and so smuggling is worth it. Along the way, everyone takes their cut and so everyone is happy. The villagers take a piece too, in a way, they get cheap tea and brandy and tobacco and anything else that comes their way.

Nik sits against the wall of the little cabin with her knees up to her chest. The cap is over her eyes and stray ginger hairs spill out the back. Richie sits alongside, his wrists are still in irons and his head is down. There's nothing in the room except for the wooden floor and the heavy locked door opposite. They were dragged up, off the boat and onboard, Richie did not make it easy, he kicked and thrashed out until one of the sailors took a cudgel and subdued him with a thud to the back of the head. It made his eyes swim.

They have been sitting like this for some minutes. The ship creaks around them as it rides the ocean. It's nothing like the narrow river boats that Nik sailed along the canal out of Beverley.

"I'm sorry," says Richie.

"So am I," answers Nik. Her voice is thin.

"It's my fault we're here," said Richie.

"You didn't expect this to happen, did you?"

"No."

"Then it's not your fault." This is the kind of thing her mother would say.

"I knew something unpleasant would happen to you, to us. It always does," Richie's voice is a whisper, as if it is his heart that is speaking. There's a faraway look in his eyes. He has lost the hat. "This is what always happens when I try to do the right thing and when I try to help. People get hurt." Nik looks up at him. He turns his face to meet hers, sees the freckles across her nose and cheeks and the earnest eyes.

"It is self-pity, Mr Turpin," she says. This is Nik's mother speaking through her, again. "You can find it all the way to the Orkney Isles and as far south as there is to go. It's not uncommon, but it is pathetic. You seem to suggest that those under your protection come to harm by being with you – this makes no sense, unless you believe in curses and you don't seem to me like a man who believes in either God or the devil." Nik added a few extra bits, but this is just as she heard it from her mother. Richie smiles.

"Anyone who joins my gang dies, young Nik. I'm glad you can meet your own death so merrily. It may not be quick, once they take that hat off your head and find out you don't stand up to piss, it may get worse, or it may get easier." There is no malice in Richie's tongue. It's just the truth.

"What will they do with us?"

"In truth, I don't know. The smugglers I've known only take time to fight soldiers of the crown. Everyone else can be paid off. You could end up as crew, or a whore somewhere."

"Then we have to get off this ship."

"Aye. You will have to."

"I said 'we' Mr Turpin."

"They'll shoot me, lass. I'm Dick Turpin no more, that man was hanged up at York, so I'll be worth nothing to them as ransom. I'm too long in the tooth to be of service to their captain, and I've already rattled a few of the crew, so they'll hate me. You'll be on your own." Again, there is no sorrow in his tone.

"What will I do?"

Richie's brow creases in a frown. He will have to distil everything he has learned in as few sentences as he can. There may be a man come through the door at any moment. He examines Nik's hazel eyes looking up at him. How is Richie to tell everything he knows, all these years on the road, every fight and gunshot, every death, every slip and cut and bruise that has led him to this point? He owes it to her to try.

"Never fight if you can run away. Be your best at all times. Don't assume anything, a friend will not always have your back and an enemy can save your life. Bullets don't always kill you and gunfights are all about luck and balls. Be brave. Listen to the world around you, a birdsong can tell you what time of day it is as well as the sun. Stand up for yourself too, if you think someone deserves a smack across the face, give it to them, no task is beneath you. Sometimes you have to lose so that you can fight another day, and not every fight needs to be settled, if you can get away running. Let the next person deal with the bastard who's done you wrong." Richie does not know if he has done a good job. Nik frowns with concern. "Being afraid doesn't mean you aren't brave."

"I think you've rather got ahead of yourself, Mr Turpin. You're not dead yet and neither am I yet a slave. I believe we can talk our way out of this. They are traders after all, and men at that." Richie smiles again. This is what he misses, level-headed reason. Where he is wont to go off on flights of poetry and drama, Nik here is grounded in the real world, as the ship around them banks to the left over the waves below.

"We'll try that first, of course."

"What can you offer?"

Richie thinks.

"I am an excellent robber, especially a highwayman. I'm good at cards and I can plough a field." Nik sighs. Even though he is much older, there is a naivety about Richie sometimes.

"My father is a merchant You know this, Sullivan of Beverley and he has connections in the port of Hull. He could send much bigger boats out to this ship than your fat friend Pollard could muster. He could pay better prices too. I'm sure the captain would rather expand his operation, perhaps we could see this as opportunity rather than our imminent death. Would you agree with me, Mr Turpin?" He feels better. Nik is razor sharp.

"You've got a brain in there," he says. "See that it doesn't run off with your heart." Now it is Nik's turn to lean forward.

"You rescued me from the Scots in Kingston Upon Hull, Mr Turpin, I am in your debt." He shakes his head.

"Not so. You killed a man for me and I agreed to bring you back for your mother, it is her who owes me, if we make it back."

"What did she promise you?"

"I would rather not say, young Nik." Richie does not want to explain it is a bullet.

"Well then," says Nik. "We should see that we get back there for you to claim your reward."

The door opposite them opens and the sailor with a chinstrap beard steps in. There's another man behind him with longer brown hair and round glasses on a ratty nose. Richie can see that the man with the glasses is thin, slightly gaunt, and better kept than the other sailor. He is clearly something aboard this ship.

"I'm the boatswain. You're not the kind of cargo we usually deal with," he begins. His accent is foreign, Dutch perhaps. "The men tell me you are Dick Turpin," he says.

"He was hanged at York," says Richie.

"Yes. I am aware. I have no real use for you on my ship and I'm afraid I can see no profit from having you aboard. Indeed, you should not have been brought on at all. There are a couple of choices you have. Stay here and do your duties on the ship, walk off when we next dock and say no more about this, or, we can put you overboard now. We're about a mile and a half out of Robin Hood's Bay. This is a working vessel."

"Are you the captain?" asks Richie.

"The captain has more important duties than this. I am one

of his officers. Have you made your decision?"

"I would wish to speak to you, Sir." It's Nik, as brave as someone who comes from wealth dares to be. "My father is a powerful merchant from Beverley, a town along the river from Hull. He may be a good business partner for you. This is why I am here." The boatswain wrinkles his thin face at this lad with a cap over his eyes.

"You're a woman," he says. "Take off your cap." Nik does so and looks up at him. He sees the prominent cheekbones and the hazel eyes, her freckles, and the look of mid defiance on her face. He sighs. "This complicates things. Who are you?"

"Sullivan, Nik Sullivan of Beverley."

"How old are you?"

"Sixteen."

"You are running from something you two, no doubt." Nik is about to explain but Richie's big right hand, still in the iron handcuff goes out to touch her, to stop her talking. "What are you running from?"

"That's none of your business," answers Richie.

"I don't have time for this," says the man with the round glasses that rest on the tip of his nose. "Mr Sykes, go back on deck and gather some of the lads, the big ones, then, come back down here and grab the tall gentlemen. Toss him overboard. We'll keep the girl for the captain." These orders are delivered as smoothly as if he were asking for the mainsail to be hoisted aloft or the deck to be washed down. Mr Sykes, the man with the chinstrap beard, nods.

"I'll not go easy," says Richie from where he sits. "Your men will be hurt, very much so." Mr Sykes looks at his superior. It is true that this man was troublesome to get into the little jail.

"How about this," says the boatswain to Richie, "if you don't cause us too much bother, we'll go easy on the girl here."

"You'll do whatever to her as soon as I'm gone." The

boatswain looks down on this man with his knees up to his chest and blue eyes under brown hair. He is not wrong, the captain will do whatever he likes with the girl.

"Very well then. Mr Sykes, bring more men. Don't shoot him either, I don't want any blood on this boat. Let's have it done right now, we'll be near Scarborough soon enough and there'll be real work to do."

The sailor with the chin strap beard has gathered perhaps ten men, three of them have wooden battens, he carries a mallet in one of his hands, the rest stand outside the little cabin in the corridor. Richie and Nik get to their feet as these men enter the room.

"Make it to the Golden Ball in Scarborough," whispers Richie. "Explain who you are, and what has happened and they will see you get back to your family." Nik behind him grips onto his tunic.

"What if I can't get there?"

"Do the best you can, Nik," he answers.

With that, the sailor steps in and makes a low swing for Richie with the mallet. It catches him on the calf and stings. This is the way this is going to be. Richie charges at him with his hands in irons and pins him to the wall by his neck. He's twice as big as the little man and left alone would probably kill him. There's the blur of movement, as other men rush in, and like ants, the sailors peel him off the man with the chinstrap beard, there are kicks and punches, batons are used on Richie and Nik stands at the end of the cell with her hand over her mouth in fear. The bravado she felt previous, with the thought that her father would go into business with these people, seems the imaginings of a child.

They drag Richie from the cell and up the stairs, there is crashing as he fights them, all six foot four of him, his big arms can't be held by one man alone. He yells also, and his booms ring out across the ship.

Alone in the cell, Nik squats down and finds the flat cap, fits it to her head and stands up again. There is no expression on her face. She'll go down fighting like Mr Turpin if she has to. She is hardening inside, there are only so many times a body can be afraid before it starts to toughen.

Richie does not quite know what is happening as they drag him on deck. There are rough hands on his body, some yank at his shoulders and others grip his legs to stop them thrashing as they move in the moonlight. There are shouts from some of the sailors, their rough musical voices call him names or obscenities in the wind. The lights from lamps flash above. There's no time for him to get his bearings amid the elbows that knock him or the wooden baton that bruises his stomach. Another strong hand grips his neck. He feels himself being lifted and the shouts of the sailors are loud around him as they chant some sort of working song, Richie's stomach turns and they rock him and then, they heft him over the starboard bow and into the clear night sky.

For a second, Richie is falling and flailing through this mist of sea air and next, he crashes into the cold water ten feet below.

It's that easy to die.

It's night. Richie is soddened with water and his limbs feel heavy as he opens the cottage door at North Burton. He knows this is not real. There's rushing in his ears. Outside it must be raining and he steps inside the little cottage just as it was all those years ago. There is Nana sitting by the fire in her chair with the big armrests. Next to her and sitting upright is Richie's sleek black whippet dog, Bess. She wags her thin tail but does not stand when she sees him. There's a sliver of moonlight from the window outside on the stone floor, and the glow from the fire does not reach far in the little room.

"I'm sorry I'm late," says Richie.

"For the first time in your bloody life, Richie Jackson, you're too early. There's nothing cooked or ready for you." Nana's hand goes out to rest on Bess's thin head and the dog looks at him with wide and mournful eyes.

"I'm cold, Nana. I'm ready to come home."

"We're all cold in this house, that's how it is in the East Riding, Richie. I thought a lad would be used to it by now. You get yourself back out there and come back when it's time."

"It's time now, Nana," he says. Richie's eyes are moist with tears. His jacket drips on to the stone floor of the cottage as he stands there.

"It's not nighttime yet, Richie," says Nana. "It's not dark outside, it's not time to come in."

"I've done enough for the day," he answers.

"Have you really, Richie?" asks Nana. "Have you done everything you had to do? Really?" Richie feels the water dripping from his hair and down his nose. "What about that young ginger lass you've left there? What's to become of her?"

"I've done as much as I can, Nana. I have. I got her out of Hull and I rescued her and I couldn't have foreseen this. It's best she's without me. Look at all the people I've hurt, I've done more wrong than good. It's best that I leave her there." Nana has that look about her, even in the dim light from the fire, that look that tells you she's about to go off on one. She'll have been storing it up all day.

"We've all of us hurt people, Richie. A body can't get through all its days doing good things to everyone. You've done as a lad has to do sometimes."

"It was me that got the Pearlman shot," he says. "It was me that robbed a hundred coaches from here to as far south as Brighton. It was me that split lips and broke noses. It was me that gathered others around me, friends I thought, and it was because of me that they died or got hung or shot or stabbed or worse. All of em gone, Big Clegg, Gibbo, Finger and even Kat. They left me here, still alive, like I was a ghost."

"What a load of shite," says Nana. "You're just like any bloody man. You think everything happens in the world because of you. There's still a lass out there, a young lass too who needs you."

"I've done all I can for her, Nana," Richie repeats. "She'll have to get by on her own."

"So you're sorry for all the folk you think have died because of you, who haven't, and there's someone you could help and you won't. Your head's clogged up like a drain full of leaves, Richie Jackson, come over here and I'll give you a clip round the bloody ear to fetch them out." Nana is beginning to get into her stride. Bess's ears go flat to her head in fear as the old woman carries on. "You shouldn't be coming in here, dripping wet when there's a job not finished. That's not how we Jackson's are, lad. We do a job right and we do it till the end, that's how it is."

"I'm not a Jackson," says Richie. He was born a bastard on the cowshed floor of North Burton house some forty-four years ago, to a woman who's second name was Turpin. Old Pennyman, the owner of the estate, wanted her to die, some say, because the bastard was his son, but Nana took the baby as her own, she brought him up as her own too.

"You've more piss in you than a pig shed floor, you're my lad alright. I raised you and taught you, and we've been through this a hundred times already," Nana is in mid bellow, she can still blow hotter than this if she has too.

"I just want to come home," whispers Richie again. His arms feel light and his head swims, he feels like he is turning over and over as he stands there, his eyes smarting and water running down his coat and off his hair onto the stone floor of the little cottage.

"It'll be time to come home when the job's done, Richie. You've never been early for anything in your life and you shan't be early for this neither. Now, there's a lass that needs you, and once that's done, once it's sorted and she's home safe, then you can come home. Me and Bess, we'll be here, we'll not be going anywhere and there's a warm bowl of milk for you and some chicken bones to suck on before you go to bed."

He tries to raise his head to look at her but there's a force on the back of his neck pushing him down. He feels his stomach turn again and cold all around him, as if he is swallowed up by ice.

"You get back out there, Richie," yells Nana as he steps backwards through the cottage door in North Burton. "Don't come back neither until you've got the job sorted," the old woman yells. He closes the front door.

Richie breaks the surface of the North Sea and gasps in gulps of air, his chest and heart struggle at the cold and his legs kick at the water below him. Beside and above, there's the dark vessel he's just been thrown off stretching upwards, with the moon like a silver coin in the sky. He can feel himself slowing down in the water. Perhaps it wasn't for the best that Kat taught him to swim off Scarborough beach, most if not all of the men on board the ship above him would have drowned by now. He looks up at the smooth side of the vessel and Nana's words ring in his ears. Even in death she isn't quiet. Richie is not sad that he's seen her, at least he knows she is waiting for him, and his Bess too. The saltwater burns his eyes as he treads water, he may see Nana quicker than he thinks, for he cannot climb up the side of the ship, even if he wasn't in such a state.

There's movement above him. Something falling in the silvery light of the moon. It hits the water with a gentle splash and Richie can see a line stretching up to the side of the ship above. A rope. He has no other choice but to grab it, with his last bit of effort, he fits the loop on the end round his foot under the water and it begins to move. With steady pulls, Richie feels himself being hauled up out of the water, he sees the rope some ten foot above his head, tight over the side.

This is being done in secret.

Nearer the edge of the fluyt, a rough hand stretches out for Richie to hold and he grabs it, another goes to the scruff of his neck and they haul him on board. He cannot stand and so Richie clatters to his knees in front of the three men who look down on him. The one in the middle has a lamp but the rest of the deck is silent. Richie can see a bald man in the middle.

"Open his shirt," he says. A sailor steps forward and pulls open Richie's wet jacket. "The Turpin that I knew has a bird scar just above his nipple, on the right." The man tugs and pulls at Richie's undershirt to show his chest, he moves the lamp forward to see. There it is, the bird scar that Richie has carried with him since he nearly fell into a fire as a little boy. The officer steps back.

"It's him," he says. "You don't remember me, Mr Turpin, but I remember you. I'm repaying an old debt. I can keep you out the way, but I'm not sure I can do anything for the lass, the captain's got wind of her." Richie looks up from the deck at a man he does not remember.

For the time being, this will have to do.

CHAPTER EIGHT

Nik sits on a chair with arm rests and a cushioned seat. She keeps her eyes fixed on the polished wood of the table in front of her and her lips are closed tight. There's a lamp burning behind a man who she believes is the captain. He has grey swept back hair and a chubby pock marked, entitled face under piggy eyes. With fat fingers, he takes a sip on a wine glass and sets it down. The ship banks to one side beneath her. Two weeks ago, if this had happened to Nicola Sullivan of Beverley, she would have screamed and cried and wept, as she did for the Scots. This version of Nik, who has shot a man to death, is getting better at holding in her fear. After they dragged Richie away, a polite lad with blond hair led her up to the deck, she heard the shouts from the stern and the splash as something hit the water far below. The man showed her down into the bowels of the ship and to a room, and this smart polished table. She has lost her cap.

"Do you know where you go for a piss on board a vessel such as this?" asks the captain. It's unnecessarily crude language for a young lass.

"Why would that information be considered important, Sir?" she asks in her best Sunday voice.

"I can find out what kind of girl you are by your answer."

"Over the side," she answers. She looks up. He is uglier when he grins.

"Looks like the spider caught a fly," he says. One of his back teeth is silver as he smiles. "What's your name?"

"Nicola Sullivan, of Beverley, you may know my father, he imports goods down the river Hull." Without the cap to hide under, she feels like the same girl who grew up in that house on Toll Gavel, the one who kept her eyes down when others were speaking and hid her hatred. The captain cocks his head as he examines her more closely.

"The boatswain said you were sixteen."

"Aye," she answers. He grins. "My father is a powerful man, Sir and you could do well to trade with him. I imagine you could fetch a better price for your goods with him than with the rough cobble men."

"I don't care who your father is, miss. Have you been with a man before?" Nik swallows. She looks at the table in front of her, at the folded napkin and the knife and fork ready to eat. Her teeth grit in fear. "Did you hear my question, girl?" asks the captain.

"No, Sir. I have not."

"Then you're a virgin." She wonders what has happened to Mr Turpin and imagines him sinking below them into the dark and cold waters of the North Sea with his eyes open in the pitch black. There is nobody to save her now. "I'm not a rough man, you understand, Nicola. Not rough at all. In fact, I'm more a tender sort. I'll explain. There's a place for you here in my bed this night, or you'll find yourself back on the floor of that cell. Which is it to be? Understand also, that you're worth a lot more unbroken as you are, so I'll not be forcing myself on you. It'll just be a bit of warmth against the cold sea air. Do you understand?" She looks up at him.

"I will go back to the cell, Sir," she answers. The captain gives her a knowing grin.

"I can see you're a well brought up young lady. A few nights on the floor in the brig will bring you to your senses. You'll not be hurt, but I'll have Mr Sykes tap you around a bit." She keeps her eyes fixed on the napkin. She wonders what 'tap you around' means.

"I'm not sure what you want from me captain, but I'm sure that my father would pay well for my safe return. Indeed, that man you threw overboard was under my father's employ to return me to his safety."

"The man who said he was Dick Turpin?"

"Yes."

"He's not going to get paid now, is he?"

"No, but someone can be."

"I think you've rather missed the point here, girl. Whatever your father could offer me would not offset the inconvenience it would cause. My ship, the Oliver does not dock on English shores, it's not an English ship. So you see, it's best if you put any thought of getting home soon out of your mind, for the time being. The best you can do is look after yourself."

"What will happen to me?"

"Depends. There are men in Rotterdam who would pay good money for an unspoiled girl such as yourself. Are you educated?"

"I can read and I know the scriptures."

"They'd pay more for a taste of the foreign."

"You would sell me?"

"Perhaps. It all depends on how favorably you treat me. I can make this as easy or as unpleasant as you wish." The Dutch captain taps his fat finger on the tablecloth. She's to remember what Mr Turpin taught her, if there's a situation then you must take charge of it.

"I would like a night to think on your offer, kind Sir," she says. "I have had a series of terrible shocks, been kidnapped, and threatened and now kidnapped again. If I am to preserve what modesty and dignity I have left, then I need time to think about my predicament." The captain's face becomes serious at this.

"Are you a lady?" he asks. He senses, as she looks at him with her hazel eyes, that there is more to this girl in her calm sense and her smooth stare.

"I'm not a lady, captain, but I would ask that you treat me as one." Nik is channeling her mother. Her shoulders are back and she is breathing evenly through her nose, in a steady and controlled manner, although she is frightened.

"Very well then. I'll see you returned to the cell, and I'll ask Mr Sykes to be lighter than he usually would be." This is a veiled threat. Nik answers as her mother would despite this:

"Thank you, captain."

The man who pulled Richie out of the North Sea says his name is Jansen, in the darkness he has taken him to the gunner's store. It's not the nicest place on board a big ship like this, but one of the quietest unless they need men to load the heavy cannons that stick out the side of the Oliver. There's the smell of gunpowder too and the acrid stink of oil. If there's a spark down here then the whole side of the boat could be blown apart. It's not as if it hasn't happened before aboard other ships. That's why Jansen has the key and keeps it on his person at all times. The man helps Richie to sit down against the bulkhead and squats in front of him. In the darkness he whispers, the accent rings of the East Riding:

"I don't know how I'll get you off this ship, Mr Turpin," he says in hushed tones. Richie's face is pale. He's sicked up seawater many times and he looks washed out, even in the darkness.

"Where's the ship bound?"

"At dawn we'll make drops at Robin Hoods Bay, then Scarborough and further up north. By tomorrow afternoon we'll be all empty after the last run at Middlesbrough, and then it'll be back across to Rotterdam to fill up again. It's the run we make every two weeks." Richie feels ill. If they get to Rotterdam then there's a good chance that he and Nik will never see home again. "Take a glug on this," says Jansen. He passes Richie a little bottle of something and he takes a swig, it's rum mixed with water and it burns all the way down his throat. They call it grog.

"I need to get off this ship," he whispers. "I have to get the girl home, somehow."

"This ship won't dock till we get back to Holland, Turpin, and there's not a sailor on board that can change that."

"Why did you save me, what was it, Jansen?"

"Aye. You'll not remember, I was just a lad myself."

"What did I do?"

"It was Pocklington way, ten years since. A hot summer. You stopped a cart that I was on. You waved us down with your pistol and robbed the constable of the peace who was taking me to York quarter sessions for pinching a pie. You gave me a shilling and told me to run and make something of my life, and I did. I saw that bird scar and I knew you were Dick Turpin. What did you do with the constable?"

"I don't remember," says Richie.

"Did you shoot him?"

"I wouldn't have in cold blood."

"Point is, Mr Turpin. I made it all the way to Kingston Upon Hull and I got on board a ship. I would never have done that without your help. Now I'm helping you."

"It's the circle," says Richie.

"What's that, Sir?"

"Good deeds and bad all have a way of coming back, like a wheel." Richie is fading.

"Aye. You'll have to rest here till the morning. Then I can bring you something."

"It will have to be tonight, I cannot wait." The strength is leaving him, he struggles to sit up.

"Trust me, Mr Turpin, you wouldn't want to go crawling around this ship in the dark, it's bad enough in the daytime. I can get you off, no bother, but it will be at Rotterdam when we unload, there's no other chance. You'll have to wait."

"No," says Richie. "The girl."

"There's nothing you can do, what will happen is out of your hands. The captain will have got hold of her."

"If she's hurt, I don't know what I'll do." Jansen swallows in the darkness of the gunner's store for he knows the kind of man the captain is.

"She'll survive, Mr Turpin. You just be thankful you have your life."

Jansen locks the door as he leaves and Richie sits in the

darkness. His chest rasps at the seawater he swallowed and his body is bruised from the punches and kicks from the seamen as they tossed him overboard. He sees Nana again in the darkness, not a dream, just a memory.

Richie will not let this girl down.

Mr Sykes marches Nik down the corridor holding her arm too tight in one hand and a lamp in the other. She stumbles at times to keep up with the pace as he navigates twists and turns, goes down another corridor and finally, to the little room she'd been locked in. He shoves her inside and steps inside after, closes the door and hangs the lamp up on a hook from the roof. She presses her back up against the far wall in the tiny cabin. There's the smell of his sweat and his foul breath. They are alone and the light from the lamp makes shadows in the corners.

"The captain said you weren't to hurt me," she whispers.

"I won't," grins the man. "I won't damage the goods at all, but it's my job to tender you up a bit. You should be more receptive to his charms, Miss, it's a lot better than having someone like me force themselves on you."

"Don't come near me," she says in her mother's best voice, all stern like a school mistress. "I know how to defend myself, Sir." Nik has some school in the art of fighting and what's known as pugilism. The Frenchman, who is her bastard uncle, showed her how to swing a punch and they took turns belting hay bales back in Beverley. It's not going to help. Mr Sykes approaches with a nasty glint in his eyes.

"We'll start with a little kiss shall we, Miss? Have you ever kissed a man before? I'm all tongues me, and I've got roaming hands as well, and my fingers like to dig in." Nik feels her hands clench in fists. She knows he is making her more afraid than she should be. So what if he kisses her, so what if he does more, she'll not be dead and she'll live to see the morning. Isn't that what Mr Turpin said? Sometimes you have to lose to fight again another day, and there's no shame in that. Mr Sykes is deliberately taking this slowly.

"Do you like to have your hair pulled, Miss, or should I give it a gentle stroke - doesn't look like you've got much of it left." He steps a little closer and she is roughly the same height. She sees the patchy chin strap beard and the gaps in his teeth, the pock holes on his forehead and sores on his arms.

"I will strike you, Sir, should you come any closer." He grins at this.

"Do you want to take your clothes off before we get started or shall I pull them off as we go." Nik feels her nostrils flare and her eyes begin to water. At least with the Scotsmen she was worth something, even if they were going to kill her. "Just so as you know," says Mr Sykes, "I'll not mark you this night, and you'll be as unbroken as you say you are, but there are all manner of unnatural things that a man can do a miss, and you'll find out all of them, just so you'll know how tender and friendly the captain can be, as opposed to a right horrible so-and-so like me." Nik takes a deep breath in. She can cry as much as she likes, she can sit down and weep, but this man will still do what he is going to do to her. He steps forward. He's enjoying it. Nik braces herself.

There's a light tap on the door.

Mr Sykes turns and huffs. He steps back and puts the key from his pocket to the lock, turns it and then opens the door slightly so he can look out at whoever is there. Like a cat jumping through a hole, a big hand grabs him by the neck and shoves him backwards. The tall frame of Richie Turpin pushes him through and pins him against the wall. The sailor struggles - he's not a pushover, and so Richie brings his other hand up in a fist to clobber him across the temple. There's a hollow thud as Mr Sykes collapses against the bulkhead, his body slides to the floor.

Richie is pale and still wet through. His angry eyes find Nik in the light from the flickering lamp swinging above them. She is frightened but steady with it. There are those who would have flown into hysterics already at their situation. Richie steps back and closes the door gently, his hand goes to the key and he locks it. He's glad she's calm, for Richie cannot afford to have her make any noise. He sees the flat cap that must have fallen from her head, and he stoops to pick it up as he approaches her.

"Put it on," he says. She takes it from him and looks confused through the fear. "Scrape back what's left of that hair and put it on." Richie's voice is gravel. She fits the cap on her head and he pulls the tip of it down lower, so it almost covers her eyes. "I need my Swift Nik," he says. It is the first time he has called her so. "We must help each other, you, and me. I need you not to break, I need my Nik to be strong, like I know you are." He sees the hazel eyes harden under the cap. Richie has used this line before, he's used it on those he needs to fight alongside him, or steal with him, or ride with him and it usually works. He is lending her his confidence – even if he's as scared as she is. Richie knows he's going to die anyway, Nik here has got a whole life ahead. Her jaw clenches when she understands the words and feels the steel of their meaning, he can see her shoulders go back and her chest inflate. "I need you, Nik. If we are going to get off this ship, I need you. Are you there?" The voice has raw spirit within:

"Aye, I'm with you, Mr Turpin."

"You stay close," he whispers.

There's a dull boom from somewhere off in the ship. Then another explosion, fiercer than the first. Then another. The boat rocks to one side with the thunder. The noise does not seem real but Richie is calm. He turns the key in the lock and looks back at Swift Nik with a tiny grin as he steadies himself from falling over.

"A spark must have got into the powder room," he whispers. "Stay close to me."

In the dark corridor, the boat is already tipping at an angle. They can hear shouts and yells from above and around them - there's another bang, Nik hears the snapping of wood as they move along the passageway to the bow of the boat. It's pitch black and she grabs onto Richie's wet jacket in front of her. The ship creaks around them. She is afraid like she has never been afraid before, like she's in the bowels of hell itself. A lamp light appears and moves towards them at speed, it's two sailors approaching with their faces and eyes twisted in worry as they come. Richie steps to the side and shields Nik with his hand behind as the sailors dash straight past them - there is nothing worse than a fire on a boat, they will not even notice these two as they run towards the sound and the acrid smell of smoke. Sailors don't swim, after all.

At the end of the dark corridor there's a ladder, Richie makes his way up it first and Nik follows. There are shouts from the sailors behind and above as they race across the ship to see the damage, loud bellows sound as men yell in Dutch and English. The boat around them continues to lurch. When they get to the next level, there's the smell of animal fat, and Richie pulls Nik into the darkness of the deserted galley, they look upwards through a grate to the cloudy dawn above them where weak light shines from a grey sky – it's already morning. The boat is moving, tipping backward, and sinking into the freezing ocean.

"We'll get through this," says Richie, and his voice is earnest. She believes him, even if he does not. Richie has experience on his side and knows that it's better not to be scared stiff by the world – whatever is going to happen to you will happen anyway. His words calm Nik. It's not just his presence that makes her feel better, it's the cap she wears low over her eyes and his belief in her. He repeated that he could not do this without assistance. This has not happened to Nik before. She's always been a child, with her hair done up in a bow, told not to speak at all, like one of the pale mannequins in Roseweather's dress shop in Beverley. She has been blank, vapid, and bland. Not now. She is red blooded and brave, her fingers curl in a fist as she stands in the deserted galley of a Dutch smuggling ship that is sinking down into the sea with sailors crawling all over it like ants.

In the pale grey of the morning, they clamber up another ladder and are on deck. The wind is fresh and the dawn clouds roll above them in a brooding sky. The bow of the ship is rising slowly as the stern is swallowed back into the sea, Richie looks over his shoulder and sees the mast overhead bending and creaking as it moves at an angle it is not supposed to be at. Nik loses her footing on the slippery deck below and Richie grabs her by the collar of her cloak to steady her. Up ahead, past the rigging on both sides of the ship is something that Richie is heading for - he noticed the jolly boat at the bow when they threw him overboard, and it hangs over the side of the ship on winches called davits, one has come loose so the little rowboat dangles with one side out of sight. There's a shout from behind them as they approach the escape vessel at the bow.

"Turpin!" Richie turns to look over his shoulder and there, running across the deck at them is Jansen, the sailor who pulled him from the water the night previous. He and Nik have reached the jollyboat and there is nowhere for them to go but overboard. Richie hits the crank handle and the boat falls from the davits into the water ten yards below where it lands with a splash.

"You bastard, Turpin, this is your doing." It's Jansen, yelling as he makes his way up the deck of the sinking ship.

"Can you swim?" asks Richie to Nik next to him. She shakes her head. Her eyes are wide with fear and her skin is white, the lips pale. With both his big hands, Richie grabs her by the shoulders, turns, and flings her over the side. There's a pause and a splash before she hits the water. This was how Richie learned to swim as well.

"I saved you Turpin," yells Jensen as he gets closer. The

mast further to the stern of the ship snaps under the pressure, it collapses backwards dragging sails and rigging with it. Figures dash up the deck of the ship. It seems that more of them are now thinking about getting off. "I bloody saved you, Turpin," calls the man again.

"You didn't save me, sailor," shouts Richie. "It was your own guilt you didn't want to live with." Before this earnest, barefoot sailor from Pocklington can get to him, Richie leaps over the side of the Dutch fluyt and into the water as well. He didn't expect to get wet again so soon. They won't follow. Like Nik, none of the sailors will be able to swim.

It's been about an hour, and the early morning mist has enveloped Richie and Nik as they sit and shiver on the little jollyboat. Ships carry them because it's not always possible to dock. They sometimes hang over the side like this one did, or sometimes they just sit on deck. Richie swam to Nik as she flailed in the freezing water of the North Sea and had to clamp his arm around her to stop the thrashing with the panic. It was a struggle to get her onto the little boat a few yards away and then more of a struggle to get himself on. He is more than exhausted. In the cold morning they drift through the mist and, against the backdrop of the noise and explosions of an hour before, the world is eerie and quiet. The sea is calm around them.

Nik leans over the side and retches sea water from her stomach, the salt burns as it comes up through her nose and mouth. She wipes her face with a wet sleeve but does not remove the cap that is tight to her head. It's a miracle it stayed on. Richie sits on the bottom of the vessel with his back against the side and his knees bent. This is the fourth boat they have been on. He grins.

"You did well," he says.

"I couldn't swim."

"Nobody swims first time, the main thing is not to drown."

"I would have drowned if you hadn't been there. Then again, I wouldn't have been in the water if you hadn't thrown me overboard." She is learning a little of the rough humour of normal folk. Nik looks down on Richie and his face is very pale, with bags under his eyes and colourless lips. "Will they all die, those sailors?" she asks.

"Lots of them will, aye. I think we're so close to shore that some of them will make it."

"What happened?" Richie struggles to sit up on the bench that runs across the middle of the jolly boat, he reaches down to take up one of the oars.

"Have you heard of a pirate called Henry Morgan?"

"Yes," nods Nik, "who hasn't?"

"It was New Year's Day, so I heard, 1669, just off the coast of Cow Island in the Caribbean." Richie fits the first oar into place at the side of the boat and reaches for the second. "Morgan had a fleet of more than a thousand men on nine ships and, in the afternoon, he called a meeting for all the captains aboard his flagship, the Oxford. All of them, and their officers, gathered in the Captain's quarters aboard the Oxford to toast the coming battle. They were set to raid the next morning, but after many drinks and revelry, and late into the evening when they needed lamp light to bring their wine to their lips, a spark found its way into the powder room. The blast killed more than two hundred men, but Morgan himself survived. That's why the Spanish thought he was in league with the devil." Nik likes stories. They drive away fear. Richie now rows the boat, due east according to the weak sun blurred out by the mist. He's not sure if he's going the right way, but it will calm Nik if she thinks they are moving to safety.

"Is that what happened?" she asks.

"They locked me in the powder room after they dragged me out the sea. Any lad who knows about black powder can make a decent fuse." Nik gives him a weak smile but this is not the same, dramatic, and frail creature that he picked up less than a week ago. Nik has gone through trials to say the least. She's becoming tough.

"I am sorry for those sailors, Mr Turpin," says Nik. She still has conscience and means the sailors who would have tumbled overboard into the freezing water.

"That's a Christian way of thinking. They were going to do you wrong, and we did it to them first. That's not a sin. It's called surviving." She looks off into the mist.

"Where are we going now?" he smiles at her and thinks back to the vision he saw of Nana under the waves. There is no doubt that without this, he would have slipped under.

"I'm hoping we're near the coast," he says.

"Then what?"

"When we make landfall, I'll get you home. This time, there'll be nothing in our way, I hope."

"Thank you, Mr Turpin."

"You're welcome, Swift Nik."

"You know that mother spoke of you, from time to time, when she knew it was just the two of us." Richie's ears prick up at this, but he does not show any outward interest. He has thought of Elizabeth Sullivan many times over the years.

"What did she say?"

"She told me she loved you." Nik is not afraid of telling him the truth. As far as she is aware, Richie Turpin is unable to be hurt, especially by words, he is too wise. Richie stops rowing, but his hands grip the oars a little tighter. For a brief second his brain thinks this might be the truth, but he's too old to be tricked by Elizabeth Sullivan who was Pike through the lips of her daughter. She did not love Richie, the world would not have allowed it. Whatever Nik heard would have been a story for a mother to tell her daughter, about her free days before she was trapped as a married woman.

"She is a fine lass, your mother. There is much of her in you."

"She is not what she once was. Do you want me to tell you

about her?" Richie goes back to rowing. He has thought of her and longed for her also. He does not want to know about the woman, for he does not want to fuel any imagination in him. On early mornings when he cannot sleep, he imagines he is with her, next to her, even now he can see the sweet curve of her neckline and her smooth shoulders, her hazel eyes looking at him, calm and playful. The dream does not become old, so, he does not want to hear of her.

"I knew her once, I don't need to know her again."

"She says that you loved her back, as a man should, and she knew it. She says you were afraid of it, and that's the reason you never returned for her." Richie answers too quickly.

"I was afraid for her. I was a wanted man, if I had returned, she would have been in danger."

"So you did love her."

"Aye." Richie tries not to look at Nik with her eyes covered by the peak of the cap. She has unpicked him.

"Perhaps that would have been better for her in the long run, Mr Turpin. The man she married, my father, Sullivan, he's a coward."

"He moves heaven and earth to get you back, Nik."

"Is he here himself?" she asks.

"I'll not defend him, lass. He's a man born rich, the kind I've robbed all my life."

"My mother hates him. She will not say but I can see the distaste on her face when he goes on and on, and the way he speaks to her is a disgrace. I know what my father is, Mr Turpin. He beats his dogs and his horses and his wives, mistresses and daughters too, and when he is too tired or drunk to do so, he will have others do it in his stead. He will want me back only to save face, if he could allow me to die, he surely would." The mist from the ocean thickens around them, and the waters are still as they drift. She has a faraway look on her young face. Richie can see what she keeps hidden somehow.

"Did he hurt you?"

"Yes, Mr Turpin, he hurt me on many occasions." She is not accusing her father, more stating a fact.

"And your mother, how does she fare at his hand?"

"I would say worse than I do." Again, there is no blame applied to the statement, it is just the truth. Nik has been through much in the last few days, it gives the reality of her life perspective.

"You will have to do something about that, my Nik, when you get home." Nik looks across the jollyboat at Richie Turpin sitting opposite. The cold sea mist is around them, freezing and without humour.

"Thank you, Mr Turpin," says Nik, "I certainly shall."

"But a word of caution."

"Aye?"

"There's no washing away blood once it's spilled, better not to spill it at all, for the damage will be on you and not on him." Nik focuses her eyes on Richie Turpin. He seems to get right to the heart of the matter and without the mess of emotion.

"I mean to kill him, Mr Turpin," she says. He nods and his eyes do not judge her. His is the voice of reason and wisdom also.

"Revenge will not bring you peace, I can promise that, and his death will be more a problem for you that it will be for him."

"It's not for me, Sir, it's for the good folk of our house."

CHAPTER NINE

The mist gets worse around them, so much so that Richie can no longer guess the position of the sun. He might as well save his strength. It is still early in the morning and, hopefully once this sea roke has swept past, he will be able to see the sun and know which way to go. Richie is dressed only in his shirt and long pants and has rolled the sleeves up so he can row better. Nik will be warmer – she's wearing the brown sackcloth waistcoat done up tight with a rope belt, she lost the cloak but she's still got the lace up shoes they bought from the stable lad.

"Do you want me to take over, Mr Turpin?" asks Nik. She looks pale in the mist but the flat cap covers any fear or worry that might be in her eyes. That's why Richie likes her to wear it – so folk can't see how frightened she is, and so she doesn't have to show them.

"There's no point. Without the sun, I can't be sure we're going in the right direction."

"Shall we just wait, then, Mr Turpin?"

"We shall."

"How far away do you think we are from the coast?"

"I'm no sailor, of course, young Nik, but these smuggler boats come as near as they can to drop off their cargo."

"We could be near Bridlington, or Hornsea," she says.

"As long as we're not as far north as Scarborough."

"Why not Scarborough. Mother says it is a fine town with fresh and healthy sea air for a body."

"I'm known well in that place, among certain types."

"Am I not rude enough for your associates, Mr Turpin?"

"I would sooner not see them, ever again. It has nothing to do with you. That part of my life is over." He reaches down to one of his black leather riding boots with both hands and begins to tug his foot out of it. "I have, somewhere within here, a few hidden coins in case of emergency. I may as well take the time to find them."

"They are fine boots."

"Aye, Sarrell's of Kingston Upon Hull. It was his lad who hid a penny in each, somewhere, at my request." Richie holds up the boot and peers inside as he shakes. A shiny object falls out and clinks on the wooden deck of the jolly boat. Nik picks it up. Just like he said, it's a dull penny.

"It seems our fortunes have taken a turn for the better, Mr Turpin, would you not agree?" He grins. Humour is a sign of spirit, especially in hard times.

"That we have. Once we reach the shore, we'll find a warm and friendly inn with a roaring fire where we'll dry ourselves off. We'll play a hand or two of the cards with a small ale while we wait for the cook to fix us a mutton supper." She smiles back at him.

"We will," she answers.

It's just before noon.

The two of them sit on the beach and watch the jolly boat get sucked out to sea on the tide.

It has been a struggle. Perhaps someone with knowledge of the sea would have done a better job, but Richie spent his youth in the fields and his middle age around a card table or on a horse. Nik can read a bible well enough and do all sorts of stitches to make pretty pictures in materials, she has ridden a narrow boat too along the beck where her father uses them to carry goods but the North Sea is not the same. They were too eager to get where they were going, so the ocean decided to take the piss; as any good sailor knows, you only reach your destination by her mercy.

When they saw the coast an hour earlier, they celebrated and took turns to row, with steady eager spirit towards land. The tide was going out which made it worse. At points, Richie wondered if it may be better to get out and swim. He was minded also of Pollard's advice that he would not be able to sail a boat back to shore. As they got closer to land, the bottom of the boat scuffed against rocks and finally, Richie stepped out into the waves, up to his waist and carried Nik with him, staggering and fighting against the swirls of the North Sea. In the struggle through the soft sand and jagged rocks, Richie lost one of his expensive boots, as if the sea wanted to take something from him if she couldn't have his life. Nik still has both her shoes and has managed to keep the flat cap too. In the right light, she does not look like she has escaped a Dutch smuggling vessel and been washed ashore. She could just be any working lad, who is filthy with hollow and hungry cheeks. Richie Turpin on the other hand, with his brown hair, quality ripped white shirt, and one boot, looks like an aristocrat who has been dragged through a holly bush after two bottles of brandy. He stretches his long legs out on the pebbly beach. Nik has her knees up to her chest.

"It'll all be fine," he says. Nik nods. "As long as we're nowhere near Scarborough."

"What about your effects, they're gone." She means his hat and the blackwood pistol, the money in the pouches, his dagger and of course, his expensive boot. He smiles from where he sits. Times of struggle are not in fist fights or running away from burning buildings or shoot outs, the real hardships of life are hunger, boredom, effort, and worry – these are the creatures that take their toll upon us. Here on the beach with their clothes sodden and nowhere to go, it is worse somehow that a Dutch smuggling fluyt, at least it was warm on board.

"They are only things, I can get more." Richie begins to get to his feet. You can fight off bad luck with words. "I'm a highwayman by trade. Whatever I want I take. There are plenty more boots, guns, and silver daggers to be had."

They trek in single file along the side of fields. The September afternoon turns grey and it begins to rain, it's light drizzle at first, but after half an hour, there's steady and sustained downpour. They continue inland. It might have been easier to stay on the ship. The rain eases up when they get to a turnpike road, Richie leads south and after a time, there's the clatter of hooves from behind them. It's a stagecoach with four horses up front pulling a big carriage, and a driver with a top hat dripping with the now light rain. He slows to a trot as he passes and looks down on the two of them, like rats, he wears a mocking grin. He sees Richie is limping and with one boot on, it makes his gait seem odd.

"Come to make your fortune?" he yells down at them in jest. Richie looks up as the man passes, he sees his red, jowly face with a big mutton chop beard. This is the kind of driver he hates, so full of hot air when there are wretches to shout at, but, put a pistol in his face, and he'll wet his fat pants.

"Which road does this lead to, Sir?" bellows Richie.

"God's city of Scarborough," he shouts down as he speeds up. Richie's shoulders drop as he watches the carriage pull away from them down the road.

Anywhere but Scarborough.

There are those who do not know this part of the world who may look upon the three great Yorkshire Ridings and say they were the same place, but they are as different as apples from a tree. One may be rotten to the core and riddled with worms and bugs, another, not yet ripe, it may be bitter and sour to the taste, the third, sweet as the open blue summer sky and crisp without being too soft. Richie knows what he thinks of the North Riding.

It's a drinker's town is Scarborough. The gin comes direct from the Netherlands and the alehouses have big breweries because they can sell more. There's fish and crabs, lobster, and all manner of treasures from the sea. This was where Richie ran to when he first left home all those years ago, he'd been told to meet someone, up at the Golden Ball on the docks, and, though he does not really want to set foot in there again, he cannot think of another place to go in this town.

It takes a good hour of walking into the afternoon to get to Scarborough properly, and they pass a great many folk about their business. On the outskirts there are farm lads and lasses away to the fields of a September day, a rider carrying post north and an old woman with a thick clump of firewood strapped to her back.

"You're missing a boot," comes to the lips of most, or some such comment. "You'll not get far like that, son." "You know they'll throw you in jail if you walk into Scarborough with the look of a beggar." Richie realises this, but he is in no mood to steal anything at present. It's hard enough just to keep moving on. Nik walks beside and is in good cheer, partly because of having two shoes but also, the sense of freedom. As a soon to be lady of Beverley, Nik has never had occasion to walk the streets and pass comment with the folk who she sees.

"There's no poor house in Scarborough," says one well-dressed man on Leading Post Street. He has a top hat and a white moustache with cracked wrinkles along his narrow face.

"I'm to sell him onto one of the ships down at the dock, Sir," says Nik with a grin. They have already crossed into the town and the rich folk of Scarborough do not have the same earthy humour that Nik is just learning to play with. He scowls back. He was not joking.

The street narrows, and they begin down long flights of steps towards the docks. Nik leads, and hears squawks from the gulls there and smells the salt from the fresh fish. At the bottom of the stairs, Scarborough beach lays before them. They turn left and walk along towards the busy dock. There are boats unloading crab and lobster pots all the way along the jetty, and crowds of people about their business, lads carry boxes on poles over their shoulders, there's a man and his wife in a big dress taking a stroll, a Jack Russell dog barks from the bow of a boat, and all around and in between, gulls dip and dive and search for tip bits and offcuts and anything else they can get their beaks around.

In the context of the dock, Richie no longer looks so out of place with his washed out face and one boot - he could be a poor and drunken sailor down on his luck. Nik follows him along the street and sees that he keeps his head down now he is here, as if to avoid the eyes of the rough and ready dock dwellers. In front, and sticking out from the other buildings, with a great golden circle hanging from the wall, is the pub that Richie has spoken of. It's the Golden Ball.

He steps up to the front door and puts his hand on the wood to push it open, before he does so, he turns back to Nik.

"Keep your wits about you in this place," he says. Nik blinks back at him, the bright, hazel, and innocent eyes look worried. Richie reaches forward and pulls the cap so it covers them up.

"They'll take you for a beggar, dressed like that," says Nik.

"Not here," he answers, "not I, and not in the Golden Ball."

CHAPTER TEN

Richie lifts the latch and they step into the little porch where there are two more doors opposite each other. The one to the right leads to the front room overlooking the docks and will be where the harder drinkers go, the worst gamblers play and where the music is loud. The left will be for the merchants and the money men, captains and those who need to get business done. Richie heads to the door on the right – the rougher side, out of instinct. He pushes it open and Nik follows.

The room is packed and deafening at first with the chatter of those at drink. Thick pipe smoke stings Nik's eyes, a dog barks somewhere, men yell, there's singing and the clatter of wooden ale pots on tables. She smells sweat, beer, mud, cooked meat, and perfume all at the same time. The floor is uneven beneath her feet. It's suddenly hot and her cheeks redden with it. Nik has never seen such a sight: it is a Saturday afternoon and the pub is in the grip of middling merriment. There's a fiddle going in the far corner, but she cannot see who is playing it, and there's the roar of many voices raised in earnest talk, storytelling, card gaming, flirting or singing, and the figures range from tall black-haired fishermen with weathered faces to fat serving lasses with dirty aprons and skullcaps; there's a couple kissing, a fellow with a red nose smoking a long clay pipe, a table of rowdy card players at the beer also. Nik has never been allowed in a pub like this.

It's mid chaos as Richie steps between two groups of men to get to the bar. He rests his big hands against the smooth wood as he waits, and Nik stands by his side feeling small. It does not take long for one of the girls passing out wooden mugs of ale to notice there is a very tall, ragged looking gentleman at the bar. She has plump cheeks and blonde hair spilling out from under her skull cap, she spots Richie and frowns in concern, she knows him and she slips off through a door leading behind the bar to the kitchens. In another second, the lass returns with a man behind her. He's a moor. Nik has seen such a fellow before at the market in Beverley a few Christmases back, this one has light skin and a shaved bald head. He wears a white neck scarf. There's a real look of concern on his face as he sees Richie standing at the bar between the drinkers. Their eyes lock. They know each other. The moor reaches for a brass ship's bell that is fixed by a wooden arm to the wall, he grabs the rope and rings it with three big, powerful clangs that sound out across the din of Saturday afternoon.

At the third dong, the voices in the pub fall silent. Drinkers stand from their card games and mugs of ale. The couple who are kissing stop and turn with confused frowns, and those figures next to Richie and Nik move away to give them space. The man with the dark skin steps forward towards Richie. His face is serious and gaunt.

"Turpin," he says. He has a soft voice that Nik imagines could be powerful if he needed it to be. "You were hanged at York."

"Not I, Omar. Here I am before you at the Golden Ball on Scarborough Docks." The moor narrows his eyes and frowns. He's not nearly as big as Richie but there is steel in his stare. His countenance is stone.

"Do you remember the promise you made when you left this place for the last time."

"I do," says Richie.

"Bring me the pistol," calls the moor behind him. Nik swallows in surprise. This is an earnest exchange and the faces of the drinkers in the Golden Ball are serious at hearing it. The fact that a pistol is involved makes it more ominous. A serving girl disappears into the kitchen and returns a moment later with a black gun, similar to the one that Richie Turpin carried before he and Nik were shipwrecked. She hands this to the moor and he holds it by the barrel. He sets it down on the bar between he and Richie Turpin.

"I'll need powder, and shot and also, a deck of playing cards," says Richie. His voice is loud enough for the folk around him to hear. The moor does not alter his expression but the crowd of now silent revelers look on in dumb confusion. It will take them a moment to work out what is going on and who this tall man at the bar is, and why he calls for powder and shot for his pistol, and a deck of cards. The four men who were actually just playing cards look down at the bits of stiff paper in their hands, they are not going to give up their deck – there's money on the game. A short woman stands on a bench to get a better view. One of the pub's black and white cats crawls along a beam and looks down on the still crowd, her eyes widen as she considers them below.

A serving lass sets a thin paper packet of black powder and two lead balls onto the counter. Another removes a card deck from one of the shelves and passes it to him. There's usually a charge for strangers to use the cards, but she knows know that the tall man standing in front of her at the bar is not quite a stranger. Richie takes the cards in his big hand and shuffles the deck with aplomb,

"Load the pistol, Nik," he asks in a whisper but he does not take his eyes from the moor who stands in front of him. Nik steps forward and takes the heavy gun. As instructed, she loads it. She rips open the packet with her teeth and pours a good measure into the barrel, then, she adds a single ball and packs it down with the ramrod from the underside of the gun. Nik adds more powder to the pan next to the flint, and satisfied, she sets the pistol back on the counter. Nik has done a reasonable job, but if there are any soldiers watching or those who know about weapons, they would have noted that this one in the flat cap is not an expert.

The dog from the corner of the room begins to bark again, the couple who were just kissing exchange a glance once more, and the pub is on the edge of falling back into the same, beautiful chaos it wallowed in a minute or so before. The moor calls out loud above the still silent, newly drunk rabble.

"Turpin here promised me he would shoot straight through a playing card." The moor does not alter his stare. "He claimed he would do this as I threw it in the air, and if he does not make the shot – he is not welcome. It was he that made the promise, not I."

"Let's get on with it, shall we?" asks Richie. "These poor folk are thirsty enough, Omar." The dark man steps forward and takes the deck then fans it out with his fingers for Nik to take a card. She looks up at him and sees that he has not stopped frowning at Richie Turpin. She chooses one from the middle, and hands it back to the moor. It's the king of hearts. Apt. The moor takes a few paces back from the bar and Richie steps back also, the crowd moves away to give him space. He holds the pistol to his nose with the barrel pointing upwards and cocks the flint with his big thumb. There is interest from the throng of still silent drinkers. Here is a spectacle as they have not seen previous. The moor, Omar, will toss the card up into the air above the bar and Dick Turpin, thought to be hanged in York, but here very much alive, is to shoot a hole through it.

"Before it hits the ground, you promised me," says the moor with the stiff card between his finger and his thumb ready to toss upwards. Richie nods at him, the tall highwayman stands with his shirt ripped open showing his collar bone, his hair is ragged and he has but one boot, with his bare foot black with muck on the other. There is steel in his blue eyes.

The moor flicks the card upwards and as soon as he moves, Richie brings the gun down and pulls the trigger. Smoke and fire erupt from the barrel in a great boom that rattles the mugs and bottles on the shelves behind the bar. There are wide eyes on the silent drinkers. The ears on the cat in the roof fold flat to her head at the noise. The bullet takes a chunk from one of the rafters overhead sending splinters into the afternoon.

Nik's stomach turns. There's no way anyone could put a lead bullet through a playing card – not a chance, but something has happened. The king of hearts flutters down from above into the awed, wordless drinkers, and a bald-headed man catches it in his grubby fingers. He brings it to his slightly drunk and wide eyes as he examines the hole in the card then passes it into the crowd behind him.

"Straight through the King's head," whispers the man.

"It's still warm," adds another lad with reverence, the playing card moves forward through the hands of the aghast revellers, inspected by the eyes of a shepherd, a butcher's boy, a serving girl, and finally to the smooth hands of the moor himself, the one they call Omar. He grins for the first time to show a row of whitish teeth with the front two missing.

"As promised," he bellows. "It is Dick Turpin come back to the Golden Ball." The roar of the drinkers is deafening.

For a minute or so there is shouting, pushing and shoving, the clattering of wooden cups against each other and the rumble of excited feet on the floorboards below them. The little black and white cat up in the rafters makes a dash higher for safety. Richie lowers the pistol with a grin. Omar lifts the hatch on the bar and steps through. The two men embrace. The moor is a good deal shorter than Richie and he buries his head in the man's chest, Nik can see that his hands are tight on Richie's back, there's emotion there. The Golden Ball is busy once more, and the spectacle of a few minutes previous is quickly forgotten as drinkers require more beer. The serving lasses fall back to dealing with them as Omar pulls Richie through the hatch and to a door in the back to the kitchen. Nik follows.

There's the smell of grease, spices, and smoke coming from the huge fireplace in the kitchen. A very large pot simmers over burning logs next to large ovens built into the walls. It's hotter here, but quieter at least. Omar moves into the centre of the room, his hand goes to his bald head in confusion. He turns on his heels. Nik can see that he is not as dangerous as he first seemed, the eyes are kind and concerned. There's even a gentle lisp to his voice as he speaks.

"Why now, Richie?" he asks.

"I was passing through."

"Passing through? There's been no word for near four years."

"I thought it best I was forgotten." Omar looks away and shakes his head. There's added drama for effect. Nik likes him.

"What about me? There was no word that you were alive."

"I told you, Omar, when I left, that I would not be back."

"It is a good job, Dick Turpin, that I did not forget about you. I kept that card with a bullet hole in it. I kept it all this time." Omar produces the king of hearts from his jacket. It's the same shiny card that Nik selected from the pack a few moments before. Like Richie, this one must be a gambler too. Perhaps that's why they appear to be friends.

"You didn't shoot through his head?" ask Nik.

"It's an old trick. Omar here switched the cards, and the one he tossed in the air already had the bullet hole in it. Any amateur card player can force someone to pick a card, like he did to you." Omar nods.

"I am sorry, Omar. I did not want to trouble you and I did not intend to return, not ever."

"Yet here you are."

"By a twist of fate only. I am not here to change anything about your situation. It was best that you thought I was hanged at York." The smaller man is passionate. His brown eyes water.

"When I heard they had captured Dick Turpin and he was to be hanged, I went there - to see you." Richie's face winces. "He was a lad called John Palmer from Essex, a pitiful man who didn't think he would hang. I knew you were still alive then."

"All those years ago, Omar, I counselled you to attend to your own affairs and the matters of this pub, rather than I. You need not look to me, you have your own family."

"You were my family," says Omar. A serving lass scuttles past in embarrassment. Nik does not know where to look. They are like lost brothers. The two of them stand facing each other in the big, hot kitchen of the Golden Ball pub. "Tell me of Kat?" asks Omar. "Is she still in your employ?"

"She's dead," says Richie. Omar's nostrils flare when he hears this and he puts his hand to his bald head again.

"My God," he whispers. "How?"

"Murdered by someone who was looking for me."

"Did she suffer?" Richie does not like to admit it, but the truth comes out of him.

"Aye, she would have." Nik did not know this and now she understands some of the pain on Richie's face. "It was my fault," he continues. "My past caught up with me Omar, and it will catch up with me again and you. If I did not need your help, I would not be here. I require only the items that I left, then, myself and my associate, Swift Nik, will be gone." The name he has given sends a shiver of power down her spine. For the first time, Omar looks down on the five-foot five figure in a flat cap next to Richie.

"Who is this boy to you?" he asks. Richie considers his words carefully, he looks down on Nik next to him and then back to Omar.

"Nik is my daughter," he answers. This saves explanation, and he wishes it were true also. The moor grins. Nik does not want to give anything away, but her chest swells as her back straightens.

"You kept that well-hidden," he says.

"I did not know myself until late. We just need what I left here, Omar, and we will be gone."

"You will share a drink with me first," he says. Omar smiles and shows his straight white teeth with the two front ones lost.

110

CHAPTER ELEVEN

The Golden Ball is full of all manner of little rooms, nooks, and corners where folk can sit, drink and be warm as evening sets in. Omar and Richie have moved to the back of the pub and taken seats in a room with a sliding door next to an open fire. It's rowdy with two big tables and benches around the outside. The little space is already packed and noisy enough to have a conversation in without being overheard. Nik has been ordered to fetch them some ale from the bar, and she carries three mugs by their handles through the busy pub. It is good to be free. She dodges past a woman with huge bosoms and a red face, around two dogs play fighting, past a gang of lads roaring with laughter and into the room. She sets the pint pots on the table in front of Richie and Omar, they make a space for her to sit in between. Omar takes a big slurp on his ale and sighs.

"What has Mr Turpin told you of the Golden Ball, Nik?" asks Omar.

"He said it was a place to watch yourself in." Omar nods in agreement.

"There are thieves at work, lass, that's for sure." In being associated with Dick Turpin himself, Nik is afforded a status here. She did not pay for the drinks and there were no cheap comments from the group of lads she passed in front of.

"Did he explain how he came to be so well thought of by the landlord here?" Omar means himself.

"He did not," answers Nik. The moor leans forward.

"Where are you two bound?"

"I'm to take Nik back to her home in Beverley. We have been on a journey and we must return there." Omar wrinkles his nose at the mention of the town.

"It's full of those Godly types there, young Nik, you want to stay here, on the port at Scarborough, there's plenty of work for a young lass like you, and plenty of drink too."

"I have promised her mother she will return," says Richie. Omar takes another sip on his wooden cup.

"What has he told you of me?" asks Omar to Nik.

"He says you are a man to trust," she lies. In truth, Richie has not mentioned this man or anything about his life at all to Nik.

"I am a man to trust indeed," says Omar. "This is my pub, but it's only my pub because of Dick Turpin. There was a time when I was a young one much the same as you are, and like Dick Turpin here, I found myself at Scarborough dock, looking for a ship to take me to the West Indies where I would not suffer as I have done here. It was such a time as this man and I became friends in the service of the road and, for a few seasons in the summer, we robbed the roadways of Newcastle, Leeds, and York. We made a tidy penny, but we were not fools, thieves of a kind, but not stupid. With all the money, we bought this place, and now, it seems, I am the only one left to keep the fires warm and brew the beer." Richie listens to the man talk.

"It's not my pub, Omar, nor Kat's neither." Omar takes his pint pot and drinks the rest of the ale in two steady gulps. This is perhaps his worry.

"So you've not come back to try and take your stake?"

"The pub is yours, Omar." He takes a deep breath.

"You'll have as much ale as you can drink this night, the both of you." Richie leans forward and his blue eyes twinkle in the firelight.

"I just need the things I left here." Omar nods.

"Get us some more ale, lass," he says.

Nik has never had a rowdy, drunken night in a pub, she has never been allowed. As a young woman in polite Beverley society, she was guarded in the guise of being protected, locked up to be secured as a prize mare from the stallions. She has never been free. Not so tonight. Nik is at the bar chatting horses to a tall and thin stable lad with ragged hair and rolled up sleeves, almost as quick, Nik is talking to one of the serving lasses about Beverley where the girl grew up, then, Nik is dancing a jig with a short haired lass in front of the fiddle player, then drinking a glass of brandy with Dick Turpin next to the big fire in the back room, then leaning over her wooden cup of ale in deep and earnest conversation to an old seafaring lad with a misty right eye. The evening becomes drunk as it gets later; it is a delicate and rowdy journey of sublime beauty and it requires all players to make the story as perfect as it can be. They all act their part, there are the squire lads fist fighting on the cobbles outside, the hot, steamy exchanges between the fisherman and the whore, the card players palming coins, the pipe smoker holding the long clay bulb cupped in his hand as smoke billows from his mouth, the mandolin player strumming, the serving lasses with their arms covered in sticky beer, Omar grinning, Richie sitting back with a hat over his eyes and a half drunken smile. It's a work in which the players are the audience.

One of the serving girls with short hair, the one who danced with Nik in front of the fiddle player earlier, walks into the back room. She looks over the faces, to Dick Turpin and Omar in the corner deep in conversation with Nik in the middle of them. The serving girl can see something there in Turpin's companion and she gives a wry grin.

The night wears on towards ten. The bells of St Mary clatter out the hour from not so far away up the hill, and the pub begins to empty of revellers. Those who have been drinking since noon are not in any fit state to enjoy themselves, it is of course Sunday tomorrow, and they should be up and dressed in their best for church. It's the law. Nik sits on the long comfy bench against the wall of the back room with Richie Turpin beside, the sash window to the street is open and the cool sea air drifts into the warm pub. There's the sound of men half-heartedly fighting a few streets away, a woman shrieking in laughter, someone close by spewing. From inside the pub, she hears the slow drawing of the fiddle and a sad tune enters the back room, she turns to Richie next to her.

"I'm going to dance, Mr Turpin," she says. He nods in agreement. Nik staggers a little passing the fire, and uses the door frame for support to walk back into the bar room. At the far end, the fiddle player holds his violin into his chest as he looks down onto it. He draws the bow over the strings and the music is mournful, it tells of late nights and lovers and lost chances. She steps forwards and there's a drunken couple, it's an old man with one of the big dock whores, they are clasped together and swaying to the ballad. The short haired serving girl who Nik danced with previous appears, she has a pretty smile and clever eyes that look up through brown hair.

"Shall we dance?" she asks. Nik nods and steps forwards. This could not happen without the drink. Not at all. There is not a chance that Nicola Sullivan of Beverley would ever, in a million years, find herself dancing with an attractive young serving lass across the uneven stone floor of the Golden Ball pub on Scarborough Docks, even though she would want to. There is no way their eyes would meet as the fiddler plays the slow and sweet tune.

"I know what you are," whispers the serving lass. She smells of sweet beer.

"What am I?" asks Nik.

"You're not what you seem to be," says the lass. There is no malice in her voice. Her eyes glisten in the orange lamp light from the corner as she moves in closer. Nik is not afraid of her. The bell behind the bar rings again and it means that the pub is closing.

"Are you staying here the night?" asks the lass with short hair as she steps back away from Nik.

"Aye," comes the reply.

"Meet me on the top corridor at one o'clock." Nik grins,

and the serving lass disappears back behind into the kitchen.

It is later yet. Now Omar and Richie Turpin lean on the bar together. There's Richie with his arm around the smaller man's shoulder and he still has one boot on, though his clothes are at least dry. The bell has been rung for closing time and most of the drinkers have left - it's that or face a kicking from the night watchman.

The lasses who work the bar are quick at this time of night, buckets are filled with hot water from the cauldron in the kitchen, mops appear for the floor and large clothes for the tables. A tall man with a big top hat appears, he has striped black and white socks pulled up to his knees and a thick ginger beard, he doesn't look drunk and carries a long cudgel in one of his big hands. Omar passes him a pouch of coins and Nik hears that this is the night watchman. He methodically searches the bar room of the Golden Ball for drunks who have fallen asleep and he will do so for all the rooms.

"There's trouble in town tonight," says the night watchman. His voice is as gruff as his appearance. "Seems like there was a bloody shipwreck a few miles out to sea, a smuggling vessel." Omar looks concerned at this.

"One of ours?" he asks.

"No, a Dutch ship, but there's a few of them made it to town here. They're looking for someone. Seems like it was sunk on purpose. I heard the powder room caught fire."

"Good God," says Omar and he looks blankly at the night watchman.

"Just like what happened to Henry Morgan," says Richie. Nik glances at him in worry.

"You'll have to tell me all about it in the morning, Watchman," says Omar.

"I will Sir, give me a minute to check the back rooms," the big man steps through the corridor and there's at once shouting. One of the dock whores runs out the pub with the watchman's voice bellowing after her.

"You girls can close up the pub," says Omar. "I'll take our guests upstairs."

Nik and Richie follow Omar through the kitchen and up the wooden back stairs of the Golden Ball, the steps are uneven and a little warped. None of them go particularly quickly for the time of night and the drink. Omar carries a lantern and they come out onto a long corridor with five doors on one side and a ladder leading upward to the roof in the darkness. This must be where the short haired lass said she would meet Nik later. Omar turns back to Richie over his shoulder.

"Can't this wait till tomorrow?" he asks.

"I need the items now, Omar." The man shuffles to the bottom of the ladder, and with the lantern in one hand, he begins to climb. They follow.

Up in the roof space, the floor is boarded out, there are rafters above them and shadows dance along the thatch of the big roof from the lantern. The smell is rich and hot up here, with the smoke from the fires below escaping through the chimneys. This is not the end of their journey. Omar uses the lantern to locate a lever on one of the far walls, he pulls it and what must be a secret door opens. He dips his head and creeps through. There's another lever on another wall, and finally another secret door that Omar goes through. Richie and Nik follow through the little spaces into a tiny room. The landlord sets the lantern on a hook on the back of the door and there's an alter and a wooden cross and a place to kneel before it.

"It's a secret Catholic chapel, they call them priest holes," says Omar.

"I know," says Richie.

"I was telling the lass," he explains. It was there when they first bought the pub many years since. Nik frowns in the darkness. There's the smell of mold in here, as if nobody has been inside for a good long time. Catholics are illegal, and worse than non-conformists even. Nik's father says they are like rats and have pointed front teeth so they can eat anything, but her uncle, the Frenchman, was born a Catholic and apart from her mother, he is the only soul in her household she can trust. Nik's father is a liar and braggard. She's learning quickly from Richie that you shouldn't take a person at face value anyway.

"There it is," says Omar. In front of them, below the little altar, is an iron chest, five foot long and perhaps three feet wide. It must be Richie's. "Have you got the key?" asks Omar. Richie shakes his head.

"I misplaced it some time ago, my friend. Anyway, the chest is just a distraction." The tall highwayman steps around the chest to the altar. He puts both hands on the wooden top under the crucifix and pulls it to reveal a long empty space underneath. From inside the hole, he removes a hessian bag which he passes to Nik, she takes a look inside. It smells of leather – they are clothes. Richie leans down and fetches more items from the bottom of the secret hole. First there is a leather rag tied tight with chords. He sets it down on the chest and unwraps it slowly in the lamplight – this is a holster with a black wood pistol tucked into it. The rag around it is oily and so the mechanism will be as good as new. Richie runs his fingers over the flintlock and smooth metal barrel, he grins.

"It was my father's," he says. He means the Pearlman. Richie unravels the belt and stands to fit it around his waist; he pulls the buckle tight. "I didn't think I'd see this again," he says. He goes back to the hole and fetches out something else – a long wooden case. He sets this on top of the chest.

"Is that it?" asks Omar in the half darkness.

"Aye." says Richie. He adjusts the gun belt on his hips and tightens the strap.

"You know you don't have to look through this now," says Omar. "It's late. It will be Sunday tomorrow and folk will be a church, as will I, you can make your preparations then." Nik cannot see Richie's face in the darkness.

"Aye, we give you our thanks, Omar." Richie stands and his great height seems strange in the little box room of the secret Catholic chapel. They are too close, the three of them, the drink has worn off Nik, there's the smell of Omar's sweet perfume and the sense that they have been in the space too long. Omar breaks the silence.

"You're always welcome here, Richie Turpin," he says. "This is your home. Without you, it might not be mine at all." Nik hears Richie take a deep breath.

"There's no need for you to say that, Omar. It has been many years and I'm a wanted man. I'm with a traveller who, in the right hands, may be worth something. You don't need to feed me the same lies that you use on the farmers, dock hands and street lasses. This is me, Richie Turpin." This makes Omar swallow.

"I have people who rely on me, Richie. As soon as you arrived there would have been talk. There are eyes that would have been on you already."

"Exactly. So why would you have me stay the night?"

"I would ask you to stay up here, Richie, right up here in the secret chapel, at least until daylight. Then, there will be fresh horses for you both and you can ride off again – like you did last time, like you did all those years ago." Omar's eyes twinkle in the lamplight of the little, stuffy room that has been closed and secret for probably more years than Nik has been alive. Richie steps closer and looks down on the man in front of him.

"We'll be gone at daybreak," whispers Richie. He reaches out and clasps Omar by the forearm. "I want to thank you, Omar, my friend. I want to thank you for your help tonight."

"You are welcome. You'll not be back then?"

"No. I wish you well."

"The horses will be ready for you in the far stable in the

livery. They will have saddles and provisions too."

"You are more than generous."

"It's the least I can do."

"No goodbyes." Omar nods.

"I'll leave you the lamp." He opens the little door behind him and then closes it behind him as he leaves.

They can hear Omar as he moves back through the passage to the roof, and his heavy steps as he walks away. Nik sits down on the floor of the little room with her knees up and her head still a little thick with drink even though she thought she was sober. Richie waits a few moments till he is sure they cannot be overheard.

"No time to rest, Nik," he whispers. "Omar will sell us out as soon as he reaches the kitchen."

"What?"

"There'll be soldiers on their way, I imagine, or at least not too far from here."

"He's your friend."

"Aye, but he's also a landlord of a busy pub and like he said, there are people who rely on him. Gone are the days when he and I robbed coaches out of York. Time moves on. We have what we came for." Nik looks up at Richie in the flickering light from the lamp.

"Mr Turpin, I am not sure I am in any state to travel." Nik has not slept properly since Kingston Upon Hull many days since, and even then, she did not sleep for she had been kidnapped. She has shot a man, ridden aboard a cobble, been captured by a smuggling vessel, and then escaped a shipwreck. She has drunk at least four big mugs of ale and made a vague and exotic agreement with a short haired bar lass to meet on the landing in the early hours.

"If we stay here, my Nik the Swift, then we will be hanged, the both of us, and I need you." It's not the hanged part that makes Nik struggle to her feet. It's his voice and that Richie needs her. She's never been needed before and the feeling is delicious somehow, despite her fatigue. "We have what we came for. I'll show you." Richie rummages through the sack at his feet, he sorts through the clothes and hats that he left there till he comes upon a pair of fine and sturdy black leather boots. He fits the left one over his bare foot, looks up and gives Nik a grin.

"We came here for a pair of boots?"

"These are from Sarrell's in Kingston Upon Hull, the best boots in the East Riding. But these are not really what we came for." He rummages around the bag some more and pulls out a flattened tricorn hat of black felt, he pushes out the crown and fits it to his head. He looks like a highwayman already with the lip of the hat sending a shadow across his face. That's not all. He draws out a grey leather holster with big straps that fit around the wearer's back and a wide hole for a gun. Richie tosses this to Nik. "This is yours," he says.

"No, it's not," replies Nik.

"It is now."

"It's for a gun. I don't have a gun, Mr Turpin."

"About that," he says. Richie goes to the long wooden case he pulled from the hiding place, he opens the two catches on the front and lifts the lid. There's a pistol within and he angles the box so that Nik can get a better look. It's a thing of beauty. Sitting on purple silk is a slender handgun, the handle is polished walnut, and carved along the metal barrel is the image of a dragon's head.

"The French and Portuguese call them serpents," says Richie in the half darkness. He takes the weapon in his big hand. "I had it made one summer out at Malton perhaps ten years ago. It packs a punch that can stop a bull, and it's not too heavy. I couldn't have understood, Nik, but I think it was made for you." He turns to her standing in the darkness. "This is yours," he says. "It's not a loan. It's forever. I did not know who would carry it. Now I do. It means also, that you ride with me by your choice. You have been rescued. You will be my equal." Nik takes the pistol and holds it pointing upwards looking at the ornate handle. Perhaps it's a little too much of a weight for the hand that has not yet grown strong, but it's not too heavy for her heart. There are twirls and spirals carved into the handle and the scales on the dragon catch the light.

"Take off the tunic, the gun belt goes around your waist and over your shoulder too. There's a knife hidden in the stitching should you ever need it." He watches Nik take off the little jacket and strap the holster on, deft fingers do the buckles on the front. She takes the gun and sets it down into the leather cup, then puts the tunic back over it once more.

"You'll need a cloak to cover it properly." It feels heavy on Nik's chest.

"I am not the same as I was, Mr Turpin. I am not young Nicola Sullivan anymore." He considers this.

"Aye. I have seen you grow. It is why you shall carry that gun and why I trust you with it." Nik looks up into his eyes. Nobody has trusted Nicola Sullivan of Beverley, she was not allowed to ride out alone, or cut firewood or read books that were unladylike. She could not take a walk without a chaperone, nor say grace before dinner, she could not clean out the horses. Like her mother, she was a trapped creature to be looked at only, and it made Nicola scared of the world around her. She was scared of the big horses in the stables and of the noise coming out of the alehouses. She was scared too when her father came into her room in the dead of night, silent and sneaky as he climbed on top of her and held her down by the throat.

That poor lass is gone.

Richie Turpin has put his trust in this one standing before him.

"I repeat. You ride with me out of choice. It's your decision whether we go back to Beverley and it is your choice also whether I deliver you to your mother, and if she pays me what she agreed." Nik moves closer still to Richie and he can feel the confidence. It is not bravado.

"I have business with my father, Mr Turpin. I will ride with you and I will make sure my mother pays the amount that she agreed." Nik does not know what was promised.

"How can I teach you all I know in such a short ride?" These words tumble from Richie's mouth without him thinking. He is frowning but more in thought in than in anger.

"I have already learned more from you, Mr Turpin, than I have in all my days yet. My mother spoke of you often and I see in you all that she told me of." Richie reaches out and puts his big hand on Nik's shoulder.

"There's no powder or bullets for these guns, yet, we'll have to find that. We'll leave the way we came, through the pub and out the back door. I'll deal with the night watchman, if I have to."

"And the livery? Will we take the horses from here?"

"No. Further down the dock and to the South Beach there is a place easier to rob from."

"There is another thing, Mr Turpin."

"Aye?"

"I have someone to meet, before we leave. I said I would see them on the top landing in the dead of night. It will take but a moment. Then I will be with you."

"Who?" Why lie?

"A lass."

"What for?"

"I don't know, to be honest, but it feels right and if I am your Swift Nik, then I must act like such." Richie reaches down in the sack, rummages for a moment and pulls out a dagger which he slips into his belt.

"Any more time than ten minutes and we'll both be swinging from the gallows, not that I don't mind that for me, but for you, it would be a right pain in the arse." Nik grins.

On the landing of the Golden Ball, the light from a silvery moon shines in through the sash window on the far wall. It is open, and the sounds of the night and the sea drift in from outside. Nik waits in the darkness with the cap pulled down over her forehead and, like a mouse creeping around a larder corner, the short-haired bar lass moves across the landing, looking one way and then the next. Nik gives a light cough from the darkness and the girl approaches, slowing when she gets a few feet away from Nik.

"You'll come to my room," says the lass.

"Not so. I have an errand to run." Nik does not want to tell this lass she is leaving.

"I know what you are," says the lass in the darkness.

"You said that before, so what am I?"

"You're a lass, the same as I am."

"Not the same as you," says Nik. "I'm free." The short haired girl in front blinks in the moonlight.

"You could take me with you, then. They say you are Nik Swift of Beverley and that you shot a man through his neck, and that you are the daughter of Dick Turpin." It's wonderful to hear she is famous.

"That I did. Why did you want me to meet you?"

"You will spend the night with me."

"Not this night." The lass moves into the darkness towards Nik, close enough to touch, and she moves her head in. Their lips meet but the kiss is chaste and simple, perhaps with more of a promise of what it could become. The short haired lass pulls back.

"You've never kissed a girl," she says.

"I've never kissed anyone," answers Nik.

Richie Turpin is waiting in the darkness at the top of the stairs and Nik hardly notices him there, still and calm against the wall.

"A good choice," he whispers when the girl has gone.

"Were you listening?"

"Only to make sure you were in no danger. The exchange is not my concern, but we have no more time to waste."

"I'm ready."

The pub is eerie in the darkness of the night. There are just embers in the fireplace and where a few hours before was noise and rowdy drinking, now there is silence as Richie walks across the uneven floor in his new boots. A figure appears from one of the rooms off the side, he's nearly as tall as Richie and has those big, black and white striped socks pulled up to his knee. He leans on his long cudgel. It is the night watchman.

"Going somewhere?" he asks Richie.

"Young Nik and I are going for a stroll." Talking your way out of a fight is preferrable to engaging in the real thing.

"At this time of night?"

"Aye. I've no need to explain myself, Sir," answers Richie.

"Omar said nobody was to leave until morning and that I was to see to that." Richie turns to square up to the man. The night watchman is just a little bit shorter, but much wider and with a nastier look on his face above his ginger beard. He grins to show uneven teeth.

"It's a pleasant evening, Sir, myself and my associate only wish to take a walk along the docks in the moonlight. There's no necessity for you or Omar to worry yourself about this." Richie's hand goes to the inside pocket of his jacket and he removes a coin. No doubt, he kept this too in the hiding place along with everything else. The night watchman eyes the coin moving between Richie's nimble fingers.

"I can't be bought," he says. "I'm a loyal lad, and stupid too, my head's as hard as a rock. That's why I'm the night watchman here."

"Indeed," says Richie. There's the scraping of a flintlock being drawn back in the darkness and Swift Nik levels her pistol at the night watchman. He sees the flat cap pulled down over the eyes and the barrel of the ornate weapon pointed at him. Not many folk have guns like this in Scarborough. Richie cuts to the quick, steps forward and brings his knee up into the night watchman's groin – if the ginger man had the same position on the docks and pubs of a city like Liverpool or Hull, he would wear a box to protect his smalls, and he would know such a move was coming. As it is, the big man of Scarborough feels Richie's boney knee on his balls, it's the sweet spot that gives a hollow pain in the stomach and makes you see stars at the side of your eyes. The watchman goes down with a groan and, before he can hit the floor, Richie has unhooked the ring of keys from his wide belt. He pulls off the nightwatchman's cloak while the man collapses against the wall, it's black and heavy wool, and it would have cost a tidy penny. Richie throws it around his neck as he turns to Nik.

"There was no need to draw your gun," he whispers. "I could have paid him off – we were about to negotiate. That weapon is your last resort, not your first." Richie steps away to the front door and Nik follows.

"I thought to scare him only."

"I'm not used to working as a pair," says Richie as he begins to try one of the long keys in the lock, then another. "We shall need to coordinate what we do in future." The third key he tries opens the mechanism and the bolt from inside the big front door slides out of the lock so Richie can push it open. They tap down the few stone steps of the Golden Ball and into the cobbled street in front of the dock. The moon is out in a clear and wide starry sky above, there's the smell of the sea from one side and the stink of ale, drains and people on the other. Riders approach, coming along the road next to the beach, Nik can see ten or so bobbing lanterns as their carriers ride in the mid distance.

"The garrison are already here," whispers Richie. "We better get off the road.

CHAPTER TWELVE

Nobody likes a thief – especially not thieves and so, the way the folk of the East Riding coast view smuggling is with a sense of moral purpose. It's parliament and the crown that have set the high duties on liquor, tea and sugar. The revenue they gain goes to fight wars off in Europe, or furnish a great castle, or dress the king in fine robes of silk. So, when a lad from Barmston helps a Dutchman unload a hoard of tea and then sells it on, they are not stealing, they are just making up for a king and a government far in the south that does not care about them. This is why there is a network of tunnels under some of these little fishing towns like Robin Hood's Bay and why you can also get a hot mug of tea or a slug of rum from any of the cottages there on a cold day. It's also the reason why Richie Turpin and Swift Nik make their way up Sandgate and past the Newcastle pub shrouded in darkness, they slip down the medieval backstreet called The Bolts. Halfway along, at Richie's request, they push open a metal grate that is barely big enough for them to slide through. Nik goes first and then Richie - if you know Scarborough as a highwayman does, then you know the tunnels too.

It's pitch-black and wet inside, just high enough for Nik to stand, Richie has to stoop. He goes first along the narrow rock passage, his feet are unsteady on the slippery floor. Nik grabs onto his cloak behind for guidance and Richie whispers back over his shoulder:

"This tunnel goes up to St Mary's and then on to the castle," his voice sounds tinny in the passageway. "Once we get to the church, we'll head out and onto the North Bay. There's a mill a mile or so up the beach." The Castle at Scarborough overlooks the North Sea from high, a hundred or so years previous, in the civil war, it was pounded by cannon fire and the tunnel that Richie walks through was lost to all but those who knew such things. When Richie and Omar traded with the smuggling boats from the dock, they could use the tunnel to move barrels from the pub up to the church and the North Bay where they'd sell them to merchant lads with horses and wagons. They used to make a heavy donation to the vicar up at St Mary's in rum or tea and he'd make sure the grate in the floor at the back of the South Lady chapel was not covered over.

The going is not so easy in the darkness. Richie slips and goes down on a few occasions, some parts of the floor are smooth and others are rough and jagged with stone. Nik slips behind and Richie hears the grunt of pain. He turns back in the darkness:

"Are you hurt?" he whispers.

"I slipped, Mr Turpin." The voice is weak and exhausted and Richie is conscious that his companion has had no rest for some time. He goes to his inside pocket and pulls out a square of cloth.

"Take a minute to catch your breath," whispers Richie. "While you were dancing last night, I pinched sweet oak cakes from the kitchen. Hold out your hand." Nik feels out for the cloth and takes it in weak hands as she rests against the damp and cold wall.

"Do we have much further to go, Mr Turpin?" comes the weak voice.

"Not so far, Nik. Eat a mouthful of the oats, and at your feet, there's a little stream of fresh water that comes from a spring up at the church." He hears her breathing is heavy and senses the weary heart. The men who approached the Golden Ball on horseback will not know of this tunnel, but Omar most certainly does, and if he is of a mind to catch Richie and young Swift Nik once he finds his night watchman with collapsed balls, then he may tell them. That's why Richie does not want to rest here, in fact, he will only be happy when he's on horseback riding away from Scarborough, in any direction.

"We must keep moving," says Richie. "Grab my hand and

we'll walk together. The steps up to the church crypt are not ten minutes from here." He feels out into the darkness, catches Nik's soft hand in his and pulls her up.

There's a loud clank from far away down the tunnel behind – a gate opening somewhere. Richie's face looks in the direction it came from even though it's black. Another noise cuts through the dank silence of the wet rock. It's the sound of dogs barking. The noise echoes down the passageway towards them. Hounds, and a good few of them by the amount of yelping. They are still a distance behind them, but it means that Richie and Nik are followed. It's Omar perhaps, or the garrison.

Time to run. Time to give it legs.

They run, but it is not easy, nor quick. Richie goes first pulling Nik behind him and there are some twists and turns in front that they cannot see, the floor is uneven and at times, slopes upwards steeply. Rough stone walls scratch at Richie's hand as he tries to feel in front of him. Behind them, they can hear the excited barks of dogs moving closer and also the shouts of men egging the beasts on with whoops and yells. Whatever hounds they have, and however big, they will tear into Richie and Nik as if they were foxes down a hole.

Nik stumbles behind, but Richie's strong grip prevents her from falling and they lumber on into the darkness. From previous trips down the passage, Richie remembers that it's not too far to some stone steps that lead up to the Church of St Mary's, and an iron grate on the floor above that opens to a crypt at the back of the church. If this grate is locked, then they will have to fight, and most likely lose. His hand goes to the dagger at his belt and he wishes that he had powder for even one shot of his pistol. It has been a long week for Richie, and he has not had many moments to think, but he has considered the person he has rescued, young Nik.

The decision to give her the pistol was not premeditated

and nor were the words he spoke - that Nik was an equal to him and his companion, the sentence and the sentiment came, fully formed from his lips. Richie has ridden with many, mostly men but some lasses, and they all had their qualities and their level of loyalty to him, but there is something different in his connection to Nik. He will protect her no matter the cost and, perhaps she would do the same for him – there is no silver involved and no contract either. He will get Nik back to Beverley if it is the last thing he ever does, and, it will be the last thing he ever does, for Elizabeth Sullivan was Pike has promised she will put a bullet through his heart and he will hold her to that. Then there will be no more running from soldiers and no more betrayals from old friends, no smuggling ships, no more tired and sore feet, and no more worries about who has died because of him. Richie has considered where he may go after his body is dead, but it cannot be worse than where he is now, and no more folk will be hurt because of his actions.

The hounds are getting closer, if they do not reach the grate soon, then Richie will have to draw the knife and fight. He will use his pistol too, if he holds it by the barrel, the handle is a strong enough cudgel. Nik clasps his hand tight from behind as the tall man moves onwards in the darkness, the grip is becoming weaker, and Richie must make a decision about what to do. His feet sting in the new boots below, his nostrils are filled with the dark mold of the wet cave around him, his heart pounds. The barks are shrill in his ears. The wall curves off to the right in front of them and he feels his way around as the passage gets narrower. He turns. This is where he'll make his stand and where only one of the beasts will be able to attack him at a time. He pulls Nik forward and moves behind her as he draws the pistol. The sound of the high-pitched barking is nearer.

"Keep on going up the tunnel," he whispers. 'There are steps that lead to a grate in the floor of the church. Get it open for me," he adds. Richie knows how people work, to an extent, he knows he cannot tell Nik to run off down the tunnel and leave him there to face the hounds and whoever is behind alone, so he has given her a job to do. Nik does not question the order and their grip unlocks. Richie uses his free hand to draw the dagger as he spins to face the other way. He bends his legs slightly, ready, and squints into the darkness of the passageway, with Nik's footsteps moving away from him. In an instant there's her heavy whisper behind:

"Light, Mr Turpin." He withdraws from his position, turns, and sees soft grey rather than black, ten yards away there's the figure of Nik a few steps up a small stone staircase leading to a wide grate where light is bleeding through. He grins and starts towards her as Nik pushes on the ironwork above, the heavy metal moves just an inch or so before thumping back into place. It will take more strength than that. Richie sets the gun back into the holster at his chest as he powers towards the steps. Now he can see, he can be more certain of his movements. Nik has the sense to stand aside as he charges up the steps towards the grate and puts his full weight against it. The iron lifts a good few feet and Nik scrambles through the opening, turning straight away to help lift the heavy metal from above so Richie can get through also.

In many ways, this is the action that defines their relationship now, for she could easily have slipped off and left Richie to the dog pack behind. Nik is not a rescued lass who cannot cope with the world, she is part of the same story. She could save herself by running into the crypt and letting the heavy grate slam shut on the tall man, but she is not that sort. They are partners these two. Holding onto the grate with gritted teeth and white knuckles, Nik struggles as Richie scrambles through. Below, the dogs are here also, the fastest is a long-nosed hunting hound with a dripping mouth and a growling chest. Its strong back and leg muscles power it up the steps towards Richie, and he kicks back at the beast with one of his new boots. The dog is too excited to be worried by this and sinks its slavering jaws into the quality leather heel made by Sarrell's of Kingston Upon Hull. Richie pulls his leg and the boot pops off as he scrambles up and through the grate that Nik has already lost grip of. As the hound charges through the opening, the heavy iron thuds into its head, knocking it back down the steps and into the path of ten or so more dogs, all whining and barking up at Nik smiling down from above.

Richie gets to his feet wearing a big and wide smirk. Yet again, he has lost one of his boots and the same mucky black foot stands flat on the stone of the church floor. The dogs bark and whine at the grate above them and there are shouts from the passageway below the little room of the South Lady Chapel at St Mary's church Scarborough.

"It's Sunday morning," whispers Richie. "We can be lost in the worshippers." This is sarcasm. Nik looks down at the filthy pants and wrecked shoes she's wearing and then back to Richie who is dirtier again, apart from the night watchman's well-made black cloak.

"We're hardly dressed for Church, Mr Turpin."

"This way," he says. There's a large, mucky dull tapestry hanging on one of the walls, Richie walks over to it, pulls up the right-hand corner to reveal a great and uneven hole. The early morning mist and grey cloud from Scarborough's North Bay peeps in. Just like the castle, St Mary's took a pounding from cannon fire during the civil war and although some of the stone walls have been rebuilt, others, like the South Lady Chapel need attention. Omar and Richie used to roll barrels through this damaged stonework many years previous. He's thankful that it hasn't been patched up.

He holds the tapestry back for Nik to step outside, they can hear the dogs move away down the passageway, and, in another minute, Richie and Swift Nik are walking down a steep hill towards a pebbly beach, blinking in the grey morning light.

They walk for a time, in silence, these two, until they get to a path that runs parallel with the beach below. The dew from the grass makes Richie's bare foot cold and there's a sharp breeze blowing mist and sea roke in at speed. Richie Turpin has lost another boot but gained many of his old items back, including a coin purse, a dagger and the Pearlman's dark mahogany gun. Nik now carries an expensive pistol also, but without powder or bullets so it's just a heavy bit of wood and iron with carvings up the barrel. More has been gained that can only be seen on Nik's face, for she is no longer that tortured girl from the big house in Beverley with an angry abusive father, and her eyes cast downwards. Nik walks level-headed and calm. In another five minutes of walking, they are lost in the sea roke around them.

It's still early in the morning. They have walked along the coastal path for an hour. At intervals, Richie turns and looks back into the mist behind them, as if there will be folk following, but there's not much to see in the fog. Nik stops with her arms on her hips and the hazel eyes staring out from under the flat cap into the mist in front. They have not spoken for some time and in his fatigue and frozen state, Richie has lost a little of his good mood. He wrapped a handkerchief around his foot but now that is wet and black with mud. A man forgets how useful a boot is when he doesn't have one.

The less people they see the better, it is Sunday after all and it is the law for a body to be in church on the Lord's Day so anyone they meet will know they are up to no good. There are other worries that run through Richie's head as he walks. Omar will not want him to get away, and there was talk of the captain of the Dutch ship also. Tongues will have been wagging in Scarborough and it will not take all sides long to realise that Richie and Nik are the ones they are after. They will have horses too and full bellies and will have had a night's sleep on a soft bed with pillows. They'll also have powder for their guns, and two boots each as well.

"We need to lengthen our steps, lass," he says as he peers into the mist ahead and then back the way they came.

"Neither of us can walk much faster, Mr Turpin. Perhaps there will be an inn further up the road."

"We'd not be welcome. You're as much wanted as I am in all this." Nik gives him a wry grin. There is something very sweet about being bad, she has never been so before. Richie bends and unties the handkerchief from around his foot, he shakes off some of the mud and folds it in half with his face in mild disgust. This will be his disguise.

"What are you doing?" asks Nik.

"We are going to do what I have learned to be good at?"

"What?" Nik wrinkles her muddy nose.

"We're going to rob someone."

Richie and Nik have moved off the road into a little copse of trees under a hill by the side of the road. Richie chose the spot because it's on a bend and part of the beach has reclaimed half of the muddy path. Anyone travelling will have to slow and go around the water. It's not the best road anyway.

A light drizzle has begun and it drips from the wet leaves on the hazel tree above and around them. Richie's hat covers his face and Nik can only see his mouth. She's glad of the rest, in truth, and leans against one of the rough trunks. Hazel is good to hide in when it's left to grow wild like this.

"Do you have anything to cover your face?" asks Richie. Nik shakes their head.

"Why would you need to be in disguise? It's not as if you have your identity to hide?"

"It's not to hide who I am, Nik, it is to explain it. A face covering will tell whoever walks or rides this road exactly who we are and what we want. It means we will have less talking to do. Further down this road is Scalby, and there was a coaching inn there once upon a time. Folk will be on their way to

Scarborough of a Sunday morning for their prayers, dressed in their best. Hopefully a big enough lad with big enough boots for me to wear."

"We've no powder or bullets."

"You can rob folk without shooting them. It's better that way. The first time I ever robbed a carriage was with an empty gun. It was just north of Beverley." Richie remembers back all those years ago, how he and his dog Bess robbed a coach near Leconfield and how he held his gun pointed at the pretty chest of a red-haired woman. "You know it was your mother I first robbed."

"She told me of it," says Nik. "She said her heart nearly came out of her chest in fear."

"Mine too," he answers. "She was a fine lass, your mam."

"She still is." Nik steps from the tree trunk so she is nearer Richie. "You can tell her so when we get to Beverley."

"That she is a fine lass?"

"Yes. You know my father is a terrible man, Mr Turpin. If you were to ask my mother, she would ride away with you." Richie smiles at the incredulity of this. As if he could.

"You would have me run away with your mother, Nik?"

"Aye. When I am done with my father, she will be a widow." The smile falls from Richie's face.

"I cautioned you on that already."

"You did. Events have only made me more steadfast in my conviction. I will kill him."

"Let me kill him for you." It's not the answer she was expecting. "I'm to hang anyway, Nik, and I would do it clean." There's no thought to the answer she gives:

"It will have to be my own hand, Mr Turpin, for I have suffered at his."

"You know that to live is sometimes more painful for a body than if it is to die. This is my warning. It may damage you more than him."

"Have you not killed a man before?"

"Aye."

"Did it damage you?"

"Some it did."

"Did you kill men that deserved it?"

"In my eyes, they did, but the act of it, why it cheapened me. I wish I had broken their noses or put out one of their eyes instead, or better still, let God deal with them."

"I will take it into my own hands, Mr Turpin. I will use this pistol and put a lead ball through my father's skull and I will leave Beverley forever and make a new life."

"And I would ride away with your mother, would I?" there's East Riding sarcasm in his tone.

"Yes," comes the reply. "I explained to you already. She loved you and waited for you, and I would say she loves you yet."

"To be young and to know how the world works is a gift, my Nik, for as age creeps up on you, it will make what is clear and simple, murky and muddy with doubt and complexity."

"You can mock me, Mr Turpin, but I will end my father's life."

"You will not find me standing in your way but, when the time comes and you have that pistol to his head, pause for a moment, just to check that you are doing what is right for you. Would you promise me that?"

"This I will promise you, Mr Turpin." Nik retreats back under the branches of the hazel wood and rests on the bark once more. The fatigue and the stress of the last few days have stripped back feelings that would have remained hidden.

"We are a strange pair, you and I," says Richie.

"How so?"

"A six-foot four highwayman without a boot and a lass in a flat cap." He wishes he had not used the word strange, for Nik is not that at all, different but not strange, this would imply something negative. Even after all these years, Richie still says the wrong thing, like he is perpetually sat in front of his Nana with his tongue-tied in knots.

"Aye. I am a woman dressed as a lad," says Nik, "and, for the first time, I feel as if I can speak my mind and walk where I wish. In the pub last night, I could come and go as I pleased. I am real. That is not how it feels to be a lass, Mr Turpin. I have been freed from my cage and I do not think I should like to be locked up once more. If this makes me strange, then so be it."

"A poor choice of words, Nik. There are people like us, those who are built differently, but we are not odd, we are just the reflection of what others may be." Clarity comes upon Richie, and when he speaks words that are true he does not need to second guess himself: "I have seen what you are, Nik, fiercer folk have buckled in the moment of real danger, but not you. Bravery is barring your teeth against fear and facing it. I have seen this on you, and I am proud of it too." Nik takes off her flat cap. In the grey morning with the light drizzle through the branches, her hazel eyes blaze with colour under the short red hair.

"I have never had a friend such as you, Mr Turpin," she says. She's not afraid of the way she feels, perhaps for the first time. "You taught me freedom. My mother was right to love you all those years back."

"She did not love me, Nik. It was an idea that she loved, a story from one of her books. I was not the man of her dreams then, and I am not now. As for you and I, our friendship will be tested these days to come, but I will do all I can to keep you safe. You have also shown me what it is to live once more."

From the road next to them there is the thudding sound of horses' hooves on the mud some way off. Richie grins.

"Look ready, my Swift Nik, I am about to show you how to steal horses." He fits the muddy handkerchief around his face and ties it at the back of his neck, then draws his pistol. Nik sets the flat cap back over her short ginger hair and pulls it low over her eyes.

"Should I draw my pistol also, Mr Turpin?" For all of her dark talk of revenge, Nik is still green around the ears.

"Not now. You'll stay here under the cover of the trees. I think I will be able to take this on my own. Stay out the way, we have no knowing who approaches." Nik nods.

Richie edges his head without hat from the foliage to get a very quick look at the cart that approaches. He hopes that it is not a stagecoach, for if it is, he will not be able to rob it in his current state - not with all the men and the guns it will have. Out of the mist comes a single black gig, it's a two wheeled cart pulled by one brown horse. There are two passengers sitting up front, and one holds the reins.

Richie pulls his head into the shadows of the bushes once more and replaces his hat. He unpicks the details from the brief glance so he might think of how best to approach this. He saw the driver on the left was an old white-haired man, with a grey trimmed beard. The woman next to him is fatter and stouter than he, with a simple green dress and a wide brimmed and fashionable shepherdess's hat. The horse that pulls them is slow and has its head down against the light rain. From this information, Richie can tell much. Neither of these two is rich, not with those clothes and that horse and that black trap, but, neither are they poor. Richie reasons that they will not be armed, for they have nothing that a normal thief would go out of his way for.

He squats down in the bushes, fits his tricorn hat tighter and waits for the horse and cart to get nearer. The voice of the thin man comes through the drizzle, nattering and complaining at his wife, it's talk of money and of those everyday chores that some couples bicker about. Sure enough, the man with the grey beard steers the horse and gig towards the bushes to avoid the part of the road that has been lost to the sea. He slows also because he's a cautious driver. This is when Richie makes his play. He steps from the bushes ten yards away from the approaching horse and makes a light whoa noise from his chest so that the animal knows to slow down, he holds up his hand in a friendly wave and his cloak is open so that both the fat woman in the shepherdess's hat and her thin, white-haired husband can see the pistol that is next to his chest. They can also see the scarf fitted over his nose and face. The man's jaw drops in fear and the woman's eyes bulge.

"I am sorry to bother you, on this Sunday morning, Sir and Madam," says Richie in a friendly voice from under the scarf, "but I have a request, I need this horse." The animal stops a few feet from Richie, and his skillful hands are already on the straps that hold the harness tight to the side of the beast. He has one undone before the man can protest.

"What in God's name is this?" calls the old fellow with his nostrils flared.

"I have money to compensate you, Sir," says Richie. "It's a matter of great importance. Allow me to ready the horse and you shall have the necessary coins."

"Now you just wait a sodding minute," continues the man with the reins in his gloves, "I'm not selling my horse. You leave those straps alone." With swift hands, Richie has undone the breeching bar and belly loops that keep the trap connected to the horse.

"You would be doing a man a great service, Sir," says Richie, "and I am to pay over the odds for such a beast, despite it not having a saddle."

"We're being robbed, Samuel," says the woman next to him who is more astute than he is. "Look at the scarf over his face and his hat - he's a highwayman I tell you. Look at his dirty britches and he only has one boot." Richie works quickly on the remaining straps on the horse to free it properly and his hand goes up to rub behind the ears so that it knows he's a friend. Now he's got this far, they will have to physically stop him from taking the animal. The two breeching bars that fit to the sides of the horse fall into the mud as Richie pulls at the bridle to make it step forward. It has been a quick job and the straps were not done up tight as they should have been.

"Samuel," calls the woman behind her. "Samuel, we're being robbed." Richie looks up and almost too late, he realises that the Samuel she is calling to is not the old man with the grey beard next to her, but a tall lad who is climbing from the back of the cart. Perhaps it was the mist, or his age that prevented Richie from seeing this crucial detail previously. This new player in the robbery, stands from the back of the cart and withdraws a stout and heavy blunderbuss, it's the short type that men who guard stagecoaches have. He levels this at Richie as he cocks the flintlock back. Richie freezes.

"You'd better hook that horse back up," says Samuel in a thick, clever voice. "And once you've done that, me and you will have words before I march you down to the constable of the peace at Scarborough." Richie does not take his hand from the reins of the horse but his other goes into his cloak, to the handle of the pistol that has no powder or bullets.

"I intend to pay for this animal, Sir," he says from under the muddy handkerchief across his face.

"I said strap that horse back up, boy, and be quick about it too. I know the constable and there'll be a half bottle of rum in this for me." Samuel grins and his teeth are crooked and blackened. Richie still does not move his hand from the reins. He answers:

"I'd wager that your shotgun is not even loaded, Sir. It's Sunday morning and you took some ale last night, that's why your nose is so red, I'd say that gun is no more loaded than the pipe in your old father's pants here. Whereas I, a man of the road, and in dire straits also, have an oiled and loaded pistol here at my chest." The man holding the shotgun takes a step to the side, and this tells Richie he has some experience, for if he pulls the trigger from the angle he is at now, he will not injure the horse with the buckshot. In a way, he is calling

Richie's bluff.

"Now you have been plain about your intentions, highwayman, I ask you to withdraw the pistol and drop it on the floor. I'm a guard by trade and I have dealt with your sort many times before." Samuel's face is level and real. He means what he says.

There's the sound of another flintlock being drawn back and Samuel senses movement from beside him. It is young Nik who steps out from the darkness of the bushes. She holds her own pistol trained on Samuel, the cap is low over her eyes and her mouth is a thin, serious line across her face.

"Do not make any sudden movements, Sir," says Richie. "My associate, Nik the Swift, does not have the same pleasant disposition as I and she knows that dead man can tell no tales, also. Do not be so foolish as to allow her hotheaded nature to get the better of her and cause you a great mischief that you may not survive." When his blood is up, Richie finds he's good at talking. He leads the horse away from the cart, slowly and turns it round so he is facing the man who says he is a coach guard. Samuel watches him with the stubby blunderbuss now not so rock steady in his hands. Richie can see that the man's nostrils are flared wide like his mother's. He is scared and that means that the shotgun is loaded. In days gone by, it was easy for Richie to show no fear in such situations, because he felt none. Today with the North Sea on one side of him, a garrison following, and a lass he cares for standing as proud as any gunfighter behind this Samuel, he feels like he has something to lose. He does not want any harm to come to Nik. For this reason, he must not let his fear show as he leads the horse towards the man. Richie can smell the stale beer on Samuel and he sees the man's watery eyes are nervous as he calculates whether to pull the trigger on the big blunderbuss in his hands. Richie leads the horse closer to him, so that they stand only a foot apart.

This is the space to test a man's nerve.

Richie has been here before.

Smooth and calm, as if he is taking a newborn baby from a worried uncle, Richie reaches out and grabs the shotgun by the barrel from the man's fingers then steps backwards. Samuel blinks at him, as if he did not try hard enough as Richie disarmed him.

"Take off your shoes," whispers Nik from behind. Samuel's face winces. It's an odd request. He does not quite know what to do. Richie levels the blunderbuss at the footman. The man stumbles as he pulls his footwear off. They are boots that slip from his feet and are made of battered brown leather, they are also wet with mud. He stands and holds them by their floppy shins. Richie stares the man dead in the eyes. There's not a trace of humour on his voice as he speaks.

"Your friends would have told you, Samuel, as a coach guard, that there is no amount of gold worth your life." Richie has heard similar from men of the road. "I promised to buy the horse." He reaches to the inside pocket of his cloak, to the leather money pouch where he pulls out a guinea with his index and middle finger. He tosses this to the woman who still has her nostrils flared, and it lands a few yards away from her in the mud. Three pairs of eyes see the coin fly and the place where it falls, the old man, the woman, and their son. Samuel watches as it glints there on the cold ground. The money will be worth more than the horse; this is the last of Samuel's many mistakes this morning. While he is not looking, Richie steps forward and swings the butt of the shotgun into his balls – it winds him and he lets out a groan as he falls to his knees. It's the second time Richie has performed such a move in less than a day, he pauses, for he does not really want to do this. Richie pulls the gun back and smacks the poor sod round the mouth with the handle, there's not much force in it, but it's enough to split his lip. Richie whispers to Samuel as he collapses to the ground:

"You should have shot me straight away, don't make the same mistake next time." Richie steps around the back of the horse, uncocks the blunderbuss and then tosses it into the bushes. He puts some of his weight on the reins and hops up onto the animal's bare back without a saddle, his heels dig lightly at the side to move it on. Nik stoops to pick up the boots, grabs onto Richie's outstretched hand above as he pulls her onto the back of the horse. It begins to trot away.

Richie clicks the back of his tongue and the horse speeds up, within half a minute, the animal and the two riders have disappeared at a canter into the mist.

CHAPTER THIRTEEN

With Richie up front and Nik behind, they ride for an hour across fields, and away from the fresh salty sea air and into the flatlands. There's a farm on the left and they keep the waters of Scalby Beck on the right. Nik has her arms clasped around Richie and her head is on his back, exhaustion has set in. It's not comfortable riding a horse without a saddle and not safe either, but both have ridden a plenty. Richie keeps a steady pace even though the horse is not fit for such a ride and won't last much longer at this speed. It doesn't have to take them much further, for Richie knows that this river on the right will take them down into the Royal Hunting Forest of Pickering, a huge and dark wood that stretches to the north almost as far as Robin Hood's Bay and west to the North York Moors. The folk local to these parts call it Dalby. Richie has been here before, many times, hunted in it, robbed those travelling through, and used it as a place to hide. He'll use it again.

The horse is beginning to slow as they ride into the forest and through two big oaks that flank the path. Its head is starting to dip and the body is beginning to slow. The beast is probably underfed and Richie can see scars on its neck from being whipped. At the first bend in the forest path, he pulls the horse up and they come to a halt. There's a carpet of fresh, fallen leaves below and a rich autumn smell from the woods around them. Nik, struggles to get down and stands uneasy as Richie dismounts. He slaps the back of the animal and it makes off, cantering away along the forest path deeper into the darkness of the trees. Her eyes are black and weary. The man grins.

"We're home," he says.

It's afternoon. If you know what you are looking for, the forest has everything. There's tinder to make a fire, at this time of the year there are mushrooms, fallen hazel nuts and the last of the blackberries the birds have not pinched. There's also cover to keep you warm from the rain and soft leaves to make a place to rest. Richie found a spot in a dip with a fallen tree covered in moss, at the roots that stick up from the ground he has made a little fire with twigs and next to this, with her back against the bark is Nik. There's some colour returning to her cheeks. Richie has filled his water bottle from the stream and Nik's throat bobs as she takes a glug. There's more. Richie has done his fair share of poaching over the years and so his eyes are quick to spot the familiar loops of traps. While he filled his water bottle in Scalby Beck a few minutes' walk away he saw the brown fur of a rabbit caught in a poacher's loop. This he has brough back to their little makeshift camp, and, with the knife from his belt he is skinning the dead animal. He's also set a flat stone in the fire to heat up.

"Why did you strike the man back there?" asks Nik. Richie looks up from cutting, she looks exhausted and has not removed the flat cap. It's the first they have spoken since the robbery.

"A kindness," he answers.

"How? They were poor. That horse was probably all they had. Striking a man without reason does not sit well with me, Mr Turpin, and I did not think you were such a person."

"He said he was a guard, if you remember. That means his job would be to protect carriages as best he can. Can you imagine how it would look if he had just let us get away with his horse without a fight? I know what happens to lads like that. They're called cowards and bastards, the folk in pubs think they're wet behind the ears and weak. With his split lip, that lad can say he put up a fight, and they'll buy him a drink for his bravery." Nik blinks up at Richie wishing she had not doubted him. "I left the blunderbuss too, it will not be his and will belong to whoever employs him. I paid for the horse and he now has experience. I think Samuel has done well. You did well also. I am thankful you were there. It takes spirit to hold a gun to someone's head, even if it is not loaded. Who would have thought that of Nicola Sullivan?"

"I will not be that lass ever again, Mr Turpin." Richie considers this serious figure sat in front of him with the cap pulled down over her eyes yet. There's defiance against the world in her. Richie has seen this anger before. He goes back to preparing the rabbit – he tries to channel his Nana, with a mixture of humour, guile, and wisdom.

"Perhaps you should let the person you are meant to be find you, Nik. You don't catch a rabbit in a trap after all, you have to make the poor bugger walk into it of its own accord."

"I feel myself with you, Mr Turpin."

"Aye, well, we have been through a lot together, and in such a short time." He cuts off a slice of meat from the rabbit and sets it on the hot stone where it begins to sizzle and cook in its own fat. Nik watches the meat spit.

"I will make my life on the road, Mr Turpin, as you have." He raises an eyebrow at this as he slices off more of the rabbit to cook on the stone.

"It's not a life you choose," he answers.

"Like catching a rabbit then, it chooses you." Nik is swift indeed, swifter than Richie.

"I don't mean it like that. You may think you enjoy the rough life, but you won't in the end."

"It's not the rough living that interests me, Mr Turpin, it is the freedom."

"Who from?"

"My father, the town of Beverley, the rules that dictate what I do every minute of the day." Richie adds more rabbit meat to the hot stone and it sizzles.

"I understand," he says. He does. Living in a place where everyone knows your business is hard, he spent his whole childhood cooped up in North Burton where folk watched his every move, but once he was free of the place, the world felt colder. Nik here is stronger than he was, perhaps. "No rush to decide anything now, Nik. You need to rest and eat, or you'll not be able to decide anything at all."

"My mother told me you had a dog once, Mr Turpin. She said you had a big and thin hunting dog with kind, sad eyes." Richie stops cutting. This one has a way of getting right to him, as if she can see his insides and the memories that swim in his heart like fish deep in the ocean.

"I lost her," he whispers.

"How?"

"You don't need to know. It was a dark time. I'd rather not remember."

"My mother said you loved that dog."

"I did. It was loyal to me." Richie is mournful suddenly.

"What was the name?"

"Bess."

"If you share your dark times, Mr Turpin, you can be relieved of them, somehow." Richie sets down the knife.

"You are a clever one, I'll give you that, and you and I have lived already through much, there'll be a tale to tell of it in times to come, but we have more road to travel and you are not home yet. I am your companion, and your friend, but do not think you can ask me to reveal my heart to you, Swift Nik, for I will not. There are many dark things there, deeds and stories, and events that have hardened me, and I will not share them. Not with you and not with anybody." Though Richie has not raised his voice, there is iron in his tone. Nik has stepped too far. Dogs are important, some more than others.

"I am sorry, Mr Turpin."

"Eat," he says. Nik uses a stick to skewer a piece of the rabbit on the pointed end, lets it cool in the fresh autumn air and then takes a bite. It's good.

For a few minutes they eat the strips of rabbit meat that have cooked on the hot stone. The taste is rich and the two need the rest and the nourishment. There's the peaceful, easy silence again, the noise of the birds flitting above and the light wind in the trees. Far away there's the shrill sound of a woodpecker drumming, a fly buzzes in front of Richie's face.

"I lost her in a card game," says Richie. He means his dog, Bess. What's the use in keeping secrets that will never be told? "I lost her in a card game to a farming lad from Fridaythorpe." He looks off into the trees around them as he speaks and his eyes are moist, faraway, and sad. "He was a terrible player, and as green as they come, and he was drunk too. I'd heard already that he was a woodsman, and his wife and he had the cottage on the estate nearby. He wasn't a drinker, and he was only at the card table because he'd had too much ale. He had steady hands and well-kept boots, good braces and stitched well to his breeches - done by his lass no doubt. I asked the landlord when I left the table if he was a man to be trusted and he guaranteed it, too quick to be a lie, and so, I went back to the table and I played big and lost hard to him - ten guineas until I had nothing left, and I offered him my dog as a double or nothing, and I made sure I lost again." Richie wipes his eyes with his thumb and forefinger. "And when he'd won, he didn't want to take the dog, nor all the money neither, he said it was too much for him and he was just a simple lad. I looked to the other gamblers at the table for help and they nodded, saying that a man couldn't lose his dog at a betting table, ten guineas, aye, but not a dog as fine as that. I drew my pistol and I held it loose at my side as I sat there, and I told him he had to take the dog, he had to take my Bess, because, a life with him would be better for her than a life on the road with me. I'm as good a card player as there is, Nik, and I can lose as easy as I can win. He knew, did that woodsman, and I made him take the money too, all of it." A single tear sits at the side of one of his eyes – that is as far as it will get. "I know that I did right, that night, maybe the only right I ever did. She was better off without me."

"Was my mother better off without you also, Mr Turpin?" It is an honest question.

"Aye. She was." He dips his head, perhaps in shame. "Those that have been my friends, Nik, have not fared well. I do not want anyone else to suffer because of me." Richie takes a strip of meat in his long fingers, he doesn't look like he wants it. "We need to rest," he says. "There will be men following us. I'd say the captain of that Dutch ship will not stop until I'm dead, or the both of us. There'll be men from the Scarborough garrison, and perhaps Omar's men too. They will not think we are so rude as to set up camp here and if they track that horse, they'll not find us, but they will in the end. As soon as it gets dark, we move." Nik nods.

They eat the rabbit meat and wash it down with water. Richie has found mushrooms which he lightly cooks on the stone also, and there's a handful of brambles. As the afternoon sun struggles through the canopy of the woods above them, Nik settles back in a bed of freshly fallen leaves that have a rich, earthy smell. Richie lays a few yards off and has covered his body with his black cloak. They lie still and the sounds of the forest come alive in the silence, the scratching of a creature some way off in the undergrowth, the faint drumming of the woodpecker and the coo of a pigeon. The wind rustles the leaves of the canopy above and it's warm but not hot. Nik's mind whirls, there is something troubling her:

"I am sorry to tell you this, Sir," says Nik. Her voice breaks the calm of the silent forest, "but I think my mother was not better off without you. I think you are wrong. I have seen the way she lives and her desperation." Nik listens for a reply, but the sounds of the forest creep back as silence returns, the rat-ta-ta of the woodpecker, the flapping of pigeon wings and the babble of Scalby beck some way behind them. Richie heard the words alright. He does not have a response. All those years ago, when he was chased away from North Burton, he vowed he would not return for her because she would have a better life without him. He was a poor farm lad, wanted for murder, with no education and no money. What could he possibly offer a woman such as she? The words Nik spoke rattle around Richie's brain as he lays with his face covered by his cloak. He feels sleep washing over him.

What if Swift Nik is right?

There's a whisper near the ground where Nik has just opened her eyes.

"Look sharp," it's Richie's voice.

"I didn't mean to sleep so long," comes the answer.

"Not so loud, lass." Her mouth is dry and there's a rumble from her stomach. She wipes the sleep from her eyes with mucky fingers and sits up. It's sunset and there's an orange glow through the trees around and above them.

"There have been people on the road not so far away," says Richie in hushed tones. He has already scouted the immediate area. "I heard their voices."

"Many of them?"

"I would say a group, aye," whispers Richie. "They were on horseback, but I didn't hear the creak of a cart. They're gone for the time being, but if they find that horse, they'll be back. I saved you some of the rabbit bones to suck on, and I found pears, a little hard but good eating." The shadows in the forest around them are getting longer and the air is colder than it was earlier in the day when they first lay on the bed of leaves. Nik's eyes adjust to the dimming light. Richie sits beside her with his knees up to his chest and the tricorn hat pulled low over his eyes.

"Are we a long way from Beverley, Mr Turpin?"

"I can't be sure where we are. West of Scarborough is all I know. If we keep south then we'll be in the right direction. Are you ready to go?"

"Aye," answers Nik. "How long will it take?"

"Scarborough is a good two days walk from Beverley and that's by road and with food in your belly, and travelling by day as well. Whatever the road may be, it will be easier than what we have already been through. I can understand that you are anxious to get back, but it will take time to do it safely, and we will have to work out how to get you back to your father. I will get you home, but it will take time."

"I'm not anxious to go home now, Sir, I would rather take all the time in the world about it. I have a job to do when I get there, and I am not sure how I will get that done either." Nik can hear Richie sigh.

"We'll need to get moving," he says.

"Once we are back in Beverley and you get what is owed to you, Mr Turpin, I would ask you to speak to my mother."

"Aye, you can be sure I will, Nik." There's something fatalistic and too quick about Richie's reply. "I thought your plan was for me to run off with your mother." Nik frown in the darkness.

"I was speaking foolishly, Mr Turpin. Now, I have my head about me, I would wish you to make a life there, once my father is gone." Richie gets to his feet without effort and his cloak swishes as he ties it around his front.

"You still plan to kill him then?"

"Yes," comes the reply. Nik struggles a little and uses the log behind her to get to her feet. At her full height, Nik stands a foot shorter than Richie. She fits that flat cap to her head and pulls it down over the red hair, as she does. It's a disguise almost.

"You'll think twice before you do it. I've said as much already," his words are thick.

"I will, Mr Turpin."

"And you will think of me."

"Aye."

"You've no need to tell me of this again, lass. Those that talk too much about what they are going to do often never follow up with the deed. I do not want you to be one of those."

Nik darkens.

"It will be done and I will say no more of it."

CHAPTER FOURTEEN

Richie Turpin walks at a steady rate in the starlight through the trees and between the tall grass. It's not quick when you cannot quite see where to put your feet. Nik has fallen in step behind his great stride and looks up to his wide tricorn hat as a dark silhouette against the pale glow of the stars in the sky above. The trees are beginning to thin out as they walk out of the great forest. Richie has explained that this is the river Derwent, and it will take them south.

It takes an hour to walk to the flat lands that Richie and Nik know as home. The night sky is wide, clear, and cold with the stars shimmering down on them from above. There's a rough path that they take along a hedge and the footing is better here so that Nik and Richie can walk side by side. There's an owl somewhere far away and the cry of a fox further into the distance. Richie keeps a steady pace and the shoes he pinched the other day squeak as he walks. In the silence of the autumn night, Nik feels like they could be the only people in the world.

"How are the shoes?"

"Too small. I had to cut a hole in the front for my toes. It was good leather too. I was sorry to do it." This seems the final comment on the subject and Nik looks down to see that Richie wears only one of the stolen shoes, the other is his own boot.

"Have you stolen a great many things, Mr Turpin?"

"I have taken what I needed and some more besides, but I'm not a rich man, so I don't suppose I have stolen a great many things."

"By that reasoning, Sir, you suggest that rich men are thieves." He looks at her in the darkness as they walk but cannot see her face because of her cap. She is quick.

"I'll not lie to you, Nik, I do believe that rich men are thieves. Either that, or they had rich fathers, or grandfathers who were thieves before they were. That's the truth of the matter. Your father is an example."

"What do you know of my father?"

"Nothing."

"Then how would you know he is a thief?"

"He's rich." Richie cannot see Nik grin as they walk.

"My father would disagree, Mr Turpin, he would say that there is a natural order to the world, with intelligent men such as he on the top, and poor working folk on the bottom, animals lower even than that. It is the will of God, he would say."

"Not so," answers Richie. His voice is sharper and more animated than usual. "I have heard a great number of men speak on this, and their reason is stronger than mine, so it is with their ideas that I will answer. A person has the right to their own body, and to govern the way in which they will live and the work that they do." He sighs. "This around us, this world and these fields, this night sky studded with stars, the mud beneath our feet, this is God's bounty and as he has given us the gift of our bodies, he has given us the world also. What we work for is rightfully ours. Your father, Nik, does not feed or water the horses that he owns, nor does he build the boats that he ships goods across the rivers, nor does he raise, slaughter and cure the leather that he ships. He is a thief to steal the time of others who do such, and a thief also to keep the money that their work generates."

"You did not craft either the shoe or the boot you wear, Mr Turpin, nor did you fashion the gun you carry."

"I did not say I was not a thief also, Nik, but I am lesser a rogue than those who do not freely confess who they are. As I recall also, you helped me steal this shoe." Again, Richie cannot see the grin that spreads across Nik's face in the darkness.

"I am one of the road, now," comes the answer.

"You are of the road until you see the hangman's noose or

a warm bed, Nik. There are no friends in this life, I mean the life that I live."

Richie slows and touches his forehead. He wishes he had not said this, for it reveals too much of who he is inside. Nik has a way, like their mother, of getting within a person and in so, teasing them out. Nik asks:

"If you and I came upon a coach now, Mr Turpin, in the darkness here, and we robbed it, and in the back was a chest full of silver and gold coins, jewellery and trinkets, posh goblets and ruby rings, what would you and I do with it?"

"I have been there, Nik, I have robbed such a carriage, and the wealth was the worst thing to happen to us, it made the gang greedy, it made us think we could be professional thieves like the rich men of this world, but there was no way we could keep it, no device by which we could say that the money was ours. We split the spoils and went our separate ways but the wealth was too much for me, so I gave it away, as best I could. Of course, I had for myself what I thought I wanted, a smart cloak and hat from Atkinson's of York, stout boots, a tidy belt and a gun fashioned to my own standards, which you now carry, Nik. All of it didn't even come close to spending the wealth I had. Beggars can only take so much, and the card table can take a good deal more, but the real money I passed to poor folk who would squirrel it away for a rainy day, the livery yard lad who knew where he could buy land for a stable, a widow who could buy an expensive house in a posh suburb of York. I tell you, truthfully, when it was all gone, I felt a relief."

They walk on. Their feet crunching on the hard mud of the road that leads south along the river Derwent back to the East Riding of Yorkshire. Nik processes the information she has heard.

"You could have bought your own land, Richie," she whispers. "You could have become a gentleman, with houses and a livery yard, and a wife, a woman such as my mother."

"I was born a poor lad, Nik, and back then I did not have

wisdom to do such a thing. There's a confidence that comes to being born with money and status that allows such men to be who they are, to own great parts of the world and sit in parliament and fight wars with folk they have never had cause to argue with."

"I do not think my father or any of his rich associates could ride or fight, or live, as you could, Mr Turpin. I believe it may only be a leap of imagination for you to become such as they are." Richie shakes his head and clicks his tongue.

"You're a swift one for sure, Nik, and wise beyond your years."

"I am also your friend on this road."

"Well, let us see about that when we get back to Beverley."

Dawn rises over the flat lands of the East Riding. As soon as the weak light appears over the horizon, there are warbles of birds in the bushes and shrill chirps as the countryside comes to life. There's the coo of a woodpigeon and the call of a song thrush. Fields of harvested and cut wheat stretch out on either side. It has been a long night of walking, Richie and Swift Nik have left the banks of the river Derwent far behind them, and continued south, nearly as far as the market town of Driffield. Richie has explained that to go through the place would be too dangerous for them, so they will have to skirt around. They have eaten the berries and nuts Richie collected in the great forest behind and Nik has been sucking and gnawing on a rabbit bone. It is the first time she has really known what hunger means.

In the distance along the straight road between the fields there appears a carriage. Two brown horses pull a large covered cab and a driver sits atop with a tall hat and a smart dark coat fastened up with golden buttons. This will be the Driffield to Scarborough stage of a Monday morning, carrying mail and possibly passengers or goods. Richie closes up his cloak to cover his pistol as he gives Nik a concerned look.

"Should we be worried?" she asks.

"I don't think so, word doesn't travel as quick as you might think. We'll just be two travellers on the way south to Driffield, looking for work perhaps. But keep that gun out of sight." Nik nods and buttons up her own jacket. The two of them walk on, side by side as the carriage approaches, Richie six foot four tall with his tricorn hat and black cloak and Nik, shorter with rounded shoulders and the flat cap pulled low over the eyes and some of the ginger hair spilling out over the ears. Details of the vehicle become clearer as it gets closer, the driver has a black beard and moustache, the cab is a smooth polished mahogany, the two horses up front are bays with platted black mains and trimmed feathers. It is a well-kept outfit that rattles towards them in the early Monday morning mist with the birds tweeting all round and a weak sun struggling up into the sky.

The driver begins to slow when he gets closer to them, he eases up the pace and gently pulls on the reins with his black leather gloves. The horses come to rest ten yards away from the two of them. This is unusual. In Richie's experience, stagecoach drivers are harsh men who need to get where they have to be, stopping slows them down, makes them late and keeps them from the large brandy in the next coaching inn. Richie approaches the driver with Nik lagging behind.

"Well met," calls the driver from his high seat.

"A fine morning to you, Sir," answers Richie from below. The driver is nervous. He is immaculately turned out and the gold buttons on his coat shine in the dull early morning sun. His dark eyes are worried and he looks back over his shoulder and then scans the horizon ahead.

"What's the word on the road?" he asks.

"What do you mean, Sir?" asks Richie.

"Well, there's been talk of highwaymen," gossip moves quickly. "There's word of some bloody fool out at Scarborough saying he's Dick Turpin, and he's not alone. He's robbed a stagecoach bound for York already." Richie takes off his hat and looks up at the driver with his earnest blue eyes under his brown hair.

"We have heard nothing, Sir. It has been a plain trip for us. Where are you bound?"

"To Scarborough, and the bloody company wouldn't give me a guard neither. They say it's all hot air and that Dick Turpin was hanged up at York years and years back. They don't have to drive these lanes like I do, and it's just me alone as well." It seems news does travel quickly, and rumour twists the truth also. The driver is one of those flighty, worried men. He takes a half pint glass bottle from his coat pocket, pops the cork, and empties a glug of whatever is inside into his mouth. Now they are close, Nik can see that his eyes are red and bloodshot like he hasn't slept.

"I don't think a highwayman would attack on a day such as today, Sir, it looks like it might be fine," says Richie. "You'll be in Scarborough before evening easily."

"I've got a family, I have, you know," says the driver. "The last thing my poor heart needs is to get robbed." Nik looks up at him with narrow eyes from under the flat cap. The man is almost unable to see the obvious as it stands right in front of him on this narrow road to Scarborough from Driffield. "They say he's six foot five the one who calls himself Dick Turpin, six foot five, he must be a giant and the lad with him is Swift Nik, a red head and called such because they'll shoot quick and ask whatever later." The driver takes out the little bottle once more and pops the cork with his finger and thumb before he takes a swig. Nik's chest swells a little in pleasure, for this is the first time she has been feared and it is a new sensation. Young Nicola Sullivan was stared at, pushed around, dominated but never feared. The driver's shaking hand puts the bottle back into his jacket and Nik feels a mixture of emotions - pity for the most part. If she were to take out the pistol from her chest, even though it is not loaded, then this man would crumple and sob, for exactly what he fears most is standing right in front of him.

"I think the day will be fine, Sir," says Richie. "I think you'll make good time to Scarborough, and from what my associate and I have seen, there are no such people on the roads. All will be well." The driver gives a smile and nods.

"It's good to meet fine honest folk on the road," he says down at them.

"Aye, you'll be in Scarborough for late afternoon." The driver tips his hat and picks up the heavy reins, gives them a light flick with his gloves creaking against the leather. The horses begin at a steady rate and speed up as they get further away. Richie and Nik watch as the carriage moves away into the morning mist.

"We needed those horses," says Nik.

"Did you see the state of him?"

"Aye." Richie replaces the tricorn hat back on his head.

"I'm a robber, Nik, but I'm not that sort of robber. The poor bastard would have dropped dead if I'd have pulled my gun."

Nik watches as the carriage gets further away.

"It seems he knew who we were."

"Aye," says Richie. "We'll have to stay off the road."

"Do you think the men from Scarborough will still be following us?"

"If there's a reward for our capture, then yes."

"For me?"

"No," answers Richie. "You will go back to Beverley, take off your flap cap, curl your hair and you will once more be Nicola Sullivan. Swift Nik will be nothing more than a rumour."

"I will not be that lass again," she says. There is no judgement from Richie:

"In that case, Nik Swift – you are wanted, and you'll be hanged if caught."

There are parts of the East Riding that are wild and untrodden, where badgers are free to roam even in the late morning, and beavers are at liberty to swim and build as they please. It's not the thick forest of Dalby, but something in between with patches of woodland amongst the fields. That's not to say this land is free – it's owned by a lord or duke or someone, either near or far away, but nobody works the soil.

A deer peers at Nik with wide and fearful eyes, frozen solid as it looks through the trees some twenty yards, ready on shivering legs to run, it thinks it has all danger within its sights. A shot rings out from the opposite side of the creature, and the birds in the trees take to the sky in fright at this. The deer does not have time to run, falls to its knees and pitches over. Richie Turpin steps out of the bushes behind it and draws his knife. He used Nik as the bait to keep the animal watching while he flanked it. There was enough powder in the pans of both pistols for a charge and Richie used a pebble for the bullet. Nik draws close, and the animal is still faintly breathing as it lays with blood running from the side of its body. Richie kneels and puts his knife to the throat gently, there's no pleasure in the movement.

He shows Nik how to gut and strip a small deer carcass, he's already shown her how to sharpen a knife on a whetstone, and how to build and light a little fire. Nik is quick, swifter perhaps because she has never been taught how to do such things before and she's eager. By ten o'clock, they have cooked strips of the meat and Richie chews on a piece as he explains how to oil the pistol and take care of the wood.

They are safe in these woods, and so the day goes as the last. Richie explains how to shoot, even though they have no balls or powder to practice, he describes how to clobber someone with the pistol handle and where to hit them round the head to get it right. They chat in whispers as the day gets hotter and then drift off to sleep until late afternoon. They eat again, and by early evening when the sun is drawing down and sending long shadows across the forest, they pack up and walk into the darkness.

Despite his size, Richie can move quietly, and he walks where it might be difficult to track, over stone or on moss. He knows too, the animals that move around them in the darkness, the moths that flutter up at the moon and the nightjar that calls eerie into the silence. In whispers, he tells Nik what he knows of the forest, where to walk and what to look out for, and when they hear the noise of a solitary poacher moving towards them, they hide in the bushes and watch his heavy boots crunch past.

At dawn, they find mushrooms on a rotten tree stump and nuts from the woodland floor, they build a little fire in a dip to cook the deer meat from the day previous. It's calm and sweet and they sleep the day out. Richie knows this country - it's where he grew up. The next night they track around the woods outside Kirkburn and onto Middleton on the Wolds. Nik's eyes are getting used to the night and the progress is slow, when it's overcast there's little they can do but wait if the going is not easy underfoot. Richie does not seem to be in any rush to get where they are bound, and it seems, they have lost those that follow from Scarborough. They speak in easy whispers. Nik tells Richie of her life in the big house on Toll Gavel and the Frenchman, Marcel, who is her mother's half-brother and how badly the house treat him, from the cooks to her own father. Nik is free to tell Richie the truth as she sees it without fear of judgement from him, for the tall man just listens and seems good at it. Nik talks of her mother and she can see that Richie listens a little keener when she does, she tells of her father too, Mr Sullivan, and how he whips the horses when they will not do as they are bid, how he whips the servants too, and his wife also, and even his daughter when nobody can see. There is no more talk of killing the old man but Richie senses it is not far from Nik's thoughts. In the dim grey of first dawn, Richie shows her how to fight with a knife and how to move in circles as his father, the Pearlman, showed him. He talks of pressure points on a man's neck and on his chest, shows Nik how to swing a punch so that it hurts. He impresses upon the youngster the few principles of street fighting, never fight when you can run, or it looks like you'll lose and never play by the rules, bite, shout, use anything you can find to stop your opponent, and if in doubt, go for the eyes. Nik is not a fighter at all, she has no experience, there's been no opportunity to rough and tumble with the lads on a summer day, but the heart is there, and the eyes are quick to spot and exploit a weakness.

The next day, they awake in the woods far south of Middleton on the Wolds. Richie has found sheep's sorrel leaves and he shows Nik that the young plant is tangy and sweet. They eat more of the venison and there are peaceful silences between these two. The few days have been calm and sweet, for Richie is an easy friend and a gentle teacher, he does not find fault with anything that Nik does. Neither of them want this to end, for in each other, they have found a strange friendship, perhaps of convenience.

Richie knows that this cannot last and that it will be best all round when he gets this lass back to her father in Beverley, then she can do as she wants; at least, there will be counsel from the mother to steer her in the right direction. There's also the price that Richie was promised, the bullet that Elizabeth said she would put through his chest. He wonders if he can go through with it for seeing the world through Nik's eyes gives him hope. Richie knows this is poison for him, for as soon as they are in Beverley, the world will go back to the way it is meant to be. He and Nik will not be highwaymen on the run and living off the woods, he will be a simple robber once again, wanted for things he has done and things he has not; and Nik will go back to being a wallflower lass with red hair who is pushed around by her bossy father – like her mother.

"We should be back in Beverley, Mr Turpin," says Nik.

"Aye. We are close, but we are not going to Beverley yet. It's too dangerous for us to just appear as we are. There is a safe house I know of, it's not far from here, just north of Market Weighton. In the village of Goodmanham. Opposite the All Saint's Church there's a pub, The Star, and behind that, in time gone by, there was a great and rich family house with seven children at the time I last heard. They go by the name of Drewton. In the woods between the pub and the house, lived a crone with knowledge for healing and she was protected for her skills too, and loved for them."

"Are we going there?"

"Aye."

"Who's the crone to you?"

"She's my mother. My Meg. If she's still there."

CHAPTER FIFTEEN

The day is starting to fade as they walk down into Goodmanham over a wide field of cut wheat. There's the autumn blaze of red sunshine behind them and the smell of ripe grass in their nostrils. Richie has taken off his tricorn hat because of the heat, but Nik has not removed the flat cap that she looks out from under, it's protection for her, no matter how hot it might get. They stop at the corner of the field and look down on the little village below them, Richie squats in the corner, in the shade and Nik joins him. He takes a drink from his water bottle and passes it to his companion.

"I have been here before," says Nik. "The crone you speak of, Meg, she's known to my mother somehow. She's a healer, the old kind."

"How long since you were last here?"

"Christmas just gone," answers Nik.

"Then she will most likely still be here. Did you see her?"

"The crone? No. My mother entered alone. I stayed outside the pub in the carriage with my father. She's not liked, Mr Turpin. My father says she is a witch." Richie nods. He's heard this before, many times. Rich ladies will ride from as far as Kingston Upon Hull to consult Meg, as far even as Lincoln or York too, but if she did not have the protection of this village, the pub and the Drewton family, she would probably be a witch. Men fear powerful women who don't need them, and they fear that which they do not understand even more.

"What ailed your mother, Nik?"

"It was not a good time for her. Come to think of it, Mr Turpin, it has never been a good time for her." Nik does not really want to tell Richie what she knows. "She lost a child." Richie's hand goes to his forehead in concern and he fits the tricorn hat back onto his head so that it hides his face and expression.

"I hope she did not suffer too much," he says.

"She suffers all the time, Mr Turpin." He dips his head.

"I am sorry to hear that."

"Things will be different," says Nik, "when I get home."

"I hope you are right. I would counsel you to act with caution and not let your hot blood run away with you when the time comes." That warning again.

"Aye," comes the answer. Nik has the security and arrogance of the young, of those who have yet to truly be hurt or injured by the crashing waves of the everyday. It's not the time to talk over this again.

"We will proceed as such," explains Richie nodding down the hill to the village. "There's a track that leads along this field and to the back of the cottages and, at the bottom there is a gate to a cow field. There's a cottage in the trees, or there was a while ago. We must enter unseen."

"Will that be difficult?" ask Nik.

"It depends if she has dogs or a cockerel."

Richie keeps behind the thick bush as they walk down the gentle slope towards Goodmanham. Dusk is falling. At the far end, over the harvested wheat, there's a flock of starlings wheeling and swooping in unison as they do before they roost. It means they feel safe. Richie watches them for a moment before following the hedge down to the village.

On the right-hand side there's a cow field with the animals in the far corner, and a cottage far off. This is the nearest they have come to civilization for the last two days almost, the only other soul they have encountered was the unknowing poacher walking past them in the dead of night. There's the smell of wood smoke, cow dung and horses. It is much the same as when Richie was last here some ten years ago, when he made the same little journey down the hill to where he knew Meg was. He had heard about the death of his Nana and returned as far as Goodmanham where he knew his Meg had set up as a healer.

The path leads to a quaint gate opening onto a little grass field with a wooden shack set beside a weeping willow and a duck pond. Last time he came here, Richie did not make it past this point. He reasoned that Meg would not want to see him after the events all those years back. Perhaps he was afraid of how she might treat him. He looks down at Nik. and she glances up from under the flat cap. There's the crack of a twig behind them, and Nik reacts first, drawing the pistol from inside her jacket, she turns on her heels and levels it into the darkness. Richie has not had time to make any movement. A tall, blonde figure steps out of the dusk and in his hand is a smoothbore musket. He carries it lightly as he moves forward so they can just make out his face. Nik uses her thumb to pull back the action on her pistol and it crackles as it cocks.

"Drop your weapon, Sir," whispers Nik. The blonde man does not seem to hear as he moves closer. He is well dressed in the country style, with shoulder length hair and a moustache, a simple tunic and riding boots. He moves as a young man, but there is something about his face that makes him look older. He does not seem to be worried by the pistol that Nik holds in an unsure hand, perhaps he knows it's not loaded.

"I saw you come down the hill, by chance," says the man. His accent is clear, smooth, and educated. "How tall are you, Sir?" he asks, for the smoothbore musket points at Richie. It's an odd question to ask with a gun trained on someone.

"I am six foot four," he answers. The blonde man nods.

"She said that you would come, eventually," he explains. "She said so many years ago, as well as last month. She said that there would be a tall man, six foot four who would come under the cover of dark perhaps, alone possibly. He would have a tricorn hat and cloak of black, and boots made by Sarrell's of Kingston Upon Hull. A man of the road."

"That is I," replies Richie.

"Have your lad put his gun away," says the blond man. Nik

does not move at all, but the heavy gun wobbles in effort as she holds it straight.

"Do as the gentleman asks please," whispers Richie. Now there is compliance and Nik puts the pistol back into the holster inside her tunic. The musket does not move from its target.

"Are you a Drewton lad?" asks Richie.

"Hardly a lad anymore."

"She knew I was coming?"

"Yes," he pauses, "but you are many years late. I thought she might be losing her mind after all. Is this your lad?" He nods down at Nik. At the suggestion, Richie answers without thinking, as if what he is about to say is the truth. Perhaps it is.

"My daughter."

"You do know who I am speaking about don't you?" asks the blond man.

"Yes, the cunning woman from the cottage over there. She's Meg."

"Aye."

"You must know, in turn, who I am, then."

"Yes," he replies and he lowers the musket. "You're Dick Turpin, you're her son."

Richie has to dip his head considerably to get through the door frame, Nik, not so much. The blond man with the musket does not enter but hangs back outside. Nik glances at him out the corner of her eye as she steps into the cottage, he is more perfunctory than friendly.

There's the smell of pine needles and smoke as they walk into the darkened cottage. At one end is a small fireplace under a wide chimney breast kitted out with an oven and little doors aside the flames. Along both walls there are shelves with hundreds of mismatched bottles and pots. There's red powder, nuts, ground up leaves, little sticks, stones, and chemicals all peeking out through the clear, green or brown glass bottles into the centre of the room. In front of the fire is a big, working table. A woman with a white headscarf lights a lamp hanging from one of the low rafters, she has her sleeves rolled up and her forearms are strong and smooth. She's hardly a crone. Nik sees her face as she turns, she is old, but still powerful and has fine blue eyes with crow's feet wrinkles at the side. Richie removes his hat as he stands there looking at the woman and her hand goes to her mouth in shock when she sees who it is, he walks towards her and she to him. They embrace, with Richie bending down so the woman can put her arms around his neck as she grips him tight. Nik sees her eyes close and the wince on her face as she holds him – she is about to cry. They keep the position for a minute before Richie steps back, now Nik can see that the woman's face is serene and calm, and all the emotion that was there within is gone. This is the East Riding of Yorkshire; a person doesn't go showing how they feel. Richie turns to Nik:

"This is my mother, Meg." Nik nods as she's seen stable lads do to old ladies, then takes off the cap. It reveals the red hair and the clever, hazel eyes. Meg gives her a smile. Like her son, there is no judgement even though she can see that this is a young woman dressed as a young man.

"I'll make us tea," she says as she goes back behind the table to the fire. From a black cauldron over the coals she scoops out hot water first into one cup and then another. She turns and sets them on the table. Richie and Nik remain standing. "Sit down will you, Richie? It's been twenty years since I last saw you, what do you want me to do, cry? There's too much water under the bridge since then. What's important is that you're here now." Richie takes the cup. Meg was always tougher than Nana, not in the words she says, but in the way that she lives. It's Meg who can amputate a man's leg with a saw while he screams in pain, and it's Meg who delivers babies and pulls out teeth, she mops up blood and stitches up wounds, she listens to the darkest stories that folk dare not tell anyone else. She's like stone on the outside, smooth and calm with the voice of reason. Richie can see in her eyes he has upset her, but it will play out in time. He sits down in one of the chairs next to the table and nervously, Nik does the same. Meg gets herself a cup and then sits opposite with her arms folded and the steam from the hot water rising in lines to the rafters above.

Richie swallows. One of the cottage cats, the long-haired scruffy one, creeps away to the dark corner sensing danger. There's the sound of a flapping bird outside. Nik licks her lips as the seconds pass.

After the shock of seeing her son, Meg is angry.

The coals flicker into a flame which dies down again in fear. Richie will have to face this seething silent fury as he sits there with his tea in front of him. Meg will not shout or cry, there will be no wailing, no stories of self-pity. There will only be the stone-cold hammer of truth. His stomach knots in fear, nobody but Meg can make him feel like this, no one else, except perhaps Elizabeth Pike now Sullivan.

"I am sorry I did not come earlier," says Richie. He must also use truth to explain. "I was afraid, after I left it so long. Then it was a longer time still, and I was more afraid."

"What were you afraid of, Richie?" she asks. He swallows again and looks down at the wood of the table.

"You. I was afraid I broke your heart." Meg responds quickly:

"The world broke my heart long before you came along, Richie Jackson of North Burton. You were the tonic that healed me, once upon a time."

"Did you not hear that I had been hanged?"

"I knew it was not you, Richie."

"How?" Richie examines Meg's face, just as he remembers it, but with more wisdom and wrinkles from the sides of her mouth.

"A mother knows these things, and I have those come to me from York, for my services. They described the man who was hanged. He was not six foot four."

"I did not want to put you in danger?"

"You have put me in danger now. This is a weak excuse, Richie. You were wanted for so many years, perhaps even so now. You were afraid to face me. Why?" Meg knows the answer to this but she must have it from Richie, to get it into the air so that they can move on from this. It has been waiting for a long time. Richie looks down at his big hands where he clutches his tricorn hat and Nik can see that he is more like a little boy, afraid of this wise and calm woman, afraid that he will have to reveal himself to her. "You will have to explain yourself, Richie." He swallows.

"It was my fault the Pearlman died. The man I called my father. He was shot at the Pennyman Estate when he and I rescued the Pike woman and her father." Tears begin in Richie's eyes and his face reddens, the words are an effort for him to force out, guilt he has carried, and the beginning of a pattern that repeated itself again and again, the loss of those he loved and who travelled with him. He takes a breath but there are no tears, just the promise of them.

"You will have to be clearer, Richie. You will have to tell me and this young lass here, just what it is you are and just what it is you are running from." He did not expect this so soon, and he is unprepared. To have himself unpicked and unraveled, to see the mess he has made of all his days laid out bare for people he cares for to see.

"He told me to go north and to run because there were soldiers following, I promised him I would. He was shot in the stomach, and he made light of it, so that I thought it was nothing." The memories are flooding Richie's brain, they come quick and rich, hot, and still with the same emotion. "He died on the hill opposite Etton village, against a fencepost, and I put his pistol in his hand, like the old ways say you should, and he didn't make a single sound while he went." Richie looks up to Meg. "I left him there, and it was because of me that he died, and it has been my punishment since, Meg. For all those who have travelled with me, all of them, the ones that I have wanted to protect… they have suffered, and it is my curse also. This is why I could not come before, I could not have this happen to you." The speech has cost Richie, for it has come from his heart.

"Yet here you are," says Meg. Her eyes are red, but the stone-cold truth speaks from her lips.

"I am here to say goodbye. I have nothing left to run from. I will stand up for my crimes and I will take the punishment, and if I hang, then the better for it. This lass that travels with me is to be returned to her mother. I am here because nothing must happen to her, and, I will be of no danger to you once I lay down my gun." Meg counters.

"I wish you had trusted me more back in those days, Richie. I would have hidden you under my floorboards like I did your father when he was a wanted man. I could have helped. And, I would have told you back then, the same as I will now, that it was not you that shot the Pearlman, nor was it you that bid him to join you that night at the Pennyman house. He was a hothead and a scoundrel, and he loved the fight more than he loved anything, and he loved you for what you did back then. So he was shot, Richie, and it was not you to blame, and I do not know your story since then, but I know it was not your fault that those you travelled with died either. You have been a fool not to come to your mother, for sense and reason is my anchor." Meg looks down into her own wooden cup and then back up to her son. He wipes his eyes with the back of his big hand because the emotion is something he must hide within him, as he's been taught. Meg looks at Nik for the first time, at the wise eyes and the red hair and the slightly frightened expression.

"You look familiar. What is your name, lass?"

"I am Nicola Sullivan, also Nik Swift." It is the first time she's used the name. It was not planned, but seems more appropriate and more polite in this setting.

"Who's your mother?"

"Elizabeth Sullivan of Toll Gavel, Beverley." Meg grins.

"Now it makes sense, Richie," she says. "Elizabeth Sullivan who was Pike, who you rescued all those years ago from the Pennyman house. Now you've rescued her daughter. Did you see her?"

"Aye."

"She waited for you, a long time too." Richie nods as if he does not quite believe this is true. "After you took off, she found me, out at Etton, and it was she who introduced me to the Drewton family here, they are her friends, and it was she who helped me move. Once Nana and you were gone, I wanted a fresh start."

"What happened to Nana?" asks Richie. He knows she is dead, she must be, it's been twenty years and she was old back then.

"She fell down the cellar stairs at the pub and hit her head on the stone floor. Philipson, the landlord, says she was drunk and it was pitch black. She didn't suffer."

"Old cow," whispers Richie with a smile.

"It took four men to lift her out the pub and onto a cart," explains Meg. "They say she was drinking a gallon and a half of ale a day, and that Philipson was close to going bust." Richie grins again. Even in death Nana was trouble.

"Did she miss me?"

"She was glad you went out into the world, she said I should have done the same years ago with your father, but she did miss you, in the way that any Nana misses her grandchildren." Richie nods. This is a comfort to him.

"Meg, I must see that Nik here gets to her mother, and no mistake. I cannot afford for this to go wrong also. Would you help me get her to Beverley?"

"I surely will. I imagine word will already have got out that you are here, and that Nicola Sullivan is here also. You know how village tongues wag. What will you do now, Richie Lad? Will you melt into the autumn darkness?"

"I made a deal with Nik's mother, and I aim to get my payment."

"Is it money you asked for, Richie?"

"No, something else." He does not like to say what.

"I am glad it's not, for that would be the worst reason to risk your life. You can both stay here the night, and tomorrow ride to Beverley. The Drewtons will see the lass comes to no harm."

"I will ride too," says Richie. His words are thick.

"Then it will be goodbye will it, Richie Lad?"

"Aye, my Meg and it will be goodbye forever."

Meg's cottage is cozy. There's light from the lamp that hangs from the rafters and the fire is low in the hearth. Meg has made up a special brew for Richie, she used her pestle and mortar, powder from a bottle on the shelf, a leaf from a pot, dried herbs from another. She mixed it with water and made him drink the lot down then led him off to the bed in the far corner and made him sit down. She took off his boot and stolen shoe. Nik listened as she spoke to him, soft and sweet, she watched as she bid him to lay down and lifted his legs up onto the bed. She rubbed his head and put a blanket over him. It did not take her long, and the tall man was asleep in next to no time, all that brooding darkness and danger turned off like a tap. Meg returns to Nik who sits at the long table yet with the cap in her hands. She takes a seat opposite.

"You know they will hang him if he goes to Beverley."

"My mother has promised him something, she will honour it." replies Nik.

"She may not be able to honour it, Nicola. The law will take charge."

"My name is Nik, Miss Meg. I am Nicola no more."

"A taste of adventure has given you a new direction, has it, young lass?"

"Perhaps."

"I don't want him to hang."

"He will not."

"How can you be so sure, young Miss?"

"I'm not a miss." There's a little darkness in Nik's eyes. "He is my friend, and he looked out for me when nobody else has. I'll not let anything happen to him. My father is a powerful man." Meg takes a sip on her tea.

"I know what kind of a man your father is, Nik, he will do what's best for himself regardless of your wishes, or a man's life."

"I will deal with my father," says Nik. Meg looks down and sees the handle of the pistol Richie gave her peeping out of the holster that is hidden inside her jacket.

"The certainty of youth." Nik has heard these words before from Richie's lips. "I'll explain. The moment Richie sets foot in Beverley town, he'll be captured and he'll be hanged. I need you to be brave for his sake. At first light tomorrow, you'll slip out the door before he awakes, I'll let the Drewton stable lad know that you'll take a horse, and you'll ride as fast as you can to Beverley town, it'll take you two hours. You'll be back in the heart of your family, and my Richie will not be captured and not be murdered. What do you say to that?" Nik looks up to Megs eyes and the wrinkled wise face, the thin once blonde hair. There is no need to think about this. Nik knows that Richie will not get whatever her mother promised, she has just not had the time to think it through. It was always up to Nik to deal with their father, and this way, Richie will be safe too.

"What of the payment that my mother promised him?"

"Depends on what it is."

"I don't know what deal they have made, but part of me

hoped that it, was…" Nik struggles at the words. "Part of me hoped that he promised to take her away, ride off with her far from Beverley and the East Riding forever." Meg smiles and her eyes twinkle in the orange firelight.

"If that is what she's promised, he'll get her in the dead of night."

"Then, I'll ride at first light."

"You're a good lass, Nik."

"What do I tell Mr Turpin?" asks Nik.

"What do you think? What's best for him?"

"It's best that I slip off without him knowing." Meg nods. That would be the best thing indeed.

"You will see him down the road, Nik, however this story plays out." Nik smiles and Meg sees the straight white teeth and kindness in the eyes.

"I believe I will see him again."

Nik is awake in the darkness of the morning. It is before the sun is up and the embers in the fireplace glow under the big cauldron, the cottage is still black but the shapes of the furniture around are gaining definition. Meg gave Nik a blanket and she sat with it over her shoulders in front of the fire with her knees up to her chest. At the foot of the chair is the holster that carries Nik's gun – there is powder in it now and a lead ball too that Meg gave, for protection. Nik loaded Richie's pistol as well while he slept.

Nik's face is serious in the darkness. It's one thing to consider what to do, but it's quite another to put that into action. Nik is afraid. Her mouth is dry. It's not the ride from Goodmanham to Beverley that will be the problem, this is a few hours on fair roads, it is Mr Sullivan, the father. Nik does not know how she will react to him in her current form and carrying a pistol at her chest. One wrong or cruel word from the man's mouth, and she cannot be sure what she will do. She will not take his insults anymore, not after what she's learned and seen. Meg told her there would be a lad along at first light to lead her to the stables.

Nik stands, takes off the blanket and reaches down to pick up the holster. She fits it around her chest and does the straps up, then puts the grey, oversized jacket on to cover it. These are not Nik's clothes, they belong to another, but they are comfortable and more real than any of the dresses bought by her mother. Nik searches for the cap and fits it on her head over her eyes, she steps towards the door of the cottage and takes a deep breath. There is no way to know how this will all play out, but one thing is certain for a start, she is Nicola Sullivan no more.

The handle turns and the door creaks as it opens slowly inwards - someone else pushes it open from outside. Grey light spills into the cottage, and Nik looks up to a familiar face. There are the fat jowls and bald head of Mr Binx, her father's footman. He carries a musket in his big hands and behind him, sneering and wearing a feathered hat with his pointy beard, is her father, Mr Sullivan. They are here.

At least now Nik knows what she will do when she sees him. She goes to draw the pistol at her chest.

Time slows. Binx and two stable lads, as well as the Frenchman, Marcel, have ridden since they first got word Nicola Sullivan was at Goodmanham. Mr Sullivan insisted on coming too. Binx has been wound up on the journey, Mr Sullivan told him many times that because he is the biggest and is better paid than the others, he'll have to do the fighting if there is any. It has made Binx angry, and scared also, which may cause him to be more dangerous. As he steps in, Nik draws the pistol and levels it upwards so that the muzzle points directly up into the fat man's face. If he knew what he was looking at, he would probably stop, but he cannot quite see in the darkness. Binx is worried also that the two stable lads, the Frenchman and Mr Sullivan himself will think him weak if he does not perform his duties as required. He shoves the musket forward, knocks the heavy pistol out of Nik's hands and pushes her back into the cottage. The weapon clatters to the stone floor as Binx bursts in. Nik stumbles backwards into the darkness – she does not yet have the experience to know how to fight, it will require more training, and a good deal more real punch ups to acquire the kind of skill that Richie has. Binx senses that the figure is weaker than he and this spurs him on, he gives a throaty grunt, stumbles on the uneven stone floor, and falls forward, on top of Nik and the weight of the musket is heavy across her chest. There's a loud cry of the wind being slammed out of her.

"I've got this one pinned," yells Binx to the others. They follow, the two stable lads next, and then the Frenchman with Mr Sullivan standing in the door so he will be the last one to get hurt.

"Don't you move, you bastard," calls the fat man. "You tell us where young Nicola is or I'll crush the bloody life out of you." Nik groans.

"It's me." There it is. Nik thought she was someone different, but it's still there, the girl's voice, high-pitched and in pain, permanently scared and in need of someone to protect her. Mr Sullivan registers this.

"Get off her," he booms and Binx scrabbles to his feet. The musket in his hands falls away as he stands, he tries to help the figure he has just fallen on top of and protestations of innocence sprout from his wet and flabby lips.

"I didn't know it were you, lass. How could I?" Mr Sullivan steps into the semi darkness of the cottage and the two stable lads move aside. Marcel goes to his knees next to the fallen Nik, he holds out one of his hands in black gloves and Nik uses it to help her sit up.

"Nicola, is that you?" commands her father. He frowns down at the figure dressed in a flat cap and lad's clothes. Nik looks up, and there, standing very still behind her father, like a shadow, is Richie Turpin, with his tricorn hat tight to his head to obscure his features. In his right hand, and held against the back of Mr Sullivan's head, is his pistol with the flintlock pulled back. Sullivan has yet to notice.

"Do not make any sudden movements, Father," says Nik. There's that girl's voice there, again. The one she thought was lost. "There's the highwayman behind you, with his pistol to the back of your head." Nik's voice is steady, as if stating a simple matter of fact.

Sullivan goes ridged and glances to the side. Sure enough, out the corner of his eye, there's a dark figure towering over him with the muzzle of the pistol pointed at the back of his skull. The rich man lets out a whimper of terror. Marcel draws his rapier as he stands. Richie Turpin is rock still.

"Just say the word, Nik," Richie whispers. "Say the word and I'll put him out of his misery. You and I both know I'm to hang, and no mistakes. At least this way, we may both be afforded a way out of our predicament." Mr Sullivan swallows and his Adam's apple bobs under his tight silk neckerchief. One of the stable lads steps backwards in fear. Binx's widens his eyes. Marcel grits his teeth under his black moustache. Nik gets to her feet and the eyes are covered by the flat cap. There's no rush for an answer.

It would be much easier this way, if Richie were to shoot her father, for everyone. Binx would not have to listen to the man shout at him for his ineptitude. Marcel feels the iron weight of the rapier in his palm. Mr Sullivan is his landlord and the man who keeps him from a house that was his father's. It would be a much quicker ride home without Sullivan.

"It would not be right, Mr Turpin," says Nik. It's not a weak voice this time, and the words are smooth and solid as a whetstone. The figure behind Mr Sullivan removes the pistol and spirits it back under the long cloak, he clears his throat.

"I am sorry, Mr Sullivan," says Richie, "by the manner in which you entered, I took you and your companions to be common footpads and reacted as such. Your man pushed my associate to the floor. Thanks to young Nik's swiftness, any accident or misunderstanding has been prevented." Richie uses the language he's learned from gentleman, with unnecessarily long words and drawn-out sentences that are as pretty as the clothes they wear and the rings on their fingers. Sullivan turns to face him and is about to launch into remonstrations when the dawn light from the open door catches Richie's face. He sees the steel blue eyes. Here is a man who Sullivan has no sway over, and despite what this highwayman says, he was ready to shoot him. Sullivan must pretend he does not quite understand what happened, for he cannot be seen to lose face.

"Who are you?" he asks though he knows who it is.

"Mr Turpin, at your service. Nik and I were to ride to Beverley this day. This was the task that you entrusted to me, Sir."

Sullivan scoffs.

"So you say now. I was alerted to my daughter's presence here by one of the serving girls who is in my employ. There is little happens in the East Riding, Mr Turpin, that I am not aware of." The last fact is a lie. Richie looks down at the man with a feathered hat and a pointed fox beard. He knows what he has done and what kind of a master he is to his family. Richie suddenly thinks of the smooth, calm eyes of Elizabeth Pike, the woman who is this man's wife, and cold fury fills his stomach. Now he sees Sullivan again with his beady eyes, the self-importance in his flared nostrils, the sense of entitlement in the manner - he would like to kill him stone dead; only, Swift Nik has said she will do the job. Richie previously counselled mercy, but this close to the man, he sees the appeal of murder. "If you have harmed one hair on my daughter's head, then you shall hang," spits Sullivan.

"It's I who you employed to bring her back." Richie is a man with little to lose. His ride to Beverley may be his last one ever, and so, there is no fear. His face wears no emotion as he looks down on Mr Sullivan. Nik breaks the silence.

"Would it not be better gentlemen, if we could stand in the light outside? We would be able to get a better measure of what we are to do next?" There's mettle in her tone.

It's a fresh autumn morning in Goodmanham. There are perhaps fifteen horses and twice as many men gathered in the driveway of the great Drewton house. It's a few minutes' walk to the cottage where Nik and Richie spent the night. Near the front door and steps leading up to it are Drewton lads, three of them blonde and carrying muskets at ease in their folded arms. Some way off stand the Sullivans, Binx holding two horses by the reins, the stable lads holding two others and the Frenchman in his dark fishtailed coat and long boots standing guard between them. Richie Turpin walks away from the cottage last of all and his face is red, behind him is Meg and her old face is bleak and grey, they will have said their last goodbyes.

Under one of the two trees that flank the drive entrance, Mr Sullivan and his daughter face each other. He has marched her away from listening ears and, once he is satisfied they are far enough, he clicks his tongue for Nik to stop.

"Take off the cap, please Nicola," he asks.

"It's a disguise," comes the answer.

"You are in safe company now. I see no reason for you to wear it." Nik swallows. She cannot defy him. As Nik removes the material, thick ginger hair spills out to just behind the ears.

"What happened to your hair?"

"The Scots cut it off."

"Why?"

"To frighten me."

"What's that at your chest, under the coat?"

"A pistol." Nik gathered it up from the cottage floor. He gives a huff that comes out as a scoff.

"Do you know how to shoot?" The tone is sarcastic.

"Yes."

"Yes what?"

"Yes, Sir." Nik holds her father's gaze. She is as tall as he is. This action is rude. She thinks about drawing the weapon and shooting him in the stomach, but that would be impossible – there are witnesses, and, as the man looks at her, she can feel the bravado and the self-confidence she learned with Richie Turpin slipping away.

"It's not a ladylike thing to carry a gun, Nicola. You'll remove it, now." Girls like Nicola Sullivan do not defy their fathers, a gaze is one thing, but an order is another. Nik begins to unbutton the jacket down to the waist.

"What are you doing?" asks Sullivan.

"I must remove the jacket to take off the gun." He glances off at the men from his household twenty yards away and sees they are watching them.

"Do not remove any clothes," he commands. "Do you remember nothing about what it means to be a young woman?"

"Are you more concerned with men seeing my arms or that I carry a pistol." He snaps his head to look at her.

"You have too much of your mother in you, Nicola. She has cooled very much as she grows older. You will need some correction, I feel. You belong to me. Like a horse or a dog, more so than these lads who are in my employ. I do not want others to see what is mine. It cheapens you, and therefore me. Keep your pistol where it is for the time being."

"Yes, Sir," she answers. The days Nik spent with Richie and the spirit he helped her develop is ebbing away in front of this man's pettiness.

"And what was that conversation that you had with Turpin in the cottage. He says he thought I was a robber. What did he mean in his question to you?"

"I do not remember. I was afraid." Nik falls to lies quickly.

"You remember that you are my property, Nicola. I gave

you your life, and I can just as soon end it as well." Sullivan is not speaking out of turn. Nicola and her mother really do belong to him in the eyes of society, the law and the church. Nik's eyes burn with anger. Sullivan removes one of his gloves by pulling first at the thumb, and then two of the fingers. He steps forward, pauses and slaps his daughter around the face with the leather glove. It's not meant to hurt, rather to shock. Nik recoils from the blow and faces her father, but with the eyes cast down this time.

"Whatever this bloody fool Turpin has shown you, you'll have to have beaten out of you, and quickly as well. I'll get Binx on the job as soon as we get back." Nik keeps her eyes fixed on the ground in front and feels the sting of the leather on her face. She dare not look around for Mr Turpin, he cannot be of any assistance now. Nik swallows and resolves - Sullivan will have to die, and there will be no clemency as Mr Turpin advised.

CHAPTER SIXTEEN

As soon as the sun comes out from behind the clouds at about half past eight in the morning, the world is back to how it was before Nik was kidnapped by the Scotsmen. The flat cap and the pistol have been removed, but not the holster, and so, Nik has been stripped of the personage that she carried for a few days. There's a group of seven riding back to Beverley up Weighton Hill with a clear blue autumn sky above. Nik rides beside her father up front with the two stable lads next and then behind, Binx and the Frenchman, Marcel. Richie rides alone at the back with his tricorn hat pulled low over his eyes and his black cloak wrapped around him. Nik dare not look back at the man, despite wanting to. Her father is pontificating. This means he is acting like a cock.

"There's been a lot of talk since you've been gone, Nicola. The cook Mrs Beasley, the serving girls, your mother, they all seem to think that when you return, the very best thing for you will be marriage. I'm not prepared to settle for just any suitor as I explained, and so, when you get back, you will discuss what steps to take. There are events and parties that you and your mother can attend, places where you can be seen in good society." Nik has always disliked him. The man is self-absorbed, worried about what others think of him, emotionally detached. He has not asked how they came to be in Goodmanham, west of Beverley, nor has he mentioned the Scotsmen who kidnapped her or the ordeal she has endured. He has not questioned her experience, and now, as they ride to the top of Weighton hill, he thinks only of himself and the future. Nicola Sullivan as she was before would have worried about marriage, about the dresses and the dances, about meeting men; she would have fretted about her husband and where they would live, how quickly she would fall pregnant, how her mother would be without her in the house. Swift Nik is not that bothered at all. Now she knows what has to happen, the words her father speaks are like dandelion seeds blowing away in the wind never to be seen again. She nods in pretend understanding when he looks at her.

"Of course, this whole episode will have to be forgotten, Nicola," he continues. "I've said we were visiting a cousin in York to account for your absence in the last week, and this has not been questioned."

"Did mother worry?"

"You know how she is. She does not have any backbone. She weeps most evenings. The cunning woman back in Goodmanham there gave her tonic that would make her sleep, but she prefers brandy. At least when you're back, I'll be able to get some rest without her blubbering and fretting about whether you're dead or not." Nik looks straight ahead. They are at the top of the hill. She knows from her trips here with her mother, that this high up you can see the flat lands far into the distance. She turns to look. There are the stable lads and Binx with his bald head and fat face, Marcel and his moustache and then, some distance down the hill, is the thin figure of Richie riding a black mare with his collars up. When he sees her looking at him, he tips his hat by pulling the front point down slightly. Nik sees this, but does not alter her expression as she turns back to ride on. Her father sees that she noticed the man.

"You know he'll be hanged," he says.

"So you have explained, father." Nik believes this is false, for Mr Turpin has explained he is to be paid off by her mother.

"Whatever happened on this little trip, and whatever you've learned will be beaten out of you." She turns to look at him. It is defiance.

"You've already said that as well," she answers. "It's a sign of weakness to repeat oneself." This is something she's heard him say before and she's pleased she managed to use it against him in context. Mr Sullivan responds in kind.

"It's your mother, I worry about, Nicola. If she cannot

control her spirits and emotions, I feel it may be necessary to have her sent away. There are convents up near Harrogate where they take women of a weak disposition, you know, they have harsh and simple lives but they are free of the day-to-day suffering of normal women." This is a threat. "If you were to marry into a good family, I could guarantee she would be cared for properly." Nik smiles and nods her head, hiding the bravado she's learned.

"I'll marry whoever you wish me to marry, father." She manages to speak with a dull tone.

"I'll provide the suitors, Nicola, but it will be your choice of whom you marry. You need not see me as an enemy in all this. Your success, after all, will be mine also."

"You are always successful, father, even when you are not."

"What am I to take as the meaning of that remark?"

"It's meant to signify that you always manage to come out on top, whatever happens." This is real insolence. "You will take the credit for getting me back when we return home."

"I shall, it was me that sought out Turpin, and my money that paid for him too."

"But it was not you who came for me. Just like it was not you who made the money you inherited, or the wealth that you married into, or the business you operate." Nik keeps her eyes fixed on the rolling chalk hills in front, and the road that will take her home. Mr Sullivan snarls back in a whisper.

"You're as bad as your mother and you'll learn to hold your tongue as she has, even if I have to beat that lesson into you."

"You don't even do the beating – it's Binx who does the whipping, is it not, when you get too tired?"

"You will regret those words."

"If Mr Turpin hangs, father, then I will hang myself also. Think of how that would look to the rich men of Beverley, how poor a father you would be judged, to have a daughter that would rather die than live under his roof." Sullivan grins.

"Do not try to be crueler than I, Nicola, it is from me that you got this trait. I am infinitely more resourceful and full of more spite than you could dream, I'll have you watched all day, locked up if I have to, worse even. It is natural for a child to push boundaries and to test her elders, I'm pleased you have at least some backbone, unlike your mother, but you will find that I am more devious than you expect. Turpin will hang, of that I am certain."

"You don't know him."

"And you do? A few days on the road and you have become a vagabond, have you? He's a low born thief. He'll hang if I have to do it myself."

"What did mother promise him?"

"Do you really want to know?"

"That's why I asked. Your language need not be redundant in its repetition. You're not speaking to some pleb now, father."

"Very well. Your mother promised him a bullet in his chest, through his heart." Nik looks at her father riding next to her, he is only just a little bigger than she is. "I'll make sure he gets the hangman's noose instead."

Nik digs her heels into the horse she rides and it jogs forward to put some distance between them. She looks down at the empty holster at her chest.

If she had the gun, she'd shoot him.

The sky above is a smooth autumn blue as the group make their way across the high point of the Wolds and down towards Beverley. There's a lane leading away from the main mud road off through fields. Nik knows this is the way to North Burton where Mr Turpin comes from. She turns back to look at him and sees that he's staring down the lane also. He has not spoken a word to any one of them over the journey and has never left his position at the rear of the group. Nik pities him in his loneliness.

They pass Bishop Burton where Mr Sullivan stops to get

off his horse at the Inn. He goes inside for a few moments, just into the front door, and then comes out again to climb back up into his saddle. He's nimble for a small man and his eyes nervously dart over the little group, ending on Richie Turpin at the back. Nik knows that he is up to something. He will have sent some message to be carried forward to Beverley about when, and who is arriving.

They move through a forest before they come to the Westwood, it's an area of common ground for the people of Beverley and their cows and horses. Windmills dot the landscape and there's the racecourse to the left. Nik can see, in the distance, the tower of the Minster. The spire dominates these rolling hills and pastures, she has lived in the shadow of it all her life. It means that she is nearly home. Nik is not sure how events will go.

The North Bar gate stands at the end of the pastures and they turn right into it. Now they are nearer town there are more people around, a shire horse leads a cart of hay, there's a group of tannery working lads dressed in their leather aprons walking in front. It's as normal as it can be. They trot through the gate and under its brick arch – Nik holds her breath as tradition dictates, for you should never breathe under the North Bar. They pass St Mary's, this is the other of the big churches of Beverley and while it's smaller than the minster, it's no less imposing. At intervals, her father, Mr Sullivan, looks back to the men behind him and to Turpin with this tricorn hat still low over his eyes. He glances to Nik. She can do precious little to help right now. Nik could warn Richie, but he will already know what is going on. He has had any number of chances to make off on the horse they've loaned him, so it means he's here out of his own volition. Nik now knows the payment his mother promised the man also.

There's the smell of the town as they reach Toll Gavel, the main thoroughfare across the middle of the town, it's the sweetness of brewed beer and excrement, the stink from the tannery a mile away, people and perfume, of moth balls from the dress shop and chemicals from the pharmacy on the corner. It is all as Nik remembered it last. They stop outside the Sullivan residence, Nik and her father dismount and two stable lads lead their horses away.

"Take Mr Turpin round the back, please, Mr Binx," orders Mr Sullivan. "He'll be fed and watered there." The man with a bald head nods and leads the way with Richie following. The highwayman does not look up as he passes Nik, his eyes are down on the road and covered by the tricorn hat, and there is no sparkle in him as he trots on. The gun at his chest clinks and he still wears the tatty shoe they stole from the man at Scarborough. Nik wants to call out to him, but he is already around the corner to the livery yard. She feels her stomach hollow and the pulling sensation of sorrow in her legs. This is not how she wanted to say goodbye.

The great door to the Sullivan house opens. Standing beside Mrs Beasley, the cook, is Nik's mother wearing a simple green dress with her hair pinned up. She looks thin and pale and her eyes are red, her face crumples into tears when she sees her daughter and she steps forward to greet her with open arms. Mr Sullivan stops her by holding up his palm.

"Nicola is filthy from the road, wife. I think we should allow her to put on suitable clothes before we conduct any greeting." Nik pushes past him. She and her mother embrace. Elizabeth whispers into her ear:

"Thank God you are home, sweet Nicola. Are you hurt?"

"I am well, mother. I am well and changed also." They hold each other.

"You will tell me all about it."

"Mr Turpin saved me, mother."

"Where is he?"

"He's around the back, wife, Binx has taken him to the livery yard," says Sullivan.

There's a sudden look of horror on her face.

In the livery yard there has been a struggle. Mr Sullivan did not want to take any chances with Turpin and so, hiding in the empty horse stalls are eight lads. There's Mr Binx too and the other stable boys. It does not quite go to plan. When Richie steps through the gates, a fellow grabs him from behind, only to be shrugged off and then flattened with a right hook. More square up to him, the heavy lad from the butcher's shop, two river sailors, a scrawny coal cart driver – Richie has fought men like this before, many times. They have strong backs from hard work, but they don't know how or where to strike, they try too hard and can't dance either. The butcher's lad attacks first, Richie, sweeps away his legs with a kick and clobbers him in the nose as he falls. He has to make this look like he is trying. He sees off the sailors with jabs until the dusty coal cart man grabs him by the waist, and Binx hits him over the back of the head with a shovel.

Many men fall on him now and they manage to pin him first against a wall, and then onto the cobbles of the livery yard, they pull his arms around his back as Binx fits iron handcuffs around his boney wrists. The tricorn hat has fallen off and he has scuffed his cheek so it's red. It's taken less than five minutes for them to subdue him. Richie Turpin looks up as Elizabeth Sullivan and Nik walk out from the house, his teeth are barred. Binx drags him up so he is standing.

"What is the meaning of this?" cries Elizabeth. "We were to pay him, not put him in irons." Sullivan appears at her side.

"He's to hang, dear wife. He's to hang for the kidnap of our daughter. I'm only thankful that Binx and I were able to apprehend him at Market Weighton."

"That's a lie," says Nik. "It was Turpin who saved me."

"You are mistaken, Nicola," he calls. "Your sex gives you to flights of fancy and wonder, your imagination has got the better of you. Turpin here kidnapped you and tried to ransom your personage to me. There are men who will testify, myself for one, Binx also, any of these lads here will swear in court it was so." The faces of the men assembled look nervously at Sullivan, he will pay them, and for that they will say whatever he wants.

"That's right Mr Sullivan," says Binx from behind Richie.

"He's to hang. Didn't I tell you, Nicola?" She shoots him a dark glare. "Take him away," he commands.

It's already dark. The serving girls boiled hot water and drew Nik a bath, so she has washed and changed. She stands at the window of her little room at the back of the house and looks down on the livery yard in darkness. The dress she has on is uncomfortable with big sleeves and pleats that hang from the shoulders. She feels out of place. There's a tap at the door.

"Come," she calls and the handle turns. It's her mother, Elizabeth Sullivan. She's calm but her eyes are angry. It is the first time they have been alone. The tall woman steps forward and the two embrace once again.

"I prayed with all my heart that you would be safe," whispers Elizabeth. Her voice is smooth and rich, and whatever Mr Sullivan says, she is not known to weep when emotion overcomes her.

"I am safe, mother. I am lucky."

"You said you were changed. How?"

"I am no longer a girl."

"Were you raped, Nicola?

"No. I would have been were it not for Mr Turpin. I would have been many times and I would be dead. Perhaps father would be happier if I were."

"He has worried in his own way. He cares for you deeply. I know it is hard to see." They step back from each other and Nik examines her mother's wide and pained face. What happened this afternoon was wrong.

"What of Mr Turpin?" asks Nik. Elizabeth swallows when she hears his name and her eyes go to the floor. Perhaps it's shame.

"What of him?"

"Where will he have been taken?" asks Nik.

"I don't know. Your father says he has gone to the jail on Norfolk Street, but that would put Turpin into the hands of the workings of the court. I don't think he will want to do that, yet." Nik nods. There's no point in talking in riddles as people of power and wealth do.

"I told Richie you loved him, mother." Her face remains impassive.

"What did you hope to gain by that?" Elizabeth turns her head to the closed door behind and winks at her daughter. There will be someone listening under the employ of the master of the house. Nik moves closer so she can whisper.

"I hoped he would take you away from this, from a man you do not love and a life that keeps you trapped like a hound." Elizabeth takes her gently by the arms and pushes her away from the door and to the back of the little room where a candle in a lamp flickers in the corner. Her mother's face is ghostly, her smooth skin is white and perfect.

"I did love him, Nicola, once upon a time, but I thought he was dead. I told you those stories of him because I believed he was gone and would never come back. They were fairy tales."

"Not so," whispers Nik with her face close to her mother's, "I've learned from him. I don't have to be trapped here, and neither do you. We could be free."

"With him?"

"Not with him, we would depend on ourselves, on each other - that is how it works, that is how the world is."

"You're yet a girl, Nicola. I know how the rush of excitement feels, how it makes you tingle and how when it is gone you crave it. Were there shots fired? Did you gallop away?" There's uncharacteristic sarcasm on her voice as she says these last two lines.

"You've been trapped in here so long, mother, that you do

not remember what it is to be free." Nik looks into the thin woman's eyes, at the crow's feet, the flared nostrils and earnest stare. "I asked him to come and take you away from this."

"I waited for five years for him to come back, and he did not. He is too late. The world has moved on too far."

"I know also, what you promised him if he returned me."

"What?"

"You promised you would shoot him through the heart." Elizabeth Sullivan was Pike blinks as she remembers.

"I would have promised him anything to get you back, Nicola, the sun, the moon and all the stars as well."

"He delivered me, and now, for his efforts, he is to hang. Is that fair?"

"There's nothing fair in this world, not when you live in the Sullivan household. These are the facts that we live with and you must get used to them once again, whatever you have learned out on the road."

"I will not. I will be free, and my father will get what's coming to him, one way or another."

"It would be foolish to go against him, Nicola. I have tried over the years." Nik moves her face closer still to her mother.

"We could stand against him together, mother; and this is what I really learned on the road out there." Elizabeth's hands squeeze her daughter's arms gently in worry.

"We will have to see."

There's a light tap on the door. They both look towards the noise. Then stand back from each other.

"Come," commands Nik and the door opens. It's a maid wearing a frilly bonnet with dark hair and wide eyes.

"With respect, my lady, dinner is to be served downstairs."

"Thank you," comes Nik's stern reply.

It is as it was. Seven o'clock of an autumn night in the dining room of the large house on Toll Gavel. The grandfather clock ticks on the far wall, between the silence, and the little fire crackles in the big hearth opposite. There's the smell of perfume, wine, spices and the sweet whiff of tobacco. At the large table there are three places set. Mr Sullivan sits at the head, Nik to the right and his wife to the left. The food has not been served but there is a measure of wine in front of each of them in tiny glasses. Mr Sullivan is dressed in a golden coloured waistcoat with a green jacket atop and frilly white cuffs. He sits back in his high armed chair with the fire behind him and a look of ease on his face though his pointed beard and moustache make him seem stern. Elizabeth sits upright in her chair, her red hair is pinned back and the expression on her face is blank. Nik sits straight also, what's left of her ginger hair has been combed back and caught in a tight bun. Though there's still some of the warmth of summer in the autumn night, the air inside the room is cold and frigid.

"It's good to have us back together," says Mr Sullivan. He leans forward and takes up the little glass, then sits back with it in his hands. "Your mother and I have been discussing your marriage, Nicola, as you know. Have you had any thoughts about potential suitors you may have an interest in?"

"I have not, father," comes the reply.

"Perhaps this is more a matter for a mother to discuss with her daughter, husband? Nicola will be shy about such things."

"There is no need in my presence, I only want the best for you, as I do your mother. There's a young gentleman out at Skirlaugh, a member of the Tranmer family, and quite one for business with a few sizable farms and a good education. Have you heard of him, Nicola?" She does not turn her head to look.

"I have not, father." He takes a sip on his wine and sets it back down on the table. Even Mr Sullivan can sense the unease from these two women.

"I feel that the both of you are being frosty in your communication, I realise that you have suffered some considerable hardship and worry, but, I may add that all is well and as it should be now. Nicola is home safe and sound, and still a young woman with her dignity preserved. We should be thankful for this." Neither woman turns to look at him.

"Where is Mr Turpin?" asks Elizabeth.

"What concern of that is yours?"

"My daughter's life. He is the reason she sits here now."

"That is not true," commands Sullivan in a low tone. "I am the reason she sits here. It was my ingenuity that sent the man to look for her, and my spies that told me where she was to bring her back before he ransomed her."

"He did not ransom me," cuts in Nik. Now she looks at her father with a frown. This is insolence, but she cannot help herself. She sees her father redden.

"Mr Binx," he calls through the open door. "Could you come in here please?" The man with the bald head and stooped shoulders steps in from the corridor, he wears working men's clothes and has big swollen hands and heavy boots. Around his neck is a red neckerchief, tied tight in the modern way. He's not the kind of footman you'd find in a stately home in the country, but here in Beverley where there are many men such as Sullivan who pretend they are richer than they are, he is acceptable.

"Close the door would you Mr Binx," says Sullivan. The big man does so and comes to stand beside the master of this house, just behind his chair. It's Elizabeth who swallows as he stands there, for Binx has put his hands on her before, under orders of course. Mr Sullivan places his palms together with the fingers resting on his nose and his elbows on the arms of the chair. He contemplates his power over the two women in front of him, women who he is meant to care for. Both of them sit still and upright looking down at the cutlery set in a square in front ready for the food to be served.

"You'll both be beaten tonight. Nothing so anyone can see of course. Your mother knows how this works, Nicola. Now it's your turn to understand. After we have dined, Binx and I will visit each of you in turn." His voice is clear and loud. "'I'll make sure it does you no real harm, you understand, I'm not a monster and you are my property."

Nik Swift grits her teeth.

She did not know the moment would come so soon. Perhaps she is not ready for it; but smooth anger is rising in her, not rage, something less hot but more dangerous when controlled.

It must be now.

As she turns to move off the chair, she grabs a silver fork from the table in her right hand. She powers herself forward towards her father, holding the fork pointing outward as she does so. It is unexpected. Her father's face changes immediately from smug concentration to perplexed horror, Binx above him is slower and just manages a frown. She is not aiming for her father. What would be the use of injuring the leader with his biggest pack dog next to him? The three sharp points of the silver fork find the upper thigh of Mr Binx, and the whole implement goes in deep. If Binx were a fighting man and not a thug, he would strike out at Nik, but he's been trained not to hurt her unless instructed and so his fat hands grab at the fork to stop it going any further in. Nik lets go as he bends to the pain roaring up his body. She takes a few steps past him, reaches up to grab his neckerchief and pulls him around. Like the circles Mr Turpin explained to her, she uses his weight against him to pull and tip him over. He seems to pause for a split second as she drags at his neckerchief, uncertain what is happening to him, and his eyes widen in his fat face before gravity gets the better of him, and his head speeds to the stone floor of the dining room. There is a crunch as he hits the hard ground below him and a great, baby's cry of pain and anguish from his flabby chest. He groans from his collapsed state on the stone of the dining room floor. Swift Nik has made it look easy, as if she were the bully to a big and dim-witted giant. Silence falls on the sterile room once more between the ticking of the grandfather clock and the fire crackling in the hearth. It's not done yet.

Nik steps over his body to the table, draws one of the sharp knives from her father's place setting and spins on her heel with the blade pointing out at the man's face. He does not move but his face is concerned. This kind of thing does not happen to men such as Mr Sullivan, not when he has servants and supposed footmen around to protect him.

"You've the devil in you," he mutters in horror, his smooth hands grip the arms of his chair in shock, but his eyes have the same cruel, piercing anger. Nik has been trained to be afraid of this man all her life, and it is not so easy to throw this off. Her hand begins to shake.

"You'll beat us no more, coward," she whispers. "Next time you do, there'll be a blade across your throat." She turns and sets the knife back to its place opposite her father's fork like she were a serving maid. Then, she makes the few steps back to her chair and sits. Nik looks across at her mother's face that is nervous with worry.

"Could you go and fetch another fork from the kitchen please, Binx," calls Nik, "once you have finished playing with that one?" This is not the haughty language her father would use, there's no arrogance in it. Binx struggles to his feet and there is a fresh red mark on his forehead, his eyes swim as he considers what to do next. Nik reaches out to the wine glass, draws it to her mouth and takes a sip, her arms shake and the liquid has no taste at all. She looks again at her mother. Where Nik thought there would be support, there is only fear. Mr Sullivan has not moved from his chair and his hands still grip the arms, only now the knuckles are white.

"Mrs Beasley," he yells. "Bring the kitchen staff into the dining room."

"Clemency, dear," calls out her mother to Mr Sullivan. "The child has been to hell and back!" Nik swallows.

She struck too soon.

They first pin Nik to the dining room floor. Mrs Beasley forces a wooden spoon horizontal between her teeth and ties this around the back of her head with a long cloth while various others hold her hands and arms. Nik fights and wriggles of course, but there are too many of them. Mrs Beasley has already decided that Nik must be possessed with epilepsy or some other such infliction, how else would a woman be able to stab Binx with one of the expensive silver forks?

They tie her hands at her front with more cloth and then her feet, the knots are too tight to be comfortable – Mrs Beasley is happy to inflict pain in the knowledge that she is following her master's wishes. Elizabeth protests until she is dragged away by Binx and her screams fill the high ceilings of the stairwell behind. It takes a good ten minutes to get Nik settled so she no longer thrashes, and then lays on the dining room floor breathing heavy through her nose and looking up at the people around her with wide, terrified eyes. What was she thinking? Her father has a whole army at his fingertips, Richie Turpin would never have made such a move, he would have waited and chosen his moment – or else disappeared altogether. Perhaps that's what she should have done. There's a feeling suddenly of regret and weakness as she lays there on the cold of the dining room floor with the eyes of the household upon her. She is again, poor pitiable Nicola Sullivan with her cruel father, and now she's gone as mad as a flea so they have had to tie her up and call the doctor. She blinks. That's not the story anymore. She is no longer Nicola Sullivan, she is Nik the Swift, and she just fired a dangerous cannon shot across her father's bow. How can he trust her now she has threaten to slit his throat? He will be afraid and so will the house, for what really happened will be on all their tongues and the threat that Nik made will have been heard by the serving girls just behind the door. This will be Nik's battle to fight her own way, she has learned from Turpin, but not to be a copy of him, rather, to be the best version of herself. If she's got this wrong, then it is just a stepping stone to getting it right next time.

Two servant girls and Mrs Beasley drag Nik up the first flight of stairs to the landing. They can hear her mother wailing and screaming behind one of the bedroom doors, then they pull her up to her room at the back of the house, and set her on the bed. Mrs Beasley stands over her looking down.

"Best get a hold of yourself, Nicola," she commands. "They've called the doctor, but he won't be back till tomorrow." Nik has known Mrs Beasley all her life. This is the woman who taught her how to cook and scrub pots and pans, who used to listen to her worries sometimes. She can see the scorn in the big head cook's eyes. Nik stares back from her bed, breathing heavily through her nose. Mrs Beasley waddles from the room and closes the door behind her, Nik hears the key turning in the lock from the other side.

Nik does not know how long she has lain on her bed. It could be an hour or two, or just twenty minutes. The pain in her legs and ankles is fierce where the cloth bonds have been pulled too tight, her mouth is dry with her teeth biting down on the wooden spoon. Her hands are tied in front of her and ache also. Each minute is a kind of struggle with the pain and to take a breath. Her brain whirs and fires in the darkness, she sees Mr Turpin riding with his tricorn hat low above his eyes, feels the waves of the great ship when they were at sea and smells the ale from the Golden Ball up at Scarborough where she kissed a girl. It's these memories that help her stay strong.

On the stairs outside her door, there are footsteps and then the key turning in the lock. Lamp light floods the little room and a figure steps in holding it in front of him. Nik sees the long hair and the moustache, it is her half-brother, the Frenchman, Marcel. He closes the door and sets the lamp down as he comes over to her on the bed.

"I told them I must check on you, Nicola." He sees the wooden spoon in her mouth tied around her head and without thinking, he reaches out to pull at the knot. It's too tight. He takes his knife from his belt and cuts through it, then removes the spoon from her jaws carefully. She cannot talk for the dry mouth and the pain. Marcel holds her by her shoulders gently.

"Do not speak, I do not have long. I am only to make sure you are not dead, the other members of the household are too afraid of you. They say you threatened to kill Mr Sullivan and that you stabbed that fat bastard Binx with one of the expensive forks. Is this true?"

Nik nods. She sees the wide smile on Marcel's face in the darkness. She has done what he would not dare, and Marcel has much to gain from Mr Sullivan's death.

"By God, you've done it this time, Nicola. The old man's angry and terrified in the same measure. In the morning they'll have you taken away to the convent near Harrogate, that's what Sullivan keeps telling everyone." Nik sees that Marcel is dressed in riding gear, and still wears his leather gloves. He leans forward so his face is close to hers, she can smell his perfume and the pipe tobacco in his hair. "I will come for you on the York Road as you leave for Harrogate – we will talk then and I will not be here this night. Mr Turpin is to be taken to Kingston Upon Hull to be interrogated, he's locked in one of your father's barges on Beverley Beck, the black one that he moors on Waterside Road. I think, to be hanged. You must rest, for they'll come for you in the morning." Nik nods and her bound hands go out to him.

"Thank you," she croaks.

"We will work this out, Nicola. I will come for you tomorrow while you are on the York Road."

She nods.

CHAPTER SEVENTEEN

Nik was trapped on the sailing ship before she landed at Scarborough, she was trapped by the Scotsman in Kingston Upon Hull, and, she has been trapped in her room before – perhaps all her life even. The house has returned to the stillness of silence and darkness. She managed to free her hands by tugging and working at the cloth that bound her wrists, now she struggles to work on her ankles – Mrs Beasley tied these and so they are done up properly. She rolls off the mattress onto the rug with a light thud, and crawls to where she hid her clothes under the bed. These were the items she wore on the road – the empty holster and the pants, the belt, the shirt, and the cap. In the darkness she fumbles for the holster and the little knife that Richie told her was hidden in the leather strap. It takes a few minutes and she uses this to cut the strips from her ankles – the pain is fierce and the skin is raw and red with marks they left, but she is free. It hurts to stand at first. There's water in the flowerpot on the bedside table – Nik takes a sip and does not drink it all though she wants to.

In her closet she finds a shirt and her riding pants, she takes her long boots from her chest, leather gloves and her belt. It does not take her long to get changed and to fit the holster back around her body, with the mucky coat over it and then, the flat cap. She can see herself in the darkness, an outline in the long mirror opposite her bed. She must take this slowly.

From her jewellery drawer she takes two hair pins and moves to the door with them. Richie detailed how this works and in the darkness she begins. One pin goes in the bottom of the keyhole and the other in the top, she fiddles to move the mechanism inside. It takes a few minutes before the little bar that holds the door in place moves. She stands, goes back to the vase with flowers in it and drinks the rest of the dirty water in two glugs. It's time to leave.

Nik knows this house. She grew up here. She knows how each stair feels under her feet as she creeps down and which step to miss to avoid the squeak of a floorboard. On the landing of the first floor, she sees three doors closed and the dim light from the morning glints from polished handles. The gun will be in her father's study downstairs. She thinks for a minute - behind the middle door, her mother will be sleeping in the four-poster bed with ratty Mr Sullivan laid next to her. There's a shiver up Nik's spine. She makes her way downstairs.

Mrs Beasley will have been in the kitchen already for a while. Nik can smell the bread cooking and something else, meat or pastry. The servants will not care about noise from the rest of the house but Nik is still quiet as she creeps along the corridor to her father's study. She turns the door handle and steps in. It's dark with just a chink of light spilling in through the shutter over the sash window to the street outside. She must work quickly. Her father may wake anytime soon. Nik goes to one side of the big writing desk and pulls open the top drawer – there's her father's pen and an ink well. She tries the next, it has only paper and paper weights, the next there is a silver crown and a silver necklace. She picks both up and slips them into her pocket. The gun must be in the drawers on the other side. She moves over in the dim light and is suddenly aware that she is not alone. Nik looks up from under her flat cap. There, standing still at the door that he has just walked through, is the silhouette of her father, with his drooping shoulders and long hair.

"What is it you think you are doing?" he whispers. "One word and I can have the whole house upon you once more." Nik opens the top drawer that only contains candles. She slams it and opens the next which is empty. "Nicola," he whispers and there is a trace of fear in his voice. "Nicola, what has got into you – how did you get out of your room?" Nik tries the next drawer and there it is, laid horizontally and the light catches the ornate designs on the barrel. She reaches down, picks the pistol up and holds it level, pointing at her father standing in the half-light in his dressing gown.

"Close the door," she commands. He steps inside and pulls it shut behind him. He will have to deal with this with his wit and guile. "Why don't you have a seat, Sullivan?" she whispers.

"You need help, child," he answers. He does not want rumours about his daughter to spread, they could make him look bad in the long run. "I am your father, Nicola, how could you hold a gun to me?"

"I am your daughter, Sir. How could you let the servants tie me up in such a way, with a spoon in my mouth so I could hardly breathe?"

"You were a danger to yourself."

"I said sit down, Sullivan, go on, sit down in your reading chair next to the fireplace." The man swallows in the morning. Her voice has a cold quality to it, and so he does as he is told. He takes a seat in the armchair where he reads correspondence opposite the dead and cold fireplace. This is out of his control. Nik steps back to the window and opens one side of the shutters. Grey morning light floods the room. Sullivan can see Nik, now, wearing the same muddy flat cap pulled low so her eyes are in darkness. She continues to point the gun at her father as he watches her from his reading chair.

"Put down the gun," he says. "We both know it's not loaded." She lifts the pan to her nose and gets the aroma of gunpowder.

"We both know it is, Father." She steps forward, close enough so that she can see his features. "Do you remember what you did to me?" He swallows and his eyes look away.

"No," he answers.

"Yes, you do. You came into my room. You came many nights when mother was asleep. Do you remember? It happened over and over." The gun makes her brave.

"I meant you no harm. You were never hurt, and you were yet a virgin, unless that bloody Turpin did something unnatural to you." She steps closer yet.

"I remember, father. I remember every second of it. I remember your breath hot on my face, I remember you telling me not to move because it would all be over in a second. I remember the wriggling and feeling sick and your grunting from the back of your neck." He does not look at her.

"You are sick in the mind, child."

"I came back here to kill you, Sullivan. I was to kill you for what you did to me and my mother also. I have no wish for myself anymore. I told Mr Turpin what I was to do and he petitioned me to be merciful. Now I think back to his advice, I see that he was right. I will let you live with the shame of what you have done." Sullivan looks up at his daughter, there is defiance in his eyes.

"You belong to me, as your mother does. You are mine to do with as I please, this is the word of the law and of God. When you are caught this day, daughter, and you will be caught whether you shoot me or not, you will be stripped and whipped like a whore. I would do it myself." Nik steps in so the muzzle of the gun is an inch away from his face.

"You haven't got the balls," she whispers. He smiles up at her showing his bright white teeth. Nik does not feel anger. She has removed her feelings from this situation. The man must be punished for what he has done, but she cannot go killing him today, not when she has to collect Mr Turpin. She pulls the pistol upwards so it is vertical in her hands.

"You've seen sense," he comments as he notes the position of the gun. "It will not get you off the hook, my darling."

There is only so much a young lass can take.

She draws the heavy pistol back to her shoulder and wallops him around the side of the head with the barrel. There's a dull thud as it hits his temple and his body collapses back into the reading chair, his eyes swim. Nik takes hold of the pistol by the end, for the mahogany stock is not just for show, it's heavy and smooth, made for clattering folk around when there's no powder or bullets left or you don't have time to reload. As her father sits up, Nik clocks him with the handle across the head, and there's another hollow thud. This time he falls back into the chair like a ragdoll, out like a light or dead.

"It was loaded," she whispers and is, at once, glad that she did not shoot him, even though he may die yet. Nik blinks down on the man who abused her at intervals, hated her, said he loved her and who trained her to feel nothing but bitterness for him. If he is not dead, and he ever gets his hands on her, she will hang and strangely, there is a satisfaction to this, for now she really will be an outlaw.

Nik closes the study door gently as she leaves. If she can get away without a racket this will be better. She looks up the stairs and there are nothing but shadows in the growing morning light. Mrs Beasley might not be so easy to get past. She does not place the gun back in the holster but holds it pointing upwards. At the kitchen door, she pauses. It very much depends on who is behind on what happens, if it's just Mrs Beasley then things will be easier. If Binx is awake, it will be ugly. Nik gives herself a little grin because this will be difficult and she is not afraid of it. She pushes open the kitchen door.

There's the smell of pastry and meat cooking, wood burning and the hot steam of boiling water in the air, the door is open to the livery yard outside. Apart from a black and white cat under the table, the kitchen is deserted. Nik steps inside and goes to the far corner next to the chimney breast where she can hide in the shadows. Mrs Beasley, wearing a tatty white skullcap, comes back through the door carrying a bucket of water which she adds to the cauldron that is over the fire. She does not notice the figure hiding in the darkness with the cap and pistol. Nik watches Mrs Beasley as she goes to the oven with a cloth in her hands and pulls out a large tray of pastries. She sets them on the counter to cool. As she does so, she stops suddenly, as if something has changed, she turns and there is Swift Nik with the pistol pointing at the old woman. Mrs Beasley's nostrils flare and her eyes widen as she comprehends.

"Nicola?" she whispers.

"Make any sort of noise, Mrs Beasley, and I will put a hole through your face." The old woman blinks in distress. "Who else is here?" asks Nik.

"Just I, Binx is off at the Beckside to fetch fruit from the boats. The serving lasses will come later. What do you want, Nicola? How did you get out of your room?"

"I picked the lock." Mrs Beasley's mean eyes do not seem as frightened as they ought to be. She looks down on the Sullivan family from a far greater height than they look down on her. Nicola here is still a little girl.

"How could you hold a pistol at me, Nicola? It was me that rocked you on my knees as a young lass, it was me that taught you to bake. Let's stop this nonsense now, little one, set the pistol down and we'll have some tea and one of these fresh rolls out the oven." Nik's face does not alter, she pulls the hammer back on the flintlock with her other hand, and is worried that there is a bullet yet inside the pistol. She wants to frighten Mrs Beasley, not kill her.

"It was you who tied those ropes as tight as you could yesterday," she whispers. "It was you who taught me I was a silly, weak little girl. My path is this now, Mrs Beasley, I am not afraid to kill you." The big cook swallows.

"What do you want?" she asks as she stands in front of the dark figure.

"I'll take all of the pastries for a start," commands Nik and her voice is smooth and low with menace. Mrs Beasley turns back to the counter. She takes a large cloth from a drawer and lays it out square. Into this she adds the pastries she's cooked.

"They're rouleau de saucisse," she mutters, "my own recipe." Nik steps forward.

"They're sausage rolls, Mrs Beasley, you old cow. Turn around," says Nik. It feels good to bully the old woman who has bullied everyone else for so long. "Hold out your hand." Mrs Beasley is still afraid, but she offers her outstretched palms. Into this, Nik places the crown and the silver necklace she stole from her father's study. It will be more money than Mrs Beasley earns in two months.

"These are yours," says Nik.

"You stole them." comes the reply.

"Hasn't my father stolen more from you, Mrs Beasley? Your hard work, the best years of your life at toil in this kitchen? Nobody will know you have them and I will not tell." The old woman quickly puts the crown and necklace into the pocket of her apron. "I will not return, Mrs Beasley, best of luck to you."

"They will hunt you down, Nicola, and you'll be hanged on Gallows Lane. Mark my words." Nik grins an open smile she learned from Mr Turpin, the one that means 'I don't care.' She grabs the cloth of sausage rolls, moves back, lowers the pistol and walks out of the back door into the morning, steps down the livery yard to the gate at the end, and opens the latch out onto Walkergate. She begins a light run towards the Minster as she puts the pistol back in the holster and behind, in the kitchen, she can hear Mrs Beasley yelling at the top of her voice.

Although it's early, there are folk about on the streets. It's Tuesday and so there will be no market in the main square. Nik makes her way up Toll Gavel and away from the house she hopes she will never return to again. She passes the Angel pub on the right and continues on towards Wednesday Market place. There's a carriage in front and Nik keeps her head down as the driver considers her from above with a scowl. She presses on, through Wednesday Market place and she can see the tall towers of the Minster in front of her over the low roofs of the houses. Nik follows Eastgate that will take her towards the canal system that is known locally as Beverley Beck, for she heard from Marcel the night previous, that Mr Turpin has been locked inside one of the vessels there and he will be transported down to Kingston Upon Hull. She walks the length of Eastgate and Minster bells peel to mark seven o'clock. She knows the members of her household will already be awake, and if her father is not dead, he will give chase. Nobody will expect her to head for the Beckside. As she passes the Sunn Inn she looks in through the open door – they will already be serving. There's a flatbed carriage out the front and a big horse with its head in a bucket of oats. On the back there are boxes of what Nik presumes will be beer. She's already nearly killed her father, and this is the life she has chosen, so, she slips past the man carrying one of the crates into the pub, hops up onto the flatbed and picks out a bottle of the beer from within. In another ten seconds, she is off down the road. If she's brave enough, she can get away with anything.

She goes up past Flemingate, and runs through a number of alleys, then back onto the cobbles and the river is in front of her. Nik knows this place too. She knows the smell from the tannery and the iron works on the bank. There are the shouts from the river lads who take goods up as far as Driffield, or go the other way to Kingston Upon Hull. They carry grain from the fields, pots and plates folk make along the river, leather and iron, and they bring in more from the big port at Hull, wine and booze from Holland and France, copper, timber, felt, cloth and it's this little stretch of water from outside the Forester's Arms to the Shipyard at Grovehill Lock where much of Beverley's industry is, and where Nik's father keeps his barges that travel up and down the water and make him rich. Nik walks down the busy side of the beck, there are working lads with their clothes black with dirt from the ironworks chatting before they start. There's a narrow boat being pulled along by a carthorse on the path. On busy days the traffic can be heavy, and there's already shouting of boatmen as they curse at each other. It's not a part of town for a lady by any means and Nik has only been down here so many times because of her father.

She carries on right to the end of the path, and there, just before the shipyard are her father's boats. The tide washes all the way up from the river Hull and so now, when the tide is high, the boats bob on the water. There are two of them moored by the side of each other, great long broad beamed barges designed to carry goods in shallow water. There's the one Marcel spoke about on the outside. Nik keeps her cap down and walks steady towards it. There'll be a watchman somewhere with his eyes on the two valuable boats, Mr Sullivan pays good money to the town cooperation to allow them to be moored here. She sees a man at the far end next to the gates to the shipyard, facing the other way, he's wearing a cocked black hat – Nik knows him somehow, she's seen the hat before. He appears to be chatting to someone through the gates so she must be quick. As soon as she reaches the stern of the first boat, she takes a little sidestep on board, and walks across deck to the back – as confident and as quick as you like. She played on this barge as a little girl many times, and she knows the ins and outs of it well enough. There's a large hatch in the deck to the main hold with a big nail through a hook to stop it being opened from inside. As quick as a rabbit disappearing down a hole, Nik removes the nail, opens up and drops down into the darkness, the hatch falls shut above her with a clack and the boat rocks in the water as she lands on a sack of something that feels like grain.

She waits for her eyes to adjust to the dim light and scans up and down in front of her. There's a layer of sacks along the bottom of the hold and the musty and earthy smell of the grain inside. A figure is laid out on the sacks about halfway down and her feet crunch as she walks along towards him. The boat is almost empty, it means that it will sail north to Driffield to fill up and then back down to Kingston Upon Hull.

He sits up when she gets nearer to him and Nik squats down in front. He has lost his hat, and his face looks gaunt in the chinks of light that find their way through the deck boards above. She removes her cap so she can see him better.

"Nik?" he whispers.

"I'm here, Mr Turpin." He leans forward and reaches out his big hand to touch hers. She holds it, but only for a second.

"You came for me?"

"It was not so very long ago, Mr Turpin, that you came to rescue me," she whispers. "Do not be so shocked."

"You should not have come. I am pleased to see you, but you should not have come." She ignores his comment.

"I've brought you food and something to drink also." She brings out the bottle of beer she stole from the Sunn Inn.

"There is no way we can escape this one."

"Did they hurt you?"

"Aye, I'm all over a bruise."

"Eat, and your spirits will be lifted. We must get off this barge before high tide proper, before they turn it round and sail it away." There is something about Mr Turpin, something a little lost about him, the tone of his voice does not have the same sparkle that it did a few days before.

"I'm to be hanged, Nik. This is how it has to end. I'm to die, I do not want to keep running, not anymore. I'm tired of it. You were my last job, and your mother promised me a bullet through the chest for it." Nik undoes the cloth with the sausage rolls, fishes one out and holds it up to Richie.

"You must eat."

"You are in danger here."

"I was in more danger at my father's house. I thought on your advice when the time came."

"Did you kill him?"

"I hit him around the head with the handle of my pistol

and it knocked him out cold. He may yet be dead."

"How did it make you feel?" She has not yet asked herself this question.

"I didn't feel anything."

"I hope he is not dead, but only for your sake." He takes the sausage roll and sets it down without interest.

"You will ride away with me, Mr Turpin and we will be free folk of the road. We will rob when we need to and sleep when we want." He shakes his head.

"I cannot live that life anymore, Nik, and I cannot put you in danger. My body and my spirit are tired. The best thing you could do for me is to draw that pistol from your chest, hold it pointing at my heart, and pull the trigger." His voice is dark. Nik gives a light snarl, but her anger is smooth and level.

"Mr Turpin, it is you who unlocked who I really am. I have come here to repay my debt to you, so, you will eat what I have brought. I heard that you were to be taken to Kingston Upon Hull, but this barge is nearly empty, so it will be going up river to Driffield where they will fill it with grain from the harvest. If we can hide long enough here in the hold, until evening perhaps…then we can make good our escape."

"Where will we go?" asks Richie Turpin.

"North. Past Scarborough to Northumberland, you will know people there."

"I do, but I am not of a mind to introduce you to them, Nik. They are real thieves who live the life because they are cruel and quick, they have learned to be so because they were born dirt poor and hungry. I do not want that life for you."

"Then what am I to do? I have already attacked and perhaps killed my father and frightened the life out of Mrs Beasley. I am a fugitive." Richie Turpin rubs his face with his dirty hand. She has him backed into a corner, and if he doesn't help her, she'll be in worse danger. There is something about young Nik that gives him hope, her red hair and her hazel eyes looking at him in the dim light of a Beverley Beck river barge.

"I'll take you as far as I can," he says. There are shouts and footsteps above on deck, the boat is being boarded, but not in threat, they are the easy insults from working lads only. Nik is right, this barge will sail down to the Grovehill Lock and ride the high tide from the Humber Estuary all the way as far as it can towards Driffield. It depends on the winds as to how far they'll get. There are shouts and the raising of the sails above between swearing yells of river lads. The hatch that Nik scrabbled through opens and a head looks down into the hold. Nik has already gathered up the sausage rolls and hidden herself under a half empty sack of grain.

"Are you dead yet, mister?" calls the voice.

"I need water," yells Richie back along the deserted hold. The man removes his head. Nik can hear him telling the other lads above that the prisoner isn't dead, but he wants a drink. Another lad says he's got his own water and they laugh even though it's not a good joke. Nik hears footsteps directly above her and a whisper through gritted teeth of a man with a deep voice.

"You keep your eyes on that hatch, when I first stepped on board, it was open. They reckon it's Dick Turpin down there."

"They hanged him up at York," comes the reply, "and they battered that poor bastard good and proper before they threw him down there. I'd be surprised if he can even walk."

"You just keep your eyes on that hatch, lad."

"Aye, Sir, I will."

"Nobody's to know who's down there either, Mr Sullivan's orders."

Back down in the hold, Nik looks at Mr Turpin slumped against the wall of the barge. The vessel begins to move off slowly, they'll be using poles to push it out into the river proper. He looks ill even in the grey light. She feels inside her chest to the pistol that he gave her.

If she has to shoot all the lads above to get him off this barge - she will.

CHAPTER EIGHTEEN

It's perhaps ten o'clock in the morning. The smell from the grain in the sacks is strong, and the hold of the river barge is getting warmer in the late summer sun. Nik guesses the little ship has passed through Grovehill Lock by now, she can feel the river water running under them and there's less shouting and walking about on deck. It's mostly good-natured banter but Nik can sense an edge on some of the men's voices above, one of them in particular is gruff with a lower tone than the others. She wonders also, if they have found her father yet and if he is dead. Now they are out onto the river and riding the moving tide north, any news of Mr Sullivan will have to wait till another day.

Nik moves away from her hiding place and goes to sit next to Mr Turpin. He's managed to sit up with his back against the side. He moves slowly and at points she has seen him touching his legs and his chest. Nik can imagine the kind of beating her father's men would have given him, but nothing will be above the neck and nothing significant will be broken. She opens the tea towel and offers him one of the sausage rolls, again, but he shakes his head. When she passes him the beer, he takes it and removes the cork very gently so it doesn't make a pop, then takes a sip and rests his head on the wood of the ship behind him. They can feel the water below and the smooth flow of the boat as the northerly wind helps them along. They cannot really speak here, if they do, the boat lads above might hear that there are two people down here when there is meant to be one. He passes her the brown bottle of beer and she takes a swig, it's bitter and sweet at the same time.

"You should sleep," he whispers and his voice is faint.

Her eyes open, and the light is dim. The air is still warm with the musty smell of the grain around her and her hand goes for the pistol at her chest - the holster is empty. Her stomach rumbles in fear, and she sits bolt upright. Above her and lightly kicking one of her riding boots is Mr Turpin, he stands with his head stooped because the roof is too low, and in his right hand, held upwards, is Nik's pistol, the one with the dragon carvings along the barrel. The boat has stopped and there's no sound from the deck. He beckons her upward with the gun. It's just before dawn. It's time to go.

Nik gets to her feet and her head spins, her mouth is dry and her shoulders are stiff. She follows Mr Turpin down the hold of the boat in the blackness and their feet make light crunching sounds on the sacks of grain below them. He is not himself, she can see from the way he carries his body, there's pain in his movements. When he gets to the hatch, he stretches up his hand and pushes to see if the catch above still holds it in place. He turns to Nik in the darkness.

"Have you got your knife?" he asks in a whisper.

"Aye." Nik pulls it from her belt and passes it up to him. Richie stretches up and slips the blade through the gap between the wood and the hatch, the tip knocks the nail out of the way. He can't tell her now, but the hatch is made this way so that lads who get trapped inside can open it up from below. It's not a jail, and anyone with more sense than Mr Sullivan of Beverley would not have dumped Dick Turpin in the hold of a barge, no matter how hard a beating they gave him. There's a grin on his face as he passes the knife back to her and she smiles also – he is not completely lost in all this.

He gives her a leg up by holding his hands together like a cup and she steps up as he lifts. Nik presses lightly on the hatch to open it up and peeps out. It's not cold but the air from outside is fresh and clean. She nods at Richie below and he pushes her upwards further for her to clamber out. Nik keeps low to the deck of the boat as she scans around them, the river sailors will have orders to keep an eye on their prisoner but it's too early for them to be awake. The barge is moored against the bank somehow, but the night is grey around her and the sky clouded over. Dawn is perhaps ten minutes away.

Nik turns back around and reaches her hand to Mr Turpin below. He takes it and she pulls but he's not as quick as he could be as he clambers out onto deck. She hears an involuntary grunt escape from his chest at the pain. Even with dawn so close, normal folk would be afraid of the darkness - not for the ghouls or the ghosts, really, but for the risk of injury and ending up in the water. She hears him step across the creaky boards of the barge without seeing where he is going for if they are not off this vessel in a few minutes, they will be seen. Nik follows the light footstep sounds he makes. He has found the gangplank already and he clicks his tongue to let Nik know where he is.

She was meant to be rescuing him.

In the darkness they walk through long grass up to their waists. Richie strides out in front making a path for her to follow. There's the smell of the night, it's manure from the fields, the sweat from Mr Turpin ahead and fresh autumn leaves rotting already on the forest floor way off. The sun is rising behind them and birds are beginning in the trees around, a cockerel announces the morning from somewhere near and his voice is shrill and earnest. He sounds again. They will be at one of the farms along the river Hull. Barges stop here and the farmers treat the sailors well for nobody else will take their wheat down to Beverley. Why on earth would her father put him on a barge to come all the way up here? It comes to her as they walk through the grass, there's a fence up ahead and in the dim light she can see a low building. Someone is going to kill Mr Turpin, he is not to be taken to Kingston Upon Hull at all, and there's to be no trial. How could there be? Sullivan would be a laughingstock if he suggested he had captured Dick Turpin, because the man has already hanged out at York.

From a low building in front of a field, there's the sound of horses moving around inside their stables, it's a livery yard.

Richie climbs over the fence and Nik follows. She can see that he is still holding her gun upright in his hand as he surveys the rows of half doors in front of him. The birds in the woods behind are making a racket now, as they welcome in the new day, and the horses are ready for the light too with their faces looking out into the dawn from the dark stables. He passes her back the pistol and Nik puts it into the holster.

"Can you ride without a saddle?" he whispers. Nik clicks her tongue back at his sarcasm, as she makes her way to a stable door. She holds out her hand and the long face of a horse comes to her so she can scratch the nose – she knows her animals does Nik. The call of the cockerel sounds again as the sun sends weak light from the east behind them. She finds the simple bolt lock on the other side of the door and slides it open. Two stalls down, Mr Turpin does the same. It's been easy thus far. Nik leads the grey cob out of the stable and into the beginning dawn. She looks up and coming round the corner is a young farm lass wearing a dark headscarf and carrying a bucket. Her expression is first one of puzzlement as her eyebrow raises at the stranger leading a horse out of its stable, then, one of worry. She drops the bucket when she sees Mr Turpin in front of the second horse behind Nik.

"Don't make a noise," whispers Nik. "You scream and I'll shoot you through the chest, lass." The farm girl staggers back in shock. If she were able to stop herself screaming, she surely would, but her instincts kick in, fear consumes her and her stomach tightens. She takes a great gulp of air and then screams into the new dawn morning with her fists clenched so tight that the fingernails dig into her palms. Nik's horse makes a frightened start, but she already has hold of it by its mane, and, as it begins to bolt, she jumps to get onto its back. Nik manages to get her foot over and her leg round so, as the horse speeds into the yard, she is in as much control as a rider can be without a bit, bridle or a saddle. There's a shout from the other buildings as the farm girl continues to scream aloud. Nik looks back and Richie Turpin has managed to get onto his horse also and is riding towards her, he is fatigued somewhat and slower than she has seen him previous. She turns her head forward, there's no way of knowing where they are meant to go, Nik will have to rely on the horse's sense of direction for the way. She's riding at speed down a track with a field on one side and pine woods on the other – the horse below is in a state of mild panic and Nik grips with her knees and grits her teeth. Riding without a saddle is bad enough, but with neither bit nor bridle to control the beast, she can do little else but hang on. Behind, Richie is a little more in control of the bay horse he rides, he is heavier and more experienced, his hand rests on the animal's neck, just behind the ear to steady it and build confidence in him – for if the horse has trust, he will be able to ride better.

There are shouts from behind them as they thunder down the track between the pine wood and the field, they are followed already, there's the crack of a whip in the air, farm lads chase them on steeds that have saddles. Nik glances behind once more and sees that Richie has control of his horse, perhaps more so than she does of hers. She grins. The light is picking up from the rising sun as the hooves thud into the soft mud of the track.

They ride out into an open grass field and up a long slope to the crest of a hill. There's a rider following on a pale horse at speed, ahead of three more behind, he's an older man with a weathered face and his teeth barred under black hair. They are gaining. Nik presses on to the top of the hill and mud sprays from their horse's hooves as they go, she's first and then Richie atop the bay with his eyes narrowed as he holds onto the neck. The rider behind him with the black hair begins to close on him, he has the look of a skilled horseman with his head down as he races after Richie.

"Bastard thieves," he bellows out into the morning. It's not so much one man on a horse that bothers Nik, more the others following behind, for without saddles neither she nor Richie will be able to get far enough away. The bones of the horse's spine are uncomfortable on Nik's buttocks, her grip is too tight on its mane, she can feel the dew from the morning mist in her eyes. She looks back once more and sees the rider atop the pale horse gaining on Richie – the highwayman is too big on the animal's back to build up speed. She draws the pistol from her chest, and her thumb pulls back the hammer above the flintlock, she slows the horse below her by tightening her legs. Richie notes what she is doing, she can see him grin as he flattens himself to the horse and steers it to the left so she can get a good shot.

It's not that she wants to kill the rider following, with his wrinkled face and gritted teeth.

Not at all.

It should just be a warning to him and the others behind, that these two riders are armed and prepared to defend themselves too. The pistol is heavy in her hand and the barrel dips as she holds it outstretched behind her with the horse at a quick, rhythmic canter below. She squeezes the trigger and the hammer falls, hits the flint and sends a spark into the powder in the pan on top of the pistol. It might not even be loaded properly. Chances are, the mist has got into the gun and the powder won't light, or maybe the ball that was packed into the barrel has come loose and fallen out somewhere along the way. These are the things that Nik hopes for as she holds the pistol level, feels the recoil and sees the blaze of fire and smoke burst from the mechanism. Thirty yards away, the metal ball from the pistol hits the man on the white horse in his chest, it breaks ribs as it goes through him, punctures a lung, and he collapses off the animal and tumbles, head over heels backwards in the grass below. Nik turns as she replaces the gun in the holster at her chest, as if she has done it a thousand times and rides on. Mr Turpin, on his bay comes up behind her and they crest the little hill and then ride down the other side. The other riders fall back after this shot.

She is rescuing him after all.

They ride for half an hour, slower than they would if they had saddles or even bridles, but fast enough to put some space between them and those that might have followed if they were brave enough. Nik's lips are an iron line across her face when they pull up inside the edge of a little wood. Richie draws next to her. From just inside the darkness of the tree line they will be able to see if anyone approaches without being seen themselves. They don't dismount.

Nik looks across to Richie and her eyes are black. They would have been set upon by now if they were still pursued. She ought to feel happy as the full morning breaks outside the wood, but there will be hell to pay somewhere. There will be hell for the river sailors who could not keep a battered and beaten Dick Turpin locked up on a barge, hell for Mrs Beasley who could not stop Swift Nik from escaping, and hell too for the man who she shot through the chest.

"Will he be dead?" she asks and Richie knows who she means, for he can see and sense her mood is bleak.

"From the gunshot, I would think so," he replies, "if not that, the fall would have broken his back." She looks sickened at these answers.

"He would have done as bad to you, Swift Nik," says Richie as he gets off the big bay. "He would have been praised for it too, celebrated even. In the New Inn Tavern at Leven they'd call him a hero." He looks back the way they rode. "This is a highwayman's life, Nik. We're outlaws, you did what needed to be done and by God in his heaven, you shot him from his horse at thirty yards, and no mistake. They'll have the fear of the devil for you now, as if they didn't already." She feels different, guilty and powerful at the same time. When you become what you are meant to be, there is no celebration. It's a piece of a jigsaw puzzle settling into place, as if this real version of you has waited patiently all along. Nik grips the mane of her grey horse as she clambers down, over the right side so she can stand in front of Richie.

"What now, Mr Turpin?" she asks.

"Not Turpin," he answers. She considers him. "My name is Richie Jackson, of North Burton. I loved your mother and I love her yet. I always shall, and to be honest Nik, there has never been another." She takes a deep breath.

"Now? You have to tell me this now?"

"Aye. You are…" he struggles with it like the words don't want to leave his chest. "You have grown up. You are the same as I, a fellow of the road, a rider, and I could not have told the young one I travelled with previous. I'm not sure I could have told anyone at all."

"You will go to her when this calms down."

"No. We'll not outrun the storm that is coming, Nik. You might, but not I."

"That's the old man speaking in you, Mr Turpin, as far as I'm concerned, I'll go on forever."

"You'll call me by my name, Nik."

"Richie," the word feels strange on her tongue.

"Aye."

"My mother told me you outran a whole battalion of soldiers back in the day, you and your dog."

"I did, but they were half drunk, and I had nothing at all to lose."

"You have nothing to lose now," she counters. "You've no money, nowhere to live, just the clothes on your back and not even a pistol to shoot. I would say you have nothing to lose at all, Richie Jackson of North Burton."

"I have everything to lose here."

"What?"

"You."

CHAPTER NINETEEN

Word has been sent down river along the banks, from mouth to mouth and boat to boat, past Eske and to ears on Hull Bridge at Tickton, all the way back to Beverley and the Beckside dock there. The details of Turpin's escape have travelled up Eastgate, and to the house on Toll Gavel, and into the ears of Mr Sullivan who is recovering at the kitchen table from the blow that nearly broke his jaw and knocked him clean out. He is bitter. Bitter for the way the servants and Mrs Beasley look at him for having been beaten by his own daughter, bitter too because he could not control her. Mr Sullivan has learned that Turpin is well, that he can ride, and there is talk that Nicola shot a lad at 100 yards while on horseback and that the bullet went clear through his heart and killed him stone dead. The story is that she and Turpin are heading west through Leconfield.

Binx stands in front of the farmhouse table and looks down at his benefactor with a mixture of contempt and horror. He should have been there to defend his master. Mr Sullivan has a wet cloth against his jaw where she hit him and he rests on his elbow. His wife leans against the wall in the corner next to the big fire in the shadows so that nobody can see her face. Elizabeth Sullivan was Pike is angry also, angry that she did not defend her daughter well enough the day previous, and that the girl did not enter into her confidence, for at the drop of a hat, she would have gone with her Nicola and left the big house on Toll Gavel, forever.

"She is a monster," repeats Sullivan. "She has the devil himself in her. I tell you. She has to be stopped at all costs." He has said this much many times already, since Mrs Beasley found him slumped on his side in his reading chair and believed he was dead. Binx has called for the constable of the peace already and he is on his way. The maid shows a man in a long coat into the kitchen, he has come through the front door. He has a moustache and black hair under a short brimmed felt hat. This is the constable of the peace, Mr Ryder, he has a cold expression and piercing blue eyes.

"I came as soon as I could," he explains as he removes his simple hat. Mr Sullivan is a wealthy man and sees to it that powerful folk like Mr Ryder get special gifts at Christmas like expensive wine or cloth, sometimes fruit or chocolate even. It's for this reason that Mr Ryder has come so quickly.

"A man has taken my daughter."

"Again?" asks Ryder. He sees at once the fierce anger in Mr Sullivan's face. He got wind that Nicola was kidnapped before, even though Sullivan tried to keep it secret.

"This is different, she is not being ransomed, she is to be hunted. I need her alive and brought back here."

"Who has taken her?"

"Dick Turpin." Ryder wrinkles his nose at this.

"Turpin was hanged on the Knavesmire at York, Mr Sullivan. I was there. I saw him swing."

"Well, this fellow says his name is Turpin. He'll need to be hunted too, and I want him brought back alive so he can face me." Ryder is dubious of this. He's not seen the usually level-headed Mr Sullivan in such a state before.

"Do you know where they are?"

"Leconfield, heading west, but they could be hours away by now. I need a group of men this minute. I need them found. There are others on their trail already from Aike. I swear that there will be a large reward for the man who captures Turpin, and more for the man who returns my daughter." This last comment changes the situation in Ryder's mind, with the possibility of money involved as opposed to his duties as a man of the law, he is much more interested. Indeed, Mr Sullivan has gone from an annoyance to a pressing concern.

"I'll have my boys ready within half an hour, Mr Sullivan and we'll ride for Leconfield. You can rest assured that we'll have your man and get your daughter back." Sullivan at the table with the wet cloth still on his jaw sees that his offer of money has altered Ryder's attitude.

"You'll do well out of this Ryder, of that I can promise. I'll join you once I have regained my senses, and I'll bring my men also."

"I'm on it then, Sir."

"Safe journey, Mr Ryder." The man with jet black hair and a long coat turns on his heels and disappears following the servant woman to the front door. They hear it slam as he leaves. The folk stay in silence in the kitchen for a moment. Mrs Beasley at the sink, Sullivan at the kitchen table with Binx looking down on him, and Mrs Elizabeth Sullivan in the shadow of the corner.

"What are you hiding from, woman," scowls Mr Sullivan from where he sits. She steps out into the light and her face is grey and serious, gone are the red eyes from tears. Elizabeth feels her father in her somehow, the man who was a captain of men and rode into war for his country.

"If that girl is hurt, husband," she whispers, "I'll kill you myself."

They are followed.

Richie sent his horse packing one way, and Nik sent the one she rode packing in the other direction, both riderless. It's easier to travel the thick undergrowth of the forest without a horse, and the animals might put the men who are behind them off somewhat.

Richie is in poor health. Now the sun is up and shining through the canopy of the forest above, Nik can see that he limps on his right side and there's a bruise on one of his cheeks. He cannot move as quickly as he could previous and he does not have the same ready smile. The beating must have been severe. Nik knows they are followed because Richie will not slow down. They travel west, north of a village called Aram and into swamplands that are muddy. This ground is too wet to be farmed properly and so it has been left as wetland forest with animals the locals can hunt. There will be deer hiding between the trees, and wood pigeons bicker in the high branches. Richie clambers over a fallen trunk and his foot sinks into mud on the other side.

"Where are we heading?" asks Nik.

"Etton." This is a village over the hill from North Burton, apart from the old church, there are only a few large farms, cottages and hovels where the workers live. Nik visited the coaching inn once on a trip to York.

"What is there?"

"A place to hide, perhaps. I don't think I can run very far. Not the way I am now." He looks back at her and she sees hopelessness in his eyes, for the first time. In all that they have been through together thus far, she has never seen despair in him, fear and worry aye, but never the crushing sensation that all is lost. Perhaps it is time for Nik to show what she has learned in all this:

"You're not dead yet, Richie Jackson, tell your face to lighten up." He stops and looks back at her again with a frown, this is out of character for her and more the kind of barbed but light-hearted comment his Nana might have made. It makes him grin. In this one comment, Nik reminds him what he has perhaps forgotten. He turns to carry on through the mud in front of him. "At least you have one shoe and one boot even if they don't match, Richie," she adds. "You would have given anything for two stout boots. You should think yourself lucky." He grins despite the pain. This is how it works out here, there is nobody and nothing that cannot be mocked, even death, for if there isn't a cheap comment to be made at your friend's expense then you might as well already be in the ground.

"Time was you wept after you'd shot a man," he calls back to her, "now you've got a swagger like a drunk." She has come a long way – he is thankful for her.

The path is not easy through the woods. The two fall silent as they walk, their feet look for soft moss and hard places to stand, and when there's a squawk from a magpie in the distance, Nik looks back behind her to see if there is anyone following. She is as nervous as he is. She has shot a man. There is no going back from this now, she will have to live a life on the road as Richie has done before her because if she does not, she'll be hanged on Gallows Lane as Mrs Beasley said she would be.

It's mid-morning by the time they reach open fields. The landscape in front of them is flat and wide and the sky is a dull autumn grey, rain clouds look to be building in the north. Richie's face is bleak and there are bags under his eyes as he walks behind Nik along the side of a hedge. In the field next to them are sprout plants as tall as her waist with the odd potato flower peeping through. She is muddy up to the top of her riding breeches and her feet hurt. The pistol in the holster at her chest is heavy. She turns to see that Richie has stopped. He looks behind to the tree line of the forest they have just come out of and then to the left.

"What is it?" she calls.

"This is North Burton," he says. "This is where I come from." His voice is faint, almost as if he's talking to himself. Nik does not respond.

They walk along the north drain, it's a little stream that flows along the side of these fields all the way back to Arram behind them, into the river Hull, and then, out into the Great North Sea and the whole wide world. Richie is returning home. His vision is beginning to dim with fatigue, his legs are sore and his head throbs. One of Sullivan's men, the big one with a bald head they called Binx, hit him with an iron poker across the ribs. It hurts when Richie breathes in too deeply.

Up ahead there's a gap in the hedge that they walk through, and they stand on a dirt road, it's much easier on their feet and legs. There's a path leading west. It has been many years since

Richie has passed this way, it is Rootas Lane, due North of his home village and leading to the mill before Etton. He best explain himself to the young lass, so she is better equipped to know how he means to proceed.

"We'll follow this road up to the mill, then cross into Etton through the fields, behind the old church there is a rundown house and a trapdoor to a crypt. If we can make it there unseen, Nik, then we can pass as many days as we can, till this all blows over our heads, best to let them do the following and think we are far away." She listens as she walks.

"How can we be sure we won't be seen?"

"We can't." His tone is not sarcastic. The road narrows ahead of them and dips. On the right, there's a little dwelling, it's a simple wooden building with a thatched roof and a big chimney. A mud track leads to it and there's a run-down low roofed barn beside. These mud, wattle and daub houses of East Riding villages look as if they could get washed away in a rainstorm. Nik leads Richie on and standing on the tiny path, there's a little old man with a thick grey beard. He's barely five foot and stooped with a walking stick and a filthy smock. They almost don't notice him and he struggles to look up at them, his wrinkled face blinks at the two in shock.

"By God," he bellows.

"What is it, old man?" asks Nik. His eyes are red and watery, his nose runs over the white and grey moustache and beard. He steps back.

"You're the two they're looking for? I heard the ghost of Dick Turpin was on the roads, and a young lass named Nik the Swift with him. He's a harrowing sight, with the flesh falling off his bones, and the lass is a pale redhead with dragons tattooed up each of her arms." The man has a gift for talking shite. "I was in North Burton this morning, at the Bay Horse, and there's a gang searching." The old man's voice crackles with fear. "They say they've killed five folk already." Lies travel faster than truth in this part of the world. "There's a reward out too, the one who says he's Dick Turpin is to be captured – and he'll hang." The old man has blurted out too much. He looks up at the serious face of Nik and at her stern eyes. Now he sees who he is talking to, he can see that these really are the folk who are being hunted. He swallows. "You'll not shoot me, will you, lass? An old man like me?"

"I will shoot you," she answers. "How many men?"

"Twenty or more."

"Where are they headed?"

"I don't recount, miss."

"Where's your horse?"

"I don't have one." She glances across at Richie standing behind her with his cloak wrapped around him and his face pale. He is tall and thin, and against the grey sky behind him, he does not look like he can walk much further.

There's a shout from the track they have just walked down, Richie sees the head of a rider from behind the hedge in the distance. He is moving at speed. There's another. They have been spotted somewhere. Nik steps back and sees his concern.

"They're here. The gang the old man speaks of." There's a look of horror and disbelief on her face.

"What now?" she asks.

"Time to give it legs."

Richie more limps than runs. There appears to be something not quite right with his ankle but he moves as fast as he can down the track and away from the old man and his hovel. When they'd kicked him to the floor, a night or so previous, Mr Binx stamped on one of his ankles and there was a crack. Richie doesn't have any choice but to run on it.

"There's a crossroads up ahead, and a farm opposite with a mill," he says as they run. "We'll make for that." To the right of them and through a gulley, they can see the square tower of Etton Church in the distance, the place where Richie had wanted to hole up. It's too far now. They begin up the hill and already, Richie's chest is panting and his heart hammers under his ribs. Nik keeps his pace easily but is already out of breath also. Fear means that neither of them is of a mind to stop.

In front looms the windmill Richie spoke of, it's a single tower and juts up into the grey sky with four sails that are turned to the wind facing the other way. Richie has been here before, many times when he was younger and he passed the sails of Etton Mill and saw them turn as they do now in the light wind. There's a farmhouse before it and, as they race across the track, Nik glances quickly at the little road sign, it reads North Burton to the right and Etton to the left. They run straight on towards the mill and the farm in front. There are shouts on the breeze from behind them, horses' hooves thud on the road some half a mile away as the first of the men following comes up the hill. The old man would have quickly told the gang who he had seen.

Richie and Nik sprint as best they can up the track that leads to the farmhouse in front of the large tower of the mill, she appraises the situation. The building has a wide door painted red and a neat garden, on the drive at the side of the house, and standing on a flatbed horse carriage with sacks of flour around him, is a man wearing an apron and with a big moustache. He frowns in confusion as he sees the tall figure of Richie limping at great speed towards him with Nik running in front. He sees her draw the pistol from the holster at her chest and he steps back in concern. Next to him a tall lanky boy carries a sack of flour from the door at the bottom of the windmill. This man is Mr Gibson, and the boy loading the heavy sack of flour onto the flatbed carriage is his son, Ross. Somewhere inside the house are his wife and young daughter. Gibson has heard already that there are wanted highwaymen on the road, but he was almost certain that this wasn't true. They look in a state these two, the tall one staggering almost as he runs and with a face as grey as ash, the younger one with the pistol seems fresher, but scared. Gibson has heard stories in the pub about her already, she is Swift Nik, the bar lady told him she's killed nine men already and strangles victims with her thighs around their necks. She looks like a frightened lass to Gibson, as he steps down from the carriage.

Nik takes in everything with her keen eyes as she approaches the man and his lad. There's the open back door of the house beside them, the flatbed carriage with a dozen sacks of flour, the man with a moustache stepping down, and the tall lad of perhaps fourteen gawping in shock. The windmill is red brick made, painted black some years ago perhaps, there are three little windows vertical up the side to the top and a big, solid wooden door at the bottom. It's open wide. She is breathless when she reaches the man:

"I need the key to your mill, Sir," she explains. He frowns in confusion. "We are chased, Sir, and your sturdy mill seems the safest place to hide." Gibson is not aware of the gang that will arrive in a few minutes on his drive so he continues to frown in confusion. Nik has no time to mess about. She lifts the pistol and holds it at the miller's son, at his chest. "I'll have the key to your mill, Sir." she repeats and her voice is clipped and cold. Here is the cruelty of her father, she knows that the miller will act more quickly if he thinks this lad may be shot.

"In the door," he answers. Nik glances to the heavy lock under the door handle and sees the key sticking out of the mechanism.

"You first," she calls to Richie. He staggers to the door as quickly as his ankle will let him and disappears into the shadows inside. Nik moves after him, goes to the key on the outside of the solid wooden door and looks down the drive; as she does, she sees there are three men on horseback at a canter towards them, she cannot make out the detail because her heart beats so heavy in her chest. They are bellowing into the grey sky because they have seen Swift Nik. She does not have time to be afraid or to get this wrong. Her hand shakes as she removes the key from outside the door.

Nik must be calm. She takes a deep breath through her nose and steps into the darkness of the mill. Richie pushes the heavy door closed from inside and it complains against the floor. The shouting from the approaching riders is louder, and the hooves crunch on the gravel outside. Nik peeps through the crack of the door as it closes and sees one of the riders jump down from his horse and make a run for the mill door. Richie pushes it shut, and Nik slips the key into the lock, she turns it and hears the bolt complete the mechanism as the bar slides into place. The handle rattles as the man tests it on the other side, then there are thumps from his fist, the shouts are muffled. She leans her forehead on the wood in the darkness in relief.

"No time to rest, Nik," says Richie. "They might have another key."

CHAPTER TWENTY

At Richie's direction, they spend a few minutes piling bags of flour in front of the door, so if there is another key then the mob outside still won't be able to get in, or at least they will be slowed in their efforts.

Chimney windmills such as this are expensive buildings, and millers are smart, technical people. Their mills connect huge wooden sails to heavy cogs, and these in turn drive a round mill stone near the bottom of the tower. It's this stone that grinds wheat into smooth, fine white flour. It's not nearly as simple as that, there are a hundred things that could break or go wrong, ropes that stiffen the sails can snap, the brake heel teeth wear out, the grooves on the mill wheels need to be just right to do the job. Nik follows Richie up the narrow wooden stairs to the next level and the noise is loud, there's the creaking of the sails outside, the rattling of the central axel as it spins, and the rasping of the mill stone grinding against the fixed bottom piece. It is a marvel how inventive and how clever the world is to Nik. She has never been inside such a place, and despite her fear for the men outside, she finds wonder in a device that converts the power of the wind into something useful.

Nearer the top, the noise is louder and there's another flight of very narrow wooden steps. Richie goes up these as well. He is not quick but he seems to know where they are going. At the top of the steps, there's a trap door that's already open. He goes through it and she follows. After she clambers up, he closes the hatch in the floor with a slam. They stand on the highest level of the windmill now, and above them are the cogs that change the turning movement of the sails outside from horizontal to vertical, the wooden and iron components creak against each other as the mechanism moves. There's a window without glass and every few seconds one of the big sails outside moves past and the little room is plunged into darkness temporarily.

Richie takes a few steps and slumps down against the wall, his legs splay out in front of him in exhaustion. There's a childlike quality to his serious face. How their roles have changed. Nik goes to the window that is just an open space to sky outside.

"Caution please, Nik," he says. "If you can look below, then they can shoot up."

"I didn't see any guns," she answers.

"They will have them."

"Did you see how angry that man was?" She means the rider who hammered on the mill door below, and rattled the handle.

"Money makes men do such things," he answers. "If your father says he'll give a big reward, they will come from many miles around." Nik stands looking at the central piece of machinery that spins from the sails outside, there's beauty in the complexity of it as the wood and iron squeak against each other. It's a marvel of the modern age. There's a bag with tools to fix the machinery and two empty beer bottles next to the wall.

"What will they do outside?"

"Wait, probably. They could smoke us out, but the miller won't want his property damaged. They know we don't have anywhere to run to." Nik looks across at the open window, she can see the grey sky and the fields in the distance. It's strange to be this high up. She gets down on the floor and creeps towards the window, gets her back to the wall and moves her body slowly so she can just peek down at the ground below. There are ten or so horses and men talking to each other. She notes a thin figure sitting on a white horse, he's wearing a big hat with a red feather in it. She moves back to safety – it's her father. Nik swallows, and is glad that he's not dead somehow. She walks to where Richie sits, and sets herself down next to him with her back against the rough wall looking at the open window. The sails swoop by and the machinery rattles as it turns.

"My old man is down there," she says to Richie. He smiles.

"How do you feel about that?"

"Relieved," she answers.

"Because it means you won't go to hell?" He is mocking her.

"Oh, I'm going to hell, Mr Turpin. It's just how quickly I get there that worries me. I'm happy my father is not dead because I'll get to kill him all over again." She does not mean this. They should not be having such a conversation in the situation they are in. They ought to be frantic with worry that they are surrounded, that both of them will be hanged for what they have done, that there is no way out of this, nowhere to run, no trick to play and no clever plan that will see them ride off. This is it. Nik looks at Richie, and her smile is genuine as they sit on the uneven wooden planks of the chimney windmill at Etton. Around them outside, they can hear the thin chattering of those gathered to capture them. Nik takes the gun out of the holster and puts it on the floor, the ornate carving of the dragon's head up the barrel seems dull in the grey of the windmill.

"How much powder do you have?" asks Richie.

"None, and no bullets either," she answers. He struggles to sit forward and fidgets at his belt for the pouch there. He reaches in to find a little leather package which he hands to Nik. She opens it and there are three long packets of powder and two iron balls.

"For emergencies," he says. Nik nods. His face is paler yet and his voice husky.

"What did my father do to you?" she asks.

"Not him," says Richie. "The fat one with a bald head and his lads. I don't need to go into detail, do I?"

"No," answers Nik. Her brow creases with worry at the thought. Of course, her father is not going to do the beating.

She considers the two lead balls and the paper packets of powder on the warped floorboards of the mill, there's the light smell of manure from the fields and a gentle breeze through the window that has no glass or frame.

"You told me you loved my mother," she says without looking at him.

"Aye," he answers.

"This might be our last chance to talk, Richie Turpin was Jackson. Do you want to tell me about it?"

"I will try," he says. She can see that his eyes have already filled up with water, and his cheeks are red. Whatever Richie has tried to hide is at the surface now, for he can conceal it no more. He trusts her, and anyway, the game is nearly over, he has to confide in this lass, to win her confidence more and help her make the right decision. Richie has thought this through already. As they closed and locked the heavy mill door below and as he walked up the tiny steps, he considered what might have to happen. It will take a lot of explaining to get the lass to do what needs to be done, and he will need to pull at her heart strings with the only play he has left – the truth.

"I kissed your mother once, out near Tickton, on the side of the river near the Crown and Anchor pub, it was a mistake on her part perhaps, for she was injured and could not walk. I carried her along the path. A woman like your mother and a village lad like me should not, by rights, have anything to do with each other, but I had rescued her and was taking her back to her father. The kiss was not long, I might add, Nik, and there was not anything more than a few seconds when our lips met." He struggles to sit up and loosens the neck tie from his cloak. "Later, we agreed we would meet in the forest, at dawn, and I would take her away, and we would make a new life." Nik knows this story, but she does not know Richie's version of it.

"My mother has told me this. You were not there when she came."

"I was there, Nik. I was hidden. I heard her call out for me, and I heard her warn me too, that there were soldiers close at hand. I knew then, that I could not take her with me, not where I was going. I was an outlaw already and a thief with nothing but a few coins to my name, and I knew of no help nor where to go. I was alone, and I did not want that life for her. Of course, part of me wanted to come back, and in the coming months, I established myself up at the Golden Ball at Scarborough, and learned the ways of my trade. I travelled all round the north and to the cities of York, Harrogate, Leeds even across the sea to Holland and France. I did not forget her, but, the more I considered the way my life had turned out, the more I knew that she was best left alone. To be with a man of the road such as I became, that is no life for a wife or someone you love." Nik blinks as she listens to this side of the story. Her mother believed herself not worthy of him because he was handsome and brave and free, and she would only weigh him down. Now she sees that he believed he was not good enough for her. This is irony.

"Do you think she fared better without you, Richie?" There is sarcasm in her voice. "With a husband who treats her little better than an animal, and a life in a gilded cage?"

"I do not know, Nik. I made that choice all those years ago and I believed, for her sake, it would be better to be without me."

"Like your dog?" she asks. "You told me you lost your hunting dog in a card game, on purpose, to a man who you thought would look after her." He swallows. This is painful for him, turning over old errors that have been buried - he has to feel the same emotions once more.

"Aye. I could not protect them, Nik. Just as I cannot protect you."

"I do not need your protection, Sir," she says. "You have already given me the gift of self-belief and, now I can shoot a gun and ride at will across the world, so I shall, and if need be, by God, I will protect you." Her teeth grit and her nostrils are flared. Richie leans forward and his eyes blaze, he is not used to asking for help and it is not easy, but the plan will benefit the lass more than he.

"Take the bullet, load the gun, aim the barrel at my chest and pull the trigger." He can see her frown, so he whispers: "Your father will do worse to me, when they storm this windmill, his lads will beat me half to death and then do it again the next day; and, if you shoot me, you will be the one in line for the reward, I mean, that you can, with the right amount of bravado, go back to being young Nicola Sullivan, just until this blows over. Then, one night when all is quiet, you and your mother can slip away on horseback, you and she can live the life she wanted, and the one that you will have. You'll be free."

"I am no longer that girl, Richie, she would never be able to do as you ask, and neither will I. I would rather die."

"But that's just it. You'll never be her again, but you can pretend, Swift Nik could do that, she could hide for a while, for the sake of her mother and for her own life." Nik frowns at the sense of this. There is no hardship she is afraid of, not even going back to that house, but the idea she could shoot Richie, Mr Turpin, the man who has brought her to life, this is out of the question.

"They'll capture us, and we'll escape, we've done it before."

"Not this time," he whispers. "I want you to think about it, not with your heart, but with your head. I'm in no shape to be the man I once was, Nik. I hoped you could help me." He has appealed to her sense of reason, now he has to try to make her see with her feelings. "Will you take my hand, Nik?" he asks. He holds out his palm. He must be brave with this and give all of himself to it - if he must break and weep as he has never done, then so be it, for there is nothing at all more important than this lass in front of him. She must survive at all costs.

"Will you take my hand?" Nik looks fearful of this because as soon as she touches him, she feels like she may cry, he will break any defence she has with the weight of his truth. Folk of the East Riding will only tell you how they feel through sarcasm, or silence or if they are drunk, and even then they will not tell you the contents of their heart. Here is Richie, holding out his hand to her, as he has never done before. "Understand this," he says. "I feel lucky to have known you, Nik. I thought all joy was gone, and you gave me a meaning and it has been the best thing, and I do not feel it has all been in vain when I see you, and I am proud of you and what you have become in such a short time." This is from his heart. It does not come easily for a man who has kept himself hidden all his life.

There's a sound from the open window and Nik turns her head. It's a thud against the brick and a hand comes over the side with the knuckles white as the body behind it grunts and heaves themselves up. Under the big spinning sails outside that whoosh past - some bastard has climbed to the top window. The bald head of Binx draws into view. His leg comes over the side as he steps onto the top level of the windmill. There are the two runs of a ladder behind him and he stands to his full height. He will have volunteered for the job because a man his size could probably swallow a bullet and shake it off. Nik stabbed him a few days ago and it doesn't look like that bothered him. Richie tries to get to his feet, and Nik holds out her hand to calm him. Binx is languid and seemingly unbothered by his situation. He looks to the clacking of the wheels in the centre of the room and then over to the two of them opposite.

"Let me handle this, Richie," she whispers as she takes his hand and gives a squeeze.

"Use your head against him, lass."

"That I shall," she answers.

She stands. There's not enough time to load the gun, Binx would be on her before she could. In previous encounters with this man, her stomach has rumbled in fear, because, like a force of nature there is no battling against him. He was there to hold her down or pin her head against the floor, tie her against the bedpost - all at her father's request. She was powerless then, now she is not.

"You'll die today, Binx," she calls across to him. This is not necessarily going to happen, Nik is only following the training Richie gave her – use your voice and your words to unnerve whoever you fight. "You do know that's why they sent you up here, so we'll waste our bullets, you fat bastard." It feels delightful to swear and Nik has to see if reason or fear can keep the fight from happening at all. He stares back at her as one of the big sails goes past behind him in the wind.

"You'd have shot me already," he says back.

"We're saving our bullets," she answers with a grin. She's not the same afraid girl he knew. Binx does not alter his expression. This is just another job - like Mrs Beasley might ask him to collect a sack of flour from the grocer's or he might have to sort one of the servant girls out at Mr Sullivan's request. Slapping people about, especially women, is one of his strong points. He notes that the real danger, the man who claims to be Dick Turpin, is sat against the wall and looks like he doesn't have the strength to lift a fork. Binx already worked him over a day or so since. He best get on with this, down below on the ground in front of the locked door, there was chatter about what to do. Ryder suggested smoking them out, but it would have taken too much time, and Mr Sullivan wants this fixed and done before nightfall. He suggested Binx go up on a ladder, slap the injured Turpin into next week and bring Nicola down the steps over his shoulder. Binx himself didn't have much say in it.

He'll deal with Turpin first and he lumbers forward towards the man sat with his back against the wall. Binx already knows the pistol on the floorboard in front of him isn't loaded, they'd be pointing it at him if it was. He can ignore

Nicola Sullivan, even with her cocky talk she's no match for his size. Binx takes a deep breath through his nose as he rushes forward and there's suddenly a sharp sensation at the side of his head and a thud, he staggers, then sees the spanner that has been thrown at him clatter against the floor. The lass at the far end of the room who threw it grins, and there's a line of blood running down Binx's face suddenly.

Perhaps he ought to deal with Nicola first.

He changes tack and moves his body towards her. There's a way to deal with lasses, in Binx's experience, a great big backhand slap usually does it. Failing that, he grabs them by the shoulders and gives them a shake, sometimes they scratch, but that soon stops once he's got hold of them. It will be no different with Nicola Sullivan here, despite her cold attitude and level eyes. Binx heard that she shot a man from a hundred yards away while on a horse, but that has to be shite.

He pounces forward to grab her in both hands. She dances backwards and there's the flash of a knife blade across one of his palms. Binx looks down to see a big gash from his thumb already spilling blood onto the uneven top floor of Etton Mill. She's cut him.

"The trouble with you, Binx, is that you've never learned to fight anyone who'll stand up to you," she calls at him as she steps backwards. "You're a big dumb child, slow, and thick witted, dull as a bucket of muddy water with your pig eyes. You should hear how the serving girls laugh at you, Binx. They say you can't even find your own little cock to piss." Nik is making this up as she goes and it feels good not to hold her tongue. The words have humour in them also, and this makes them sting all the more, for she is not angry. It works, Binx feels fury rise in his flabby chest.

The cogs of the windmill spin and rattle as the sails outside turn them. It's as if they're laughing at him. Nik sees the flimsy but closed trapdoor next to Richie, she considers also the open window behind her. She moves around the room, keeping the spinning and clacking mechanism of the windmill at the centre between her and this big man. Binx gives chase. His face is red and the cut on his hand is nasty and weeping blood down his pants and onto the floor.

He starts forward once more, his dumb flabby face is angry. He is not used to being hurt by anyone, except perhaps Mr Sullivan, and he is not well practiced at putting his feet in the right place either, he isn't a boxer, he doesn't have to worry about keeping out of the reach of anyone. All Nik has to do is step lightly back. He follows. The window is very close behind her and the air bristles, the light breeze from the autumn fields blows in, there's the whoosh of a sail as it moves past. Nik's heart beats heavy in her chest but there's calm here in the eye of the storm. Binx has hurt her many times, but this close to him, she is not afraid.

"Is it that difficult to catch me?" she whispers, "I'm a sixteen-year-old lass." He lurches forward in red-faced flabby anger. Nik sidesteps.

His big, heavy body is languid as it falls from the top window of Etton Mill. He falls past the ladders hastily joined together to make a longer one, and past the other two windows with glass, but manages to avoid the sails as they spin in the wind. Binx doesn't have time to look up as he thuds against the floor of the yard, face first, with a huff, and his head splits like a ripe pumpkin. His body slumps uneasy on top of his head, as if it was an afterthought. It's gruesome. There's a gasp from the men gathered. Up top, Nik kicks the ladder away so that it crashes into one of the sails and breaks. They wouldn't have seen how he fell and she keeps herself out of sight.

Nik turns to look at Richie and sees that now he sits more upright against the wall, he has the pistol in his hand. It's held pointing at the open window.

"Why didn't you shoot him?" she asks.

"I didn't need to," he answers, and his eyes twinkle.

"Did you load it?"

"No," he answers. "I believe in you."

In the yard below, there is hell to pay.

"Get that bloody door open," screams Ryder. "Enough of these games." There's a lad with a crowbar jammed into the side of the wooden door of the mill, he splinters the oak as he works to rip the lock open. There is frenzy. Orders bellow out. Horses rear, nervous at the shouts. The pigeons nesting in the barn fly away into the trees. Mr Gibson, the miller, holds his hand to his head.

Richie's lips are pale and his eyes water. She moves to him and goes to her knees beside.

"You fight well," he says. "The footwork and the obscenities, the speed, it's all good, and you did not need me at all."

"I do need you," she says. She tries to change the subject. "Soon enough they will have that door at the bottom open, and there will be ten men running up those stairs. We can only keep them away for so long." Richie shakes his head. He holds the pistol out for her.

"You have to shoot me," he says. "Through the heart, here," he taps on the thin white cotton of his shirt with a long finger. She leans forward without taking the weapon.

"How could I? You are the only one who believes in me. Do you imagine it is possible?"

"Because, I believe in you, Nik. I believe you will help me, and yourself. I have been on the road too long, and when I close my eyes, I can see my Nana, sat by the fire and my hunting dog, Bess, and they are waiting for me to come home." A tear runs down his face. "I know that they will welcome me, as long as you're safe."

"It's blackmail," she whispers.

"I'm a highwayman, it's what I do," he answers. There's

shouting and banging far below as Ryder's men continue to crack open the heavy mill door. She hears her father's voice above the throng and the shrill authority of it sets a barb of fear through her. Richie Jackson, who has been Dick Turpin for many years, is right. They will kill him slowly, that is the vindictive nature of her father, and Nik will be stripped and thrown into the stables where her father will whip her himself to show he does not need Binx.

Reason weighs heavy on her. Nik is not a fool.

She collects the pistol from his hand and picks up a packet of powder, rips off the top with her teeth and pours some into the barrel. She adds the lead ball. Nik's eyes stream and her hands shake, her nose begins to run as her brain tells her body what to do. When she's loaded it, with two hands she holds the pistol pointing down at his chest. Her teeth clench together, tears spill from her eyes and down her red face.

"This is how it must be, Nik," he whispers. He struggles with the words he dare not say, words that sound so trite and foolish, and yet, they are the only words he can think of.

"I love you," he whispers, "and I loved your mother also." She pulls back the hammer with her thumb, and her chest heaves, she grimaces, her stomach rumbles, the gun rattles in her unsteady hands. On the stairs below she can hear footsteps and yells getting closer as men pour into the mill.

"Goodbye Richie Jackson,"

"I will see you along the road," he answers. She pulls the trigger and sees the spark light the powder. There's a flash and a huge plume of smoke as the gun recoils in her hands, sulfur burns her eyes and nose.

Nik has done what her father could never allow, she is her own master. It comes to her as she reaches down for the other packet of powder, that perhaps the only way she can beat the man is to become like him, at least in some way. There are heavy boots on the stairs below her as she loads the gun once more. She spits out the bullet into the barrel and packs it down, then stands. The flimsy trapdoor smashes open and with his gun held high, Mr Ryder storms up into the room.

"Hold there," yells Nik. She points her pistol at him.

"Drop your weapon," he commands.

"You drop your bastard weapon," she bellows. Through the smoke, and as he moves up into the room, Ryder sees the body of the man who said he was Dick Turpin slumped against the wall. The chest is a mess of burned blood and his head lolls to the side. "He's dead," she explains through bitter lips. More men follow Ryder up onto the top floor and she is glad they are there to see. She moves back with her pistol trained on Mr Ryder.

"I shot him," she calls. "I was tired of waiting for you or my bloody father to do something, and so I fought my way out of his hands, and I shot him in his chest." Ryder appraises the situation. He's instantly worried about the reward. The girl, Nicola Sullivan, is earnest and looks tearful, but her teeth are barred and she has the way of her father about her, all orders and certainty. "I swear to God above, Sir, I'll put a bullet through you as well if you don't lower your gun," she orders once more. Other men see the body with the chest blown open, they see the burn marks, Richie's pale face and his body laid against the brickwork at an unnatural angle. Ryder sets his pistol back into his holster. His eyes smart from the smoke.

"You shot him yourself did you, Miss Sullivan?"

"I did, Sir," she answers. He nods. If Ryder delivers her to Sullivan, there might be the reward he's looking for.

"Step back lads," he calls. "I'm bringing Nicola Sullivan home."

Nicola Sullivan walks with her chest proud, she goes down the stairs and out of the splintered door of the mill following the tall figure of Mr Ryder. Three lads carry the dead highwayman's body behind her. The gang of men that chased them but an hour ago, parts to let her through. They are unsure what's happening. Mr Ryder stops in front of Mr Sullivan who has not yet dismounted from his white horse.

"Your daughter, Sir," he says as he presents her. "It seems she shot the fellow, and with his gun as well. She might have injured herself if I hadn't been there." Nik stands behind. Mr Sullivan wrinkles his nose. It's not common knowledge that she escaped from his house and he has alluded to the fact that she was kidnapped. Perhaps this has been a lesson for her after all, she certainly has her mother's spirit, and she's got his ruthlessness as well - it can only be a good thing.

"I want the body taken back to Beverley along with Binx," she orders up to her father. Her voice is clipped and she has taken off the flat cap so that her bright hazel eyes twinkle as she speaks. He nods at this.

"Marcel will see that the bodies are delivered, Nicola." The man with the foxlike beard is at a loss for words. The last time he saw this girl, she half killed him, and yet, he cannot mention this for all to see. The shame of his own daughter attacking him would be too much for him to live down, he has a reputation and a business that would suffer because of this. Nik does not have anything to lose, and bile rises in her chest.

"I see you haven't bothered to get off your horse, father. Brave Mr Ryder here was first up the stairs with his pistol ready, and Binx there, your strongest fellow, lies with his head split open. Just when were you going to show your mettle, father?" She is mocking him in the same way that he mocks others. Mr Ryder smiles to himself and there's a gentle titter from the back of the group. The best thing Sullivan can do is get this over with.

"Bring my daughter a horse," he calls as if he is still in control. Without his wealth, Mr Sullivan would not enjoy his position at all. She clambers up onto a cob that one of the stable lads leads to her.

"If it were not for Mr Ryder here, I may never have got out of that mill alive," she adds. This is not true, and anyone who was up there knows it, but it suits Nik to assist Ryder and it suits him to corroborate the story.

"I will see that he is thanked in the right manner, daughter."

"See that he is, father. It will be so good to get home, and so good to see mother," she adds. Mr Sullivan rides a little ahead of his daughter. He swallows.

It's not hard to work on the story.

It tells itself.

It began to develop as Nik walked down the thin steps of the windmill at Etton. The man who kidnapped her was not Dick Turpin, for the great highwayman was hanged at York. This man who kidnapped Nik, not just once, but twice, was a lad from North Burton, and he was infatuated with her. It was he who shot the farm hand from horseback near Aike, and it wasn't at ten yards and it only grazed his shoulder. It was that man who pushed Binx out the window from the top of Etton Mill so that his fat head popped on the hard ground below. Nicola Sullivan, alone and trapped in the highest part of the windmill above had come to the end of what she could bear, and she took up the robber's pistol. She shot that man in the chest at point blank range through his heart.

It was she who killed him in the end.

You wouldn't want to cross Nicola Sullivan, not after what she's been through.

CHAPTER TWENTY-ONE

Richie opens the door and steps inside out of the night. He is dressed in his black cloak and he takes his tricorn hat from his head. There's Nana, in her winged chair beside the fire in the cottage at North Burton. Bess, his hunting dog, has her thin head resting on the old woman's lap as she strokes the ears. Nana looks up and Bess moves only her eyes because she does not want to stop having her ears scratched.

"What's going on, Richie?" says Nana.

"I've come home," he says. The old woman does one of her sighs and rolls her eyes.

"Have you brought us anything?" Richie pats down his pockets and feels at the pouches on his belt.

"I've not Nana. I thought I'd be welcome… after all this time." Nana huffs.

"It's fine for you to be off and about, up at York and on the river at Beverley, and with that Elizabeth Pike and in your fine and dandy clothes, but you've never given a thought to your Nana here and your loyal dog, Bess. There's not a thing for us to eat here, Richie and it's as cold as freezing with the draught coming down this chimney." The fire blazes. There's the smell of chicken or turkey boiling in the pot on the fire, and on Nana's top lip, there's a tiny red line from drinking port straight out the bottle.

"The road's been long, Nana," he counters. He's tired. You should not show Nana weakness, this only makes her stronger.

"You young uns only think about yourselves. Last time you were here you were wet through and worried about some young lass you said you couldn't help. What's happened to her?" Richie takes a breath in and his lungs rasp in pain, he looks down and sees the blood red of his chest, splattered open and burned by the powder. His stomach turns when he sees it. He remembers looking up into Nik's eyes as she cried, with the barrel of her dragon pistol at his chest, then the smoke and the pain. He draws the left side of his cloak over himself to cover the wound.

"That lass will be fine now, Nana. I've come home. I've come home for good." The old woman stops scratching Bess behind her ear, but only so she can waggle her finger at Richie.

"It's not bloody time to come home," she says. "You've come back with nowt at all. You've to get back out there and bring us back something." Richie frowns.

"You've got everything already," he mutters.

"I can't be having you back here if you're going to be in some sort of mood. I mean Bess won't stand it, she goes all a tremble when I raise my voice, and she's got a weak heart, just like I have. You can't come home, Richie, it's not time, you're not ready. You're not settled." She shoos her flabby hand at him. "You'll have to go if your being like this, with that bloody long face, I've had enough trouble in my life, Richie Jackson, without you bringing all your moping and miserable ways into the house. You're not ready to come in yet."

"Then what am I to do, Nana?"

"I don't bloody know," she says. "You'll not be dead till you're at peace, Richie Lad. You'll have to find it. If I knew how to give it to you, I would have done all them years ago, and you'd have saved me and Bess here so much worry. You're a right pain, it's fine for you to break a lad from Walkington's jaw in a fight or gamble away a month's worth of pennies at the cards, but real decisions, why, you've been shite at them. You've been second guessing yourself and thinking that whatever you want must be a mistake all your life. It can't carry on, Richie, I'm too old to keep worrying about it. You'll know when you're ready to come home…because you won't want to."

"I could just take a rest for a minute, Nana. I'd not be long. Just till my bones warm up and my chest stops hurting. You can tell me what's been happening in North Burton since last." Nana has been holding back, but launches, full-bore into him:

"I didn't bring you up to have a sit down before the job's done," she says, "that's not how Jacksons do it, Richie. I didn't get where I am now by sitting on my fat arse all day and talking about things whilst I warmed myself by the fire taking slugs of port. Now, just like before, you get yourself out there and come back when you're in a better mood." Richie steps back. The black dog by Nana's side shivers because the old woman has become angry and raised her voice. "Look what you've done to poor Bess here," she calls. He swallows and turns to the door behind him, then puts his big hand on the latch to lift it. Before he opens up, he looks over his shoulder at the old woman next to the fire with the head of the big dog on her lap.

"Perhaps I'm not welcome here after all." he says. Her face softens. The lad is so easy to hurt. She can't bear it sometimes.

"You've to let someone love you, Richie. I know I've been horrible to you, I know I have. It's just my way. Other folk have been horrible back to me, like your granddad, but you... you've not to be afraid of kindness." Nana's wrinkled face attempts a smile and it makes her look oddly evil with the gaps in her teeth.

Richie opens the door.

He gasps, and the pain in his chest is real, like his lungs are full of needles and each of them digging in at the same time. He tries to move his arms but they are stiff. His eyes flicker and open but the light is too sharp. There's the instinct to sit up and run - scream even, but he resists, experience tells him to take a minute before doing anything.

He's been shot through the heart after all – Richie saw Nik do it, heard it too and felt the blast on his chest. There's the smell of sulphur and cooked flesh in his nostrils. He's on his back with a blanket across him, his shoulders are bare. Richie opens and closes his right hand because it's the only one he can move.

"You're safe, Richie." It's a familiar voice. "You're home… finally." The tone is thin and sharp. He knows it, but he cannot place who it is. Despite his pain, he moves his hand to his chest and there are bandages wrapped around his front and back. He's in no shape to move quickly as he struggles to open his eyes and sit up. Nana would say she's had worse hangovers.

"My physician cautioned on any sudden movements," says the voice. "You'll live, but the burns on your chest are extensive. It seems you were shot with powder only. You've got enough scars already, Richie, another few won't make a difference." The voice is unfriendly, with a pinch of sarcasm. He knows who this is. It is Miss Charlotte Pennyman. When he was a lad, it was she who lived in the great manor house at North Burton, she who said she was his half-brother, she who said Richie's father was Mr Pennyman who let his mother die in childbirth on the cowshed floor. He opens his eyes and the light in the room is sharp, he's already propped up by pillows at his back and he looks out over a long four poster bed, down white sheets and across to a mirror and Miss Charlotte Pennyman in a chair in the corner. She has aged greatly, her face is a mess of wrinkles and her eyes droop, her mouth is a permanent scowl. Her hair is grey and pulled up in a bun.

"I thought you'd be dead from the drink," says Richie. His lips are dry and his chest aches. She gives a wry grin.

"I found God," she answers.

"Pity," says Richie. He doesn't like her. Now he's a man, and a dangerous one at that, he doesn't have to pretend. One of the reasons he never came back this way was in case he saw her. Given half a chance, he'd put a bullet in her chest. He scans the room. There's a long dark table against the wall with a vase of pink chrysanthemums, on the right is a window to the blue autumn afternoon sky outside. The heavy red curtains are open. The door is closed beside the chair where Miss Pennyman sits and the handle is shiny polished brass. This is a rich household he reasons. He must be in North Burton, and this must be Miss Pennyman's house. There's the smell of iodine in his nostrils and a hint of the old woman's perfume. However bad he feels, he has to get out of here, and he has to find Swift Nik, and her mother also. He blinks.

He feels clarity.

"Do you remember the last time you were here?" ask Miss Charlotte Pennyman. He nods. He and his father, the Pearlman, battled robbers in the study downstairs. He tries to sit forward and there's pain in his hips and back, he wiggles his toes, still in odd shoes under the sheets, to make sure they still work.

"I've been looking for you for a long time," she says. "You're a difficult man to find. I paid a substantial amount of money to a very good man to hunt you. I expect you met him already, since I have found you and I haven't heard from him." Richie understands now, he was the grey-haired man who hunted he and Nik down on the banks of the river Humber, the one who chased him in York, and the one who killed his friend, Kat. There's a little snarl on Richie's mouth when he realises it was Pennyman who caused that.

"I met him. His body's in the Humber," he says.

"He assured me he would kill you."

"He would have. I had help."

"You got lucky then. Here's where your luck has run out, Richie Jackson." He manages to sit forward, and he tries to move his legs to the side of the bed but pain shoots through him.

"You always did say too much. Why not just kill me while I was asleep?"

"I wanted to talk to you Richie, there's no one else left from the old days."

"Why have me hunted, Miss Pennyman, I was never going to come back?"

"How was I to know? You're the only other heir to this

house and my father's money and when I'm gone, you'd have found your way back here and tried to take it all for yourself."

"Do you honestly think, after all this, I would want your money or your house? You can leave it to whatever family you're left with."

"That's just it, Richie, there's no one." Miss Charlotte Pennyman was once a pretty and kind lass, she married a wealthy man from London, but he was cruel and wicked. When he'd broken her heart, she shriveled up into the angry creature she is now. "Because I have nobody to leave all this to, there might be a slim chance you could get your hands on it." Richie shakes his head and he moves his body to the side of the bed under the sheets, his feet feel heavy.

"That's not it," he says and he looks at her now he is sitting on the side. "You might as well tell me the truth, if you're going to kill me anyway."

"Spoken like a Pennyman, Richie, straight to the point. I'll tell you why I wanted you found, it's because you got away. You managed to run from here, this village and the gossiping folk, you're just a poor farm rat and you could be free, but me, with this big house and all the horses and fields… I was trapped here. I wanted to show you, Richie Jackson, that you're just as trapped as I am." He pulls the cover off him and looks down and sees that he's still wearing his pants. With his legs over the side of the bed, he tries to stand and then sits back down in pain.

"You have what you wished for then, Miss Pennyman. I hope you are happy." She beams at him and her teeth are off white and straight.

"I will be when I see you buried, Richie." He tries to stand again.

"How did I get here?"

"The Sullivan girl's men brought you, the one who thought she'd shot you in the chest. I offered to keep your body and the fat one with his head popped open. I said I'd put you in the church opposite. She agreed, and I thought you were as dead as she did, until I felt for your pulse."

"How did you get me up here?"

"Farm lads will carry anything they are told too, Richie, you of anyone should know that." He tries once more to stand but his legs are too weak.

"What now?"

"I'll have something else wrapped up and pretend it's your corpse, then it will be buried. You can stay here."

"What for?"

"To die."

"You mean to shoot me here?"

"I won't shoot you, Richie. I'm not going to do anything to you, I won't have to in the state you're in. You been asleep for two days and your body is already wasting away, another week or so, and you won't even be able to open your eyes, and then, it will be you that's trapped and I'll be free." She smiles at him from the corner. "Make yourself at home, Richie, you won't be here too much longer. You're in the west of the house. Nobody will hear you shouting, at least, I've told the servants not to."

He watches her struggle to get up and move to the door, she is older than she should be, and her movements are stiff, but she seems pleased with herself. It seems an age before he hears the lock turn in the keyhole.

It takes Richie a few minutes, but he gets to the vase of flowers, pulls out the five pale pink chrysanthemums and drinks the water therein. He takes it slowly, with sips at first. There's grit in the water but he feels it going down his chest and through his windpipe. The sensation is divine. He chews the leaves from the flowers between sips. You can eat chrysanthemums, he's seen Meg make them into tea and she says it helps with heart problems. Richie crunches on the little petals as he sits on the edge of the bed. They taste peppery.

The light outside is fading into early evening. He can hear starlings outside.

Richie is not really sure why he is eating flowers. He should just accept this and lay back on the bed to die like Miss Charlotte Pennyman wants him to. He thought he'd been killed already, now he's got a real chance to get it all over with, he ought to let it happen. Strangely, he sees clarity, again. Now that he knows Nik can look after herself, he feels better. There's a smile on his thin lips as he remembers her fighting Binx, the look of anger on the man's face, and Nik as smooth and as calm as the morning wind.

He weighs up the glass vase in his hand. If he had enough strength, he'd smash it on the next person through the door. He will see how he feels in ten minutes or so, perhaps the flower petals will give him energy. Richie finds himself sinking back onto the bed with fatigue. He did not expect to go out like this, so serene and lazy. His mind wanders as his eyes flicker, he thinks of the ins and outs of what has happened.

Nik shot him with powder only. Perhaps she did not load the ball properly, perhaps it fell out. These things do happen, and Richie has fired powder alone from guns before – there's even a saying for it these days, just a flash in the pan. He sees the girl's eyes looking down on him through his tears, she's not the sort to get things wrong. He tries to sit up as he realises.

Perhaps it was her intention to shoot him with powder only and if this is the case, then the story is far from over.

There's the sound of something moving in the lock. It's familiar to him, and not the noise a key makes at all, rather the clack of two pins inserted into the hole at the same time. It does not take long for the lock to succumb and the bolt inside to slide back. Richie sits up on the end of the bed. The door opens and a figure steps in.

It is his Swift Nik.

She grins down at him and he can see she is different as

the light falls upon her. She is ragged but the clothes are no longer cast offs. The black pants and dark overcoat are tailored to her frame. Under the waistcoat is the handle of the gun that Richie gave her. Her face is calm and her nose now has a kink in the middle where it's been broken and there's swelling around her eyes. It's recent. To see her makes his eyes water in pride, and to see how well she stands and how unafraid she is to be herself. It is Richie who is to be rescued by her, again.

"I am pleased to see you well, my Nik," he whispers. "You were meant to shoot me." Richie's mouth is dry.

"I did," she answers.

"You've been fighting?" He's concerned for her, but there's no room for emotion.

"It was my father's doing," she says as if it were nothing at all. "I see you managed to survive the gunshot. I thought it might have done more than just wound you."

"You meant to shoot me without the ball, did you?"

"Aye, Richie. You didn't watch me load it. I believe we can live to see another day." He shakes his head and there's that smile again. It's the one he saw on Nik's face as she fought Binx and the one he's done himself on so many occasions when he ought to weep with anger or shiver with fear.

"We have to get out of here."

"There's no rush," says Nik. "My mother is down in the main house, discussing God's work with Miss Pennyman."

"She's here?"

"Aye. Much has happened in the two days since you had your chest blown apart, Richie Jackson. Can you walk?"

"I believe so, but not quickly. I wouldn't want Elizabeth to see me like this." Nik's eyes sparkle when she sees Richie is worried. His face becomes paler than it was, despite it being pale already. The prospect of contact with this woman is alarming to him. Nik knows when he is scared – and he is always afraid when he talks about her mother.

"Why am I here, Nik? What's happened?"

"I had my father's men deliver your body here to North Burton. My mother and Miss Pennyman have been friends, in the way women of society are known to each other, for many years. The serving lass told me you'd been locked up in a bedroom in the west of the house. Mr Sullivan turned a little mean when I got back home." Nik steps inside the room. Her eyes have more wisdom in them since last they spoke.

"You should have let me deal with him."

"I wish I had."

"Was it he who did that to your face?" Nik wants to explain the horror of what her father carried out when they got home, how he had the livery yard men strip her naked, how they threw her into a stable, how he whipped her till she bled and how, when she shivered, bare in the corner he told the lads they could take turns to have her like the bitch she was. Nicola Sullivan would have wept while it happened to her, she would have called the name of God to bless her with strength. Not so, this Swift Nik. The first lad who entered the stable and tried to touch her had his cheek bitten in half, and he broke her nose as he battered her afterwards. Mr Sullivan told them to leave her, but none of them would have tried anything after that anyway. In the morning he would have killed Nik for certain, but, there was one other player who kept their hand close to their chest. Elizabeth Sullivan was Pike paid Mrs Beasley five crowns to leave the house that very evening. She took a sharp meat knife from the kitchen and, when the world was quiet in the dull light of morning, she pushed the blade through Mr Sullivan's throat while he slept. As he bled and coughed up onto the sheets, she held his face in her hands and explained why – she had promised she would kill him if he hurt their daughter and here it was. She told him too, of the highwayman she had once loved and that he was not dead, that Marcel the Frenchman had delivered his body to North Burton and the house of Miss Charlotte Pennyman.

"Was it he who hurt you?" asks Richie.

"One of his lads."

"Did you kill him?" She shakes her head.

"My mother did. She cut his throat." Richie forces himself to stand. He is a little wobbly at first but he manages.

"Who knows what she did?"

"Nobody yet. I believe we are on the run, just like you are." There's no sense of urgency in her voice.

"We'll need horses," whispers Richie. Nik taps the handle of the pistol peeping out from under her jacket.

"We have two," she answers.

The last light of the autumn sun shines through the many tiny square panes that make up the study window. Miss Charlotte Pennyman sits at the big table and Elizabeth Sullivan was Pike sits opposite. There's a teapot on a tray and two elegant cups with saucers. Around them, are leather bound books on shelves, most never opened and next to the far door there is a writing desk. Elizabeth has been in this room many times on her visits to Miss Pennyman, they are not close, but, twenty years ago, Richie saved both their lives in this very room. Miss Charlotte says she has the bodies of their man Binx and Richie Jackson in the church opposite, but Elizabeth and Nik have already heard that her man is locked in a room upstairs. Nicola Sullivan has remained outside to see to the horses and take some air, or at least this is what she has told Miss Pennyman. It has given her a chance to look around and for Elizabeth to keep Miss Pennyman busy with chatter.

The journey from Beverley this morning was hard, of course Elizabeth can ride much further and faster, but it was what she left behind that worries her. She killed her husband. It's a crime against God, she knows this, and she does not care. She looked into his eyes as he died and watched his red life blood gush out all over the patterned stitching of the pillow, and she was pleased she killed him. The aftermath of what she has done, saving the judgement of the Lord, is a concern. She found her Nicola in the stables outside, gagged and naked with her hands bound in front of her, on her knees in the corner and dried blood all over her face. As Elizabeth cut the bonds and removed the gag, she expected the lass to cry out in pain but she was as calm as the dawn. There was no time to get her washed properly, and so, in the house, Elizabeth listened to her daughter explain how they would proceed, that they were to dress in riding clothes. When the livery yard lads arrived, Elizabeth was to tell them that Mr Sullivan was ill in bed after all the events of yesterday, and that Nicola and her mother were going for a horse ride so they could talk over her problems. In half an hour they were riding through the North Bar Gate with St Mary's and their house on Toll Gavel, Beverley behind them.

Nicola took all of it in her stride, the beating, the kidnapping, and it struck Elizabeth then, that her daughter was cut from cloth something akin to her grandfather, Captain Pike, with the dogged resilience and the internal resolve. They both of them, mother and daughter, weathered life in the house on Toll Gavel, with a man cruel and weak at the same time. Elizabeth took the beatings and the mental torture as well, and in the end, there was nothing left for her to do but kill her husband. She has everything in her satchel, her jewellery in a metal box, a purse full of coins and a little bible.

Now in North Burton, Elizabeth listens to Miss Charlotte explain the ins and outs of village life, the new roofing plans for St Michael's across the road, and the poor lazy farm workers who can do nothing but drink. Elizabeth has explained that they are out for a ride to get air after what has gone on. Perhaps someone has already found Mr Sullivan's body in the house in Toll Gavel. Perhaps they have already gathered men to look for Elizabeth and her daughter. Perhaps Mr Ryder is eager to see that justice is done, for there's been too much blood spilt in Beverley town of late.

Elizabeth sets down her cup and her hand is shaking

gently. The cup rattles against the saucer. She is afraid and electrified, for Nicola has explained she did not shoot Richie Jackson. They need to collect the highwayman and then be off to wherever they are going, wherever that may be. As much as Elizabeth feels sick with worry, she is free. She is free at last.

"You've been through a great deal," says Miss Charlotte Pennyman. She has aged badly, her teeth are yellow and her eyes piggy and mean.

"I believe some time in the country will do myself and my daughter the power of good, Miss Pennyman. You have been a great friend."

"It's my Christian duty to be so, Elizabeth." They are not friends. Pennyman has gone from being a drunk to a shriveled zealot. "I am always here for you." The grey-haired old woman manages to make the words sound disingenuous.

There are footsteps down the corridor, and the door opens without a knock. It frustrates Miss Pennyman, for those who do not know manners are not welcome at the estate. Nik enters. It's the first time the lady of the house has seen her today. She's shocked by her appearance in men's pants, riding boots and a flat cap over her ginger hair. The young girl's face is smooth and serious, bruises cover her eyes and she is dirty, more like a stable lad. Richie Jackson steps in behind her and closes the door. He is dressed in the long cloak Miss Charlotte left at the end of his bed. She was going to bury him in it. The old woman stands.

"What is the meaning of this?" she commands. Nik withdraws the pistol from inside her coat and levels it at Miss Pennyman.

"You know a woman your age wouldn't get over a bullet wound. Open your mouth and shout, and I'll put one through your chest." It feels good to be free to say such things to someone as horrible as Miss Pennyman - there's something of her father in Nik's tone, with the faint trace of humour. The effect of the sentence chills Miss Pennyman to silence.

Richie looks down on Elizabeth as the woman stands. She is dressed in a simple riding jacket with her ginger hair tied at the back of her head. His stomach gurgles and there is something between these two, instantly. She walks a few paces to him and her nostrils flare. Electricity crackles.

Miss Charlotte scoffs.

"You tried that on twenty years ago," she whispers. "He left you then, Elizabeth, he'll leave you again. I see now why you're here, you and your little bitch daughter have contrived to leave poor Mr Sullivan. I've heard he's a monster but that doesn't give you the right to leave him. Richie Jackson here is my guest."

"I'm not afraid to kill you," says Nik. "If words keep coming out of your mouth, I shall." She speaks softly over the hammer of the pistol. Miss Pennyman swallows, she is afraid of her. "Where is the key to this room?" asks Nik. Pennyman takes it out of her apron pocket and holds it out in her palm for the lass to collect. "I'm going to lock you in here," explains Nik. "We're going to leave out the front door, and if I hear you make a noise or shout, so help me, I will come back here and break your jaw with the handle of this pistol so that you shall never speak properly again and will only be able to eat soup." Nik has had so many mean things said to her over her short life, that she has an almost endless menu of insults to choose from. She would never attack this old woman, but like Richie says, words are weapons too, they can choke you with fear and hold you fast as well as ropes. "Do you understand? Nod your head only if you do." Miss Charlotte Pennyman nods. She likes this version of Nicola Sullivan, in another life they could be friends, she gets things done and doesn't take any nonsense. It's almost a thrill to have her here. Miss Charlotte nods again.

Elizabeth goes out first and Richie backs out behind her. He can see from Miss Charlotte's eyes that she is angry as well as afraid, just a few hours previous she had won, and now, once again, she will be trapped here in the Pennyman House at North Burton, wrapped in her own misery and self-pity, while poor farm lad Richie Jackson is free. She holds his gaze and he gives her a tiny wink before he turns and goes down the corridor and into the darkness. Nik closes the door and locks it shut. Miss Charlotte Pennyman, contrary to the wishes of Nik, bangs her thin fists on the wood and shouts at the top of her frail lungs.

In a minute, they are through the front door of the great house and there are two horses waiting. Nik skips to the first, a mottled grey cob, undoes the reins from the post and clambers on its back. Behind, Elizabeth attends to the much bigger bay. There's shouting from inside the house, and a footman appears at the front door with this face a confused frown.

"We've ridden together before, Richie," says Elizabeth. He puts his foot in the stirrup and heaves himself up despite the pain, then winces as his other foot goes over the side and he sits down in the saddle. He holds his hand out and Elizabeth takes it, he hauls her up and she sits behind him, her hands go around his waist and clasp together. The footman on the steps calls out to them, the obvious:

"What the bloody hell's going on?" Richie gently digs his heels into the horse's side and they power away after Nik, the hooves crunch on the gravel of the Pennyman House driveway as they head off.

They are away.

It's early evening. There's the sweet smell of cut hay from the fields and a nightingale still calls in the last rays of the dying day. They ride out of North Burton along the road to York, past farms that Richie once knew well, and then north towards Market Weighton to Wold Top where on a clear night you can see the stars bright above you. Nik is a sleek and able horse rider, especially on a saddle and an animal she knows well. She looks back over her shoulder to see Richie with her mother holding on to his waist and her ginger hair in a ponytail bouncing in the wind. They look like a couple.

The horses are tired when they get to the top of the hill. There's perhaps ten minutes left of good light and Nik pulls up her horse next to Kipplingcoats Lane. There's a big oak on the hill. Richie stops behind and Elizabeth climbs from the back. Riding double is hard on a horse as well as the pillion, she is happy to get off. Richie turns the horse and looks down, over the grey rolling chalk fields they have just ridden through. There are lights on the road below them, torches move in the distance, they are riders following no doubt, perhaps half an hour away.

"It will be Ryder," says Richie. "He'll have found the trail already." Nik squints down at the dots of yellow light moving far away. It would have been very simple to track the Sullivan women from Beverley. Miss Charlotte would have helped also, perhaps with a reward offered.

"How would they know we've come this way?" asks Nik.

"People saw us," answers Richie. "Which road would you come by if you wanted to get away quickly."

"This way," says Nik. "The road's wider and smoother."

"Aye." She's already as smart as he is, with all his years on the run, smarter even. "I'll head back down," he adds and then details his plan to Nik in the saddle opposite and Elizabeth standing below. "I'll meet them coming and give them something to think about also. Ride south, past Newbald and on to Ferriby. In the morning there will be a ferry across the Humber. You can be on it and into Lincolnshire, and away." There is a little of his old music in his voice. He dare not look down at Elizabeth because he is afraid of her. He would rather face Ryder and his gang, and be done in once and for all, than have to explain how he feels about her. Nik walks her horse nearer to the tall man.

"Not this time, Richie." He cocks his head at this stern lass with a flat cap over her head covering her eyes. She removes it so he can see her. "I said, not this time, Richie Turpin was Jackson. Your run is over. This is my fight now, and you're showing off to my mother anyway."

"You are being impetuous, Nicola," says Elizabeth.

"I am not she anymore, mother. I am on a different path now. You see, Richie, it is I who will ride down the hill, not you. There are many reasons. You have neither powder nor bullets nor a gun, you're injured also, and they would catch you, then they would catch my mother and me. I shall ride down with these two horses, and I'll ride a hole through a big hedge, so they'll know where I've gone, and then, I'll draw them all after me, up to Dalton Park, and I'll lose them in the woods."

Richie grins and, without reason, his eyes begin to water with tears. She is complete; brave, competent, swift and honest, and it is everything Richie admires. He takes a deep, shaky breath and looks down to Elizabeth.

"You cannot," she says as she stands with her hands held in fists at her side.

"I have to mother. It's you two who will go south to Ferriby, and it's you who will catch a morning boat across the Humber. I will see you again. What shall we say Richie, which alehouses do you know in Lincoln?"

"The Horse and Groom, Carholme Road on the west of the town. Why Lincoln?"

"It's far away," she answers. "I'll be there in four days,"

"You have seen too much, Nicola, this is not some game, this is your life and those men will kill you after they have done whatever they will do."

"You're going to have to trust me," she says back. Richie clears his throat.

"She has us." He addresses Elizabeth. "There is no way I could outrun them, not in this state, and she rides well, she knows the roads, and she knows how to shoot. I have trusted her with my life already."

"I cannot let my daughter go, Richie Jackson, you do not understand."

"There is no time for this," says Nik. "I need your horse, Richie, or they will not follow if they think it is just I." He gets down off the horse and hands her the reins.

"Four days," she says. "The Horse and Groom, Lincoln." Nik puts the cap back on her head, clicks her tongue and the horses move off.

In a few seconds she is lost to the darkness.

They leave the road and Richie follows Elizabeth into the dead of night and across the fields, there's a track by the hedge just passable under the light of the stars. She does not walk quickly because she knows that he struggles.

"She will make it," he says.

"How can you be so sure?" comes the answer.

"I can't, but I don't know what I would do if anything happens to her." Elizabeth stops and turns to him.

"Now you know how I feel then, Richie Jackson." She's just under five foot ten, too tall for a lass to be considered pretty in polite society, but just right for Richie. He steps closer as he examines her face with the smooth eyes and high cheekbones. Experience has made this woman more beautiful and the eyes are keen and intelligent.

"She rides well, she can shoot and she's strong. You taught her much."

"You also taught her, Richie."

"As she taught me. Did she explain to you… what I said before she shot me in the chest with a gun loaded only with powder?" He told her he loved her.

"Yes," says Elizabeth. There's the sound of an owl off in the distance and the stars twinkle high in the sky, the breeze from the south ruffles her hair and she can hear him breathing. "Why did you not come back, Richie, all those years ago?"

"I thought I was doing right by you. I thought a life with me would not be best for a woman as fine as you. This is the truth." He swallows. There's more, and he might as well say it. He's back from the dead. "I was afraid also, that I am not good enough for you, Elizabeth Pike."

"I waited for as long as I could, and I married that man to please my father before he died. You were everything I needed, Richie, brave and honest and a little daft too, tall and with strong hands."

"I kissed you once," he says. She is close to him and his stomach rumbles, his pulse begins to rise and his mouth is dry, his skin prickles.

"I know. Near the Crown and Anchor at Tickton. You were injured, worse than now, with a stab wound in your side."

"I thought about it, a lot, over the years, about you. It made my legs weak and my heart bang in my chest." Elizabeth Pike is still as fine as she was, her hazel eyes are level and steady. Gone is the life she lived all these years suddenly and the man who hurt her.

"Is your heart banging now, Richie Jackson?"

"Aye," he answers. She steps closer still and he lifts his hand so he can touch her face, his thumb rests upon her cheek.

"It will have to be forever, Richie," she says. "I mean it. It will have to be you and me forever, until the end of the world and until the sun stops burning and falls out of the sky."

"Aye," he says. "It will have to be. I think it has always been so for me."

He leans forward and their lips meet.

Four miles north, just before Dalton Park Woods, Swift Nik splits from the horse she has been leading across the fields. She's covered in a light sweat and can hear the shouts of the men on horseback in the distance as they follow. It has been a fine ride. She tucks her body into the saddle and grips the animal with her knees as they jump the fence in front, for a moment they are at one with the air, smooth and free, calm and effortless before the hooves thud back into the stubble of the cornfield on the other side and then power on. Swift Nik glances back over her shoulder, she sees the light of a torch in the far distance.

She is free.

For the first time she makes her own choices, and trusts herself to do so, knowing that Richie trusts her as well.

It makes her strong.

In four days, she'll be in Lincoln.

#

Printed in Great Britain
by Amazon